"I don't want wo
that I hired you
Lewis said.

Lexie propped her ha

"Don't you think that they're going to work it out when you start looking a whole lot different after spending concentrated time with me?"

Lewis paused. His lips curved up on either side. "Well, maybe not so much if people thought we were dating and you steered me in another direction, clotheswise or something. If word got out that we were dating, would that be so bad?"

"Yes. You're a client," she reminded sternly.

"But people here don't know that," he insisted, looking her square in the eye.

"But I do," Lexie shot back. "And I don't date clients, Lewis."

Not any more. Not since she had found out mixing business and pleasure with a sexy available man was the worst mistake a single woman could make.

Lewis paused to come up with a new strategy. "Then we'll just have to tell people we're spending time together because we're friends."

Available in August 2007 from Mills & Boon Special Edition

Blame It on Texas
by Cathy Gillen Thacker

The Perfect Wife
by Judy Duarte
(*Talk of the Neighbourhood*)

Outback Baby
by Lilian Darcy

Celebrity Bachelor
by Victoria Pade

Acquiring Mr Right
by Laurie Paige

Rightfully His
by Sharon De Vita

Blame It on Texas

CATHY GILLEN THACKER

All the characters in this book have no existence outside the imagination of the author, and have no relation whatsoever to anyone bearing the same name or names. They are not even distantly inspired by any individual known or unknown to the author, and all the incidents are pure invention.

First published in Great Britain 2007
Harlequin Mills & Boon Limited,
Eton House, 18-24 Paradise Road, Richmond, Surrey TW9 1SR

ISBN: 978 0 263 85641 5

23-0807

Printed and bound in Spain
by Litografia Rosés S.A., Barcelona

This book is for Mary Thacker,
for her love and support over the years.

Don't miss our new bonus Special Moments section at the end of the story, where we have horoscopes, author information, a sneak peek at a story that's in the pipeline and puzzles for you to do!

Chapter One

A full moon shone and stars twinkled in the velvety sky overhead. It was shaping up to be a beautiful October evening, Lewis McCabe thought, as he strode briskly up the steps of the Remington ranch house. Before he could press the doorbell, the front door opened. Jenna Lockhart Remington stepped across the threshold, the look on her face anything but welcoming. "I know why you're here," the elegant older woman said firmly.

"You do?" Lewis McCabe murmured. Darn it, had his four brothers phoned ahead to make his plan public before he put it into action? If so, there was going to be heck to pay, he decided grimly, and then some.

"And although—" Mrs. Remington paused to shrewdly peruse Lewis from head to toe, none of her customary hospitality evident "—I can see your need is dire—"

How could she have known how long it had been since he'd had a date? Lewis thought in irritation. Then again, this was Laramie, Texas, where everyone was family, and nothing stayed secret for long.

"Lexie is here on vacation."

"Exactly," Lewis said, glad they were no longer talking at cross purposes. "I figured since your stepdaughter's in town again I'd use the opportunity to—"

"Take advantage of her kind and generous nature?" Mrs. Remington scolded, clearly annoyed.

Was Mrs. Remington intimating he was a pity date? That Lexie would only go out with him if she felt sorry for him? "I assure you, Mrs. Remington, I have nothing but the utmost respect for Lexie," he said sincerely, determined to do whatever it took to get an audience with the woman he'd had his eye on for what seemed like forever. "I hold her in highest regard."

"Which is, of course, exactly why you are here," Mrs. Remington interrupted. "Because Lexie *is* so successful."

Given the fact this conversation had started off on the wrong foot, and had been going down the wrong path ever since, Lewis wasn't sure what to say to that. "Of course I admire what Lexie has done professionally," he admitted. "Everyone around here does." Thanks to her stunning fashion sense, she'd become every bit the celebrity her clients were.

Footsteps sounded in the background. Jake Remington, Lexie's father, appeared at his wife's side, his tall, lanky frame filling the doorway. Jake nodded at Lewis. "McCabe."

"Mr. Remington." Lewis stuck out his hand. After a moment, Jake shook it. Encouraged, Lewis continued, "I was just telling Mrs. Remington that I—"

"My wife is right," Jake Remington interrupted imperiously "There is no way Jenna and I are going to let Lexie see you. Because if we do and you ask her what darn near everyone else around here wants to ask her right now—"

Lewis swore inwardly. "Other guys have been here ahead of me?" He thought he'd gotten the jump on this, since Lexie had only arrived here from London, via her father's private jet, earlier in the day.

"Let's just say you're not the first to come calling," Mrs. Remington replied. "And the answer to everyone was the same. Lexie is not receiving guests at this time."

"Well, then when will she be?" Lewis asked, doing his best to maintain a positive outlook. Not easy, given how unfairly he was being shot down.

Jake and Jenna looked at each other. "As far as we're concerned, never," Jake said. "At least during this visit."

The thought of letting Lexie leave town without seeing her—again—did not sit well with Lewis, maybe because so many chances to connect had already passed them by. Deciding he wasn't going to let the Remingtons's assessment of his chances with Lexie decide the matter, Lewis insisted as politely as possible, "I just need a moment of her time. I won't stay. I promise."

Jenna sighed, looking thoroughly conflicted. She ran a hand through her short red-gold hair before frowning at Lewis. "She'd say yes, you know. All it would take is one look at you, and she'd be agreeing to whatever you asked."

"And that would not be good for her," Jake Remington clapped a firm hand on Lewis's shoulder. "You need to go, son."

Lewis dug in his heels. He did not want to leave it like this.

"Maybe the next time she's home," Mrs. Remington offered gently before putting an abrupt end to the conversation. The door shut and silence fell on the wide front porch of the elegant limestone ranch house.

Lewis stood there a moment longer, aware he hadn't felt this foolish since he was twenty-three and failed to get up the nerve to talk to Lexie when she was home from college on fall break. Eight years had passed…and apparently little had changed. Swearing silently to himself, he turned and started down the porch steps to his SUV. He was almost there when he heard what sounded like a tapping noise. He turned in the direction of the house and saw Lexie Remington framed in an upstairs window, looking as heart-stoppingly beautiful as ever. She motioned to him, and pointed urgently toward the rear of the house. Then, with one last glance over her shoulder, to see if he were following, she disappeared from view.

A mixture of anticipation and excitement rippling through him, Lewis strode around the ranch house. At the rear of the house, Lexie was standing in an open second-floor window in what appeared to be an old-fashioned white lawn nightgown, with a high neck and long, billowing sleeves. Her strawberry-blond hair flowing in untamed waves around her slender shoulders, she looked like a princess in a turret. All she was missing was the tiara and he wouldn't have been surprised if she'd had one of those around some place. Arms on the sill, she leaned down toward him and invited in a soft, mischievous voice that further fueled his dreams, "Come on up."

Lewis didn't know whether to laugh or try and wake himself up from what was obviously the wildest fantasy he'd ever had. "How?" he whispered back, aware it was only seven-thirty and Lexie was already dressed for bed. Another anomaly in this increasingly bizarre situation. The Lexie he recalled had always been as much of a night person as he was. No way she would have gone straight from dinner into bed, even if she had just crossed the Atlantic Ocean. No way she would have worn such a ridiculously old-fashioned nightgown.

"Climb up the trellis," she urged merrily, her alluring lips curving into a sexy smile.

Blood rushed through Lewis's veins. Had her breasts always been that curvaceous and full, her features so delicate and sensual? "You're kidding." He couldn't take his eyes from her face.

Her lovely features took on an air of challenge. To his disappointment, she tossed her head and shrugged as if it didn't matter to her in the least. "Do you want to meet me with me or not?"

Lewis didn't have to be asked twice.

LEXIE STOOD GUARD in her dimly lit bedroom while Lewis McCabe climbed up the trellis with a great deal more ease than she expected. By the time he hauled himself over her windowsill and into the bedroom she had inhabited during her youth, her heart was pounding. Why exactly, she couldn't say. It wasn't as if the two of them had ever meant anything to one another. They'd barely spoken to each other, although, it had been hard not to be aware of Lewis McCabe. He was just so darn smart. And, when he let his guard down, witty. She had lived for his subtle wisecracks and droll sense of humor.

Not that he had ever cared. Or noticed.

But he was here now. To see her. And how time had changed them both. He was taller than she recalled. Much taller. At least six-three. And *buff.* His shoulders were broad, his arms, chest, abdomen and legs—solid muscle. His face had filled out, too, giving him a ruggedly masculine appeal, a big departure from the hopelessly nerdy boy she recalled from her youth.

These days, his well-defined lips had a confident slant, and his angular jaw emanated power and determination. And yet, despite the fact that Lewis McCabe was now very much a man's man, some things remained almost the same. His lively blue-gray eyes were still framed by the wire-rimmed glasses she had always found oh-so-sexy. His spiky light brown hair had hints of chestnut and gold woven throughout, although Lewis still hadn't found a good barber. His clothes were…well…horrendous, but that was why he was trying so hard to see her. Because he knew he needed her help retooling his image. And he might not know it, yet, but she needed his help, too.

Lexie decided to cut straight to the chase. "I heard you talking to my parents and I know what you wanted to ask me. The answer is yes."

Lewis couldn't seem to stop looking at her long, white

nightgown. Good thing he didn't know how little she had under the deftly camouflaging fabric.... Now if only she could get her body to stop reacting to his presence.

"You're serious," Lewis said incredulously.

He didn't have to look so surprised, Lexie thought irritably, as she brushed her hair away from her face. "I know you need my expertise in this area, and I am perfectly willing to help you come up with a personal style that better suits your position as CEO and president of McCabe Computer Games. You're not just a computer genius, Lewis, you're a successful executive now. You've got to dress the part."

To Lexie's surprise, Lewis wasn't looking as pleased by her offer as she had expected. Perhaps because he had taken offense? Call it a hazard of her profession, but she did tend to be a tad blunt when summing up a client's style woes. She flushed self-consciously and forced a smile. "I'll waive my regular fee."

Again, Lewis McCabe didn't appear to know whether to be pleased by her generous offer, or insulted.

"Instead," she forced herself to continue matter-of-factly, "I want something much more valuable from you."

Having apparently recovered from the sight of her in the impossibly chaste nightgown, he strolled past her and settled confidently on the edge of her four-poster bed. He flashed her with a challenging half smile. "Okay, I'm all ears," he prodded dryly.

Lexie swallowed, trying hard not to notice how at home he looked in her bedroom. "I heard you and your brother Brad have a ranch now—with horses."

Lewis nodded, interest clearly piqued. "The Lazy M."

Lexie raked her teeth across her lower lip. Her heart pounded at the implacable note in his low voice. "I want to go riding tonight." The brisk October weather was perfect for an evening ride.

Lewis shrugged, unconcerned. "Put your jeans and boots on. I'll take you."

She edged close enough to inhale the brisk masculine scent of his cologne. "It's not that simple," she said, keeping her voice low enough so they wouldn't be overheard.

Some emotion Lexie couldn't quite identify flickered in Lewis's eyes. "Of course it isn't," he replied knowingly.

Lexie felt the heat in her chest spread upward to her face. She told herself it was tension—and not his proximity—causing her heart to pound. "I can't just walk out of here."

Lewis cocked his head. "I don't see why not," he told her frankly. "You are a grown woman."

Yes. She was. Unfortunately, not everyone around her accepted that. "My parents want me home tonight." *And every other day and night for the next two weeks.*

"I gathered that." Lewis rubbed the flat of his palm across the underside of his closely shaven jaw. Still keeping his eyes focused firmly on hers, he added playfully, "The question is why are they locking you in your little tower up here?"

"I'm not locked in! Well, not literally anyway," Lexie amended hurriedly, as his gaze trailed lazily over her hair, face and lips before returning to her eyes. "And the reason Jenna and my father are working so hard to keep me home and undisturbed is that they have gotten it into their heads that I need to catch up on my rest."

Lewis couldn't mask the concern in his eyes. "You want my opinion?" he asked. "You are looking a little…peaked."

Lexie knew her skin didn't have the sun-kissed glow of his. She rolled her eyes. "Give me a break. I've been in London, where it's done nothing lately but rain."

He narrowed his assessing gaze even more. "A few cloudy days don't cause skin to be that pale."

How was it that Lewis saw what those who were supposed to be close to her had failed to notice? "Then it's the nightgown," Lexie argued back, refusing to admit to the real reason behind her pale skin and tense, agitated state. "The white color washes out my skin."

He grinned, all mischief again. "I was wondering about that," he teased, getting slowly and deliberately to his feet. "You used to be such a tomboy." He sauntered closer, inundating her with his size.

Her pulse racing, Lexie leaned her head back, to better see into his face. "Still am, at heart," she drawled right back, knowing that much was only too true. As a child, she'd played outdoors constantly and rarely wore a dress—and then only under protest.

Lewis fingered the stand-up lace collar. "Then why the frilly getup?" he teased.

She drew a breath and stepped back before his hand brushed the delicate skin of her throat, or the equally sensitive underside of her chin. "All the clothes I brought with me from England are in the wash. So I had to pick something that was still in my closet here to wear when I got out of the shower."

A muscle worked in his jaw. "You really wore something like this?" he asked, doing a double take.

Lexie huffed in irritation. "I had a romantic phase, years ago." It had been a time when she had wanted to be swept off her feet. Fortunately, she was no longer the foolish young girl she had been when she had left Laramie on the arm of Constantine Romeo. "Don't worry. It passed. Never to return."

Lewis stepped back to regard her. "That's too bad. I kind of like it. It's…sexy…in an innocent sort of way."

Lexie's body tingled. She wished she'd at least had the foresight to put on a bra or a bathrobe before inviting him up to her lair. "Listen, if we're going to work together, you can't say things like that," she chided, backing away from him again.

He matched her, step for step, until the backs of her knees

hit the side of her bed. Clearly trying to push her buttons, he asked, "What if we're just fooling around together? Can I say it then?"

To her dismay, Lexie could imagine playing around with Lewis McCabe way too easily. Resolved to keep her guard up, Lexie feigned immunity to his teasing. "I'm serious, Lewis."

"So am I." Desire, pure and simple, was in his eyes. "If we're going to be spending time together, for whatever reason, why can't I tell you what's on my mind?"

Determined not to put herself in an emotionally vulnerable position with him, she said, "Because it makes us aware of each other in a way we shouldn't be...and that does not make for a good work environment."

He flashed her a contemplative grin. "Voice of experience talking?"

Hanging on to her composure by a thread, she revealed, "I got romantically involved with a man who also ended up being my client."

Lewis grimaced. "Constantine Romeo."

Years later, people were still talking about the way she had simply picked up and run off with the handsome actor, much to the chagrin of her parents and stepmother. Lexie pinned Lewis with a glare. "That's not a mistake I intend to repeat."

"Hmm. Well, if you're worried about that," he said, his low, sexy voice doing strange things to her insides, "then maybe you and I shouldn't work together."

"We have to!" Lexie countered emotionally, before she could stop herself.

He paused and eyed her thoughtfully. "Why?"

Aware she was revealing far too much of herself to a man she barely knew, Lexie gave him a flippant look. "Besides the fact that you desperately need my help?"

"Yes."

"Because unless I do a favor for you, then I can't ask you to do a favor for me," she explained before turning away.

Lewis clamped a hand on her shoulder and turned her back to face him. "Why not?"

His strong, capable fingers radiated warmth. "Because then we won't be even."

He angled his head. "Why does it have to be even?"

Frustrated, Lexie threw up her hands. "Because that's the way the world works."

"Maybe that's the way Hollywood works," he agreed, as he caught both of her hands in both of his. "It isn't the way Laramie, Texas, works. Here, you can do a favor for someone without worrying about whether or not you're going to get paid back. And vice versa. People just naturally help each other out. They don't keep score."

"Well, I'm not comfortable with that," she retorted, not about to get drawn into any sort of flirtation with him, no matter how desirable she found him. "If I ask something of someone, I give something in return. That way, I don't have to worry about owing anyone anything."

Lewis let her go. "I see."

"You disapprove." The question was, why did it matter to her what he thought?

His lips took on a reassuring curve. "I think you need to relax, take it down a notch."

So did she. "Which is why I asked you to climb up here, Lewis," Lexie explained with a grimace. "I've only been here a few hours and I'm already going stir-crazy in this house. I have to get out. I've got to have some fresh air and moonlight…and the feel of freedom I get when I ride, or I'm *never* going to be able to sleep."

Lewis gave her a seductive smile that was enough to make her stomach drop. "Makes sense."

Finally, they were on the same page!

Lexie surveyed his vintage '80s clothing that were not exactly ranch ready. She bit her lower lip. "You do ride, don't you?"

Lewis nodded.

"Well enough to keep up with me?" she asked.

"Only one way to find that out," he drawled.

Her curiosity about him intensified. The Lewis she recalled had been awkward with the ladies. The Lewis in front of her seemed to know his way around. "Good. So meet me at midnight," she urged hurriedly, trying not to think what his newfound confidence was doing to her. "I'll be waiting at the end of the drive, down by the road."

Lewis resisted her efforts to push him back toward the open window. Instead, he linked fingers with her. "Why can't we just tell your parents what you want to do and go now—via the front door?"

She unlinked their palms, not sure how much she could trust him to do what she wanted if he knew everything there was to know about her current situation. "Uh...long story."

His expression guarded, he studied her. "I have all the time in the world."

She scoffed, aware far too much time had already passed. "That's what you think."

Lewis quirked an eyebrow.

"Do you really want to face my father when he realizes you're still here?"

Recognition dawned. "I gather he wouldn't appreciate me spending time in your bedroom," Lewis remarked, a look of distinctly male satisfaction on his face.

Refusing to consider what it would be like if Lewis really were there for amorous reasons, Lexie stepped away from him. "You gather right."

He lifted both hands in surrender. "Say no more. I'm out of here."

Relief flowed through her. Much more of this two-stepping around her bedroom and she'd be thinking about kissing him. She let out a slow breath. "I'll see you later."

"Lexie." Lewis paused, one leg thrown over the windowsill. He looked deep into her eyes. "Are you sure everything is okay?"

Lexie shrugged, unable to admit just how wrong her life had gone as of late. "I'm fine," she lied. "Now scoot before someone catches you with me and we really have a lot of explaining to do."

"WELL, LOOK WHO DECIDED to join us after all," Riley McCabe teased, twenty minutes later.

All eyes were on Lewis as he strolled into the kitchen of the "fixer-upper" his youngest brother, Kevin, had just purchased.

Brad continued removing the sink and its fittings after looking at Lewis with obvious sympathy. "Struck out, huh?"

Unfortunately, they all knew where he had been and why. Lewis'd had to tell them why he was opting out of the kitchen demolition party at the last minute, after promising to help the financially tapped-out Kevin and the rest of his brothers with the task.

Lewis picked up a hammer. "What makes you think I didn't get a date?"

"Did you?" Kevin asked, unable to stop being a detective even when he wasn't working for the Laramie County sheriff's department.

"Yes." Lewis lent a hand, prying off the ancient laminate countertop. "And no."

Will McCabe narrowed his eyes, looking every bit the former fighter pilot he was. "You either did or you didn't. Which is it?"

Lewis unscrewed the plywood cover from the base cabinet. "Lexie agreed to spend time with me. Starting later tonight, as a matter of fact."

Brad knelt to remove the doors and drawers from the lower units. "I hear a catch in there."

Together, the guys carried the trash from the growing junk pile to the pickup parked just outside the back door. "She got the mistaken impression that I wanted to hire her to transform my image."

Guffaws, all around.

Riley scrutinized Lewis as they all tromped back inside to continue gutting the spacious country kitchen. "So you're going to be paying her to pay attention to you?"

Not in money. "That's the good part," Lewis said, fully aware of just how bad this arrangement he had struck with Lexie sounded.

Kevin scoffed as they worked to remove the base units from the wall. "For whom?"

"We're bartering services. She wants me to take her riding tonight. At midnight."

"And then what?" Brad, still the most cynical of them all, asked.

"If all goes well, I intend to keep seeing her," Lewis said.

Will helped them remove the rest of the unit without tearing out the drywall behind it. "Then I presume you're going to set Lexie Remington straight when you see her tonight, tell her all you intended was to ask her out."

Lewis shrugged. "She seems to think I need an image makeover."

More groans, all the way around. "That may be true," Kevin said as the guys finished extracting the bottom units. "But once you let a woman start telling you how to dress and what to do, it's all over. Unless…you want to be with a woman who runs the show in the relationship?"

"Besides, I thought you already did that," Riley continued helpfully. "You know, hitched your wagon to a woman who couldn't seem to stop 'improving' you and cutting you down."

He paused, as compassionate a brother as he was a physician. "Didn't do much for the union, as I recall."

"And yet here you are—enthusiastically signing up for that all over again," the now happily married Brad said. "Don't you know that's the kiss of death for any relationship, trying to make each other into what you want them to be instead of accepting them for who they already are?"

"We're talking about a few dates," Lewis said impatiently.

"A few dates built on a lie," Kevin corrected, all law-and-order again.

Guilt flooded Lewis. That was not something he had intended.

Will looked at Lewis with obvious pity. "How do you think Lexie's going to feel when she finds out you never had any intention of contracting her professional services? She's going to think you made a fool of her on purpose, letting her assume something that wasn't true."

Lewis hadn't thought of it that way. He hoped Lexie wouldn't, either. Aware there was only one solution to this problem that would keep Lexie's feelings from being hurt, he put down his hammer and clenched his jaw. "Lexie isn't going to find out."

Riley scoffed. "How do you figure that?"

Lewis narrowed his eyes. "'Cause none of you are going to tell her."

Easy to see all four of his brothers thought he was making a big mistake. "Look," Lewis said firmly, laying down the law as only a McCabe could, "Lexie's only going to be in Texas for two weeks before she jets off again. I finally get to spend time some quality time with her. I'm not mucking with that, and none of you are going to ruin it for me, either."

LEWIS FELT LIKE an intruder as he slowed his Yukon in front of the entrance to the Remington ranch. Lexie glided out of the shadows, right on cue, and slipped into the passenger seat beside him. She looked pretty as could be in jeans, boots, a red cotton turtleneck and denim jacket. Her thick strawberry-blond hair had been pulled into a bouncy ponytail on the back of her head. Vibrant color lit her cheeks and eyes.

"What is that delicious aroma?" Lexie demanded in her usual carefree manner. She looked at the paper bag balanced on the console between their seats.

Lewis drove the short distance down the farm road to the entrance of his own ranch, the Lazy M. "A little late night supper. I figured we might want to grab a bite before we saddle up."

"You figured right," she said, a mixture of devilry and excitement sparkling in her turquoise eyes. "I'm starving. If my nose is correct, that's chili from your aunt Greta's restaurant."

Lewis gave her an amused glance, aware how much hadn't changed about her. Lexie was still the most exciting tomboy around. Quick-witted, fun-loving and sexy as all get-out. Trying not to imagine what it would be like to finally have her in his arms, he said, "Extra spicy, just the way you like it."

"Mmm." Pleasure radiated in her low tone as she kicked back in the passenger seat. "What else is in here?"

With effort, he kept his glance away from the graceful way she moved and her long, denim-clad legs. "Coffee. Nice and strong. And jalapeño cornbread." He knew from experience it really packed a punch. "I figured I would show you something while we eat." Lewis took a separate entrance to the Lazy M Ranch house, near the south edge of the property. Perched on a hill was a bulldozer and several piles of dirt. He parked in the lane and cut the engine.

"What are you building here?" Lexie looked around curiously.

He adjusted the interior lights on the truck, so they could

see each other clearly. "A second ranch house—this one is just for me."

Lexie took off her seat belt and swiveled to face him. "How big is it going to be?"

Lewis unhooked his, too. "Haven't decided yet. I'm still working with the architect."

"Where do you live now?"

Aware how cozy it felt to be here with her like this, he handed Lexie a thermal cup of chili and a spoon. "I was bunking in the main house, and Brad had the guest cottage. When he married Lainey Carrington, and she and her son moved in with Brad, it made sense for us to switch places. Now they have two preschoolers, and another baby on the way."

"So I heard."

The presence of kids had his yearning for a family of his own growing by leaps and bounds, which was why he'd decided to go ahead and build his dream home, in the hopes that a special woman would follow.

"Anyway, it makes sense for us to spread out a little more now." He could still have meals with Brad and Lainey and the kids whenever he wanted, but he could have more privacy, too.

Lewis watched Lexie work off the lid, being careful not to spill it, and balance her square of cornbread on her bent knee. He licked a drop of chili off his thumb. "So how come we're sneaking around like a couple of teenagers?" he asked.

Lexie swallowed the spicy concoction and arched her eyebrows at him flirtatiously. "Aren't you having fun yet?"

Reminded of how reckless Lexie had always been, Lewis nudged her knee with his and grinned. "You know what I mean. What's going on between you and your folks?" He'd been wondering about that all evening. From what he recalled, they had always gotten along, until Lexie ran off to California to make her fame and fortune at the tender age of nineteen.

She licked the back of her plastic spoon. "Let's just say they are overreacting, as usual."

"They seemed awfully protective," he noted as he munched on cornbread.

In a way that didn't make sense. Jake Remington was an accomplished businessman, known for identifying fledgling businesses and turning them into hugely successful operations. Jenna Lockhart Remington was a successful clothing designer known for her one-of-a-kind couture bridal gowns and formalwear, as well as her boutique line. They were respected members of the community, renowned for their big hearts and Texas hospitality. Yet earlier, they could hardly have been more unwelcoming to him and, apparently, to everyone else who had dared appear at their front door since Lexie arrived home that morning.

She shrugged, took another bite of chili and followed it with a big gulp of coffee. Lewis saw her looking around.

He grimaced. "Sorry. I forgot to bring any napkins."

"That's okay." Lexie dabbed at the corner of her lips with her fingertip. She went back to eating. "So what kind of horses do you and your brother have out here?"

It was all Lewis could do to keep his eyes off her. "You're going to ride Lady—she's a sweetheart."

Lexie's eyebrows drew together. "She sounds tame."

"She is," Lewis assured, not sure how long it had been since Lexie had actually ridden. "You won't have any trouble with her."

She paused and put her chili aside. Frowning, she swallowed hard and shook her head in outright disagreement. "I wanted a challenge," she argued.

Brad's horse was just that. The problem was, no one rode the stallion but Brad. Lewis's cautious nature came to the fore. "It's going to be dark, Lexie."

"So?" Lexie shot him an aggravated look and put a fist to her sternum.

"So even with the lanterns I brought for us to hang on our saddles and the full moon, we're going to have to be careful."

Lexie got out of the cab of the truck and began to pace.

Not sure what was wrong, Lewis climbed out after her. Quickly, he circled around to her side. Then he watched as Lexie bent forward, perspiration dotting her forehead, her hands on her knees. Light spilled from the interior of the truck, bathing them both in a yellow glow. Lexie straightened again, her face ghostly pale. "Are you okay?" he asked, not sure what was going on with her, just knowing it wasn't good.

Lexie nodded. "I'm fine," she said, in a voice thready with pain. And then she fainted.

Chapter Two

"I can't believe you called my parents," Lexie fumed.

"What was I supposed to do?" Lewis was glad her anger with him had brought a renewed flush of color to her cheeks. When he had carried her through the automatic glass doors of Laramie Community Hospital, she had been white as a sheet. "Bring you to the hospital and not tell them?" That would have won him some points with her folks!

"You weren't supposed to bring me to the emergency room at all!" Lexie folded her arms in front of her.

Before Lewis could defend himself, the door to the examining room was opened. His brother Riley, the family doc on call, and Lexie's parents filed in. Jake and Jenna Remington looked as if they had been awakened from a sound sleep and dressed hastily. Their hair was still tousled. Jake needed a shave. Jenna's face was pale with worry. They rushed to Lexie's side and hugged her, being careful not to dislodge the IV taped to her left arm. "Thank you for calling us," Jenna told Lewis.

"Although what you were doing out with my daughter that time of night is still a question that needs to be answered," Jake said grimly.

"Don't blame Lewis, Dad," Lexie interrupted. "I asked him to take me riding."

Jake's gray-brown eyebrows climbed even higher. "In the middle of the night?"

"It's not as if you were going to let me go if you knew about it," Lexie challenged.

Riley looked at Lexie sternly. "Your father told me you just got out of the hospital in London, Lexie."

Lewis did a double take. "Is this true?" he asked her.

Lexie flushed and waved off the concern of all those around her. "It was nothing."

"It wasn't nothing," Jake Remington said gruffly. "You passed out over there, too."

"So I'm a little run-down." Lexie shrugged.

"You were having chest pains tonight," Lewis said, repeating what he had already told the staff upon her admission. "Before you passed out. At least I think you were, the way you were pressing your hand to your chest."

"Acid reflux," Riley explained.

"You can give her medication for that, right?" Jenna queried, the picture of motherly concern.

Riley nodded. "But you're still going to have to lay off the spicy food, caffeine and highly acidic things like tomatoes and citrus until you heal, Lexie. And we still have to deal with your exhaustion. You need lots of rest, no stress. And you need to start eating right."

Lexie rubbed the back of her neck, looking as if all that sounded impossible to her.

"How long before she's back on her feet?" Lexie's father asked.

"Two weeks of R and R ought to do it," Riley said.

"I want to go riding," Lexie grumbled.

"Not for at least another week," Riley cautioned. "We don't want you passing out in the saddle."

"So when do I get out of here?" Lexie asked, impatiently.

"As soon as the IV is finished," Riley said. He wrote out

a prescription for her and handed it over. "Provided you promise me you really will take it easy."

She nodded. "I promise."

"Okay, I want to see you in my office in one week, for a recheck. Call and make an appointment with my receptionist tomorrow. In the meantime, if you have any questions, don't hesitate to call." Riley accepted thanks from everyone, then exited the room.

Jake Remington turned back to his only daughter. "Okay, young lady, you heard the doctor. No more reckless inattention to your health. You're going home with us, and this time, you're staying on the ranch."

"No, I'm not." Lexie reached out and took Lewis's hand firmly in hers. "I am going home with Lewis!"

THE SILENCE IN THE examining room was deafening.

All eyes turned to Lewis.

He was used to seeing his brothers in this kind of trouble. Not him. Never him.

"Lexie, you already had one disastrous relationship," Jake said. "If you think I am going to stand by and watch you rush headlong into another, just to get back at me for never approving of Constantine Romeo—"

"I knew you were going to bring that up!" Lexie interrupted.

"Stop!" Jenna stepped between warring father and daughter. "This is the kind of stress Riley just suggested that Lexie avoid."

"Well, I'm not letting her go home with someone she barely knows," Jake protested.

"Well, I'm not going back to the ranch, either. I can't breathe there!" Lexie glared at her father.

"Then how about staying in the apartment above my shop?" Jenna suggested gently. "It's small, but private. And right down the street from the hospital, should you feel ill again."

"Fine," Lexie said. "Provided Lewis drives me there and you two go on home and get some sleep."

Jake Remington looked as if he wanted to punch him, Lewis noted uncomfortably. But her father finally agreed and the Remingtons left after bidding Lexie a tense good-night.

Lewis went out in the hall to wait while the nurse helped Lexie get ready to leave the hospital. Riley handed the chart he had been writing on to the medical records clerk and strode over to Lewis. He clapped a brotherly hand on Lewis's shoulder. "I meant what I said about Lexie needing to limit her stress right now. Especially given the way Jake Remington feels about his daughter seeing anyone."

"Shutting her up like a princess in an ivory tower is the wrong approach to take with Lexie," Lewis declared.

His brother frowned. "You're an authority on her? After what—one-fifth of one clandestine date?"

"She asked me to help her out. I'm going to do that," Lewis insisted stubbornly.

Riley's gaze narrowed. "And I'm telling you this—make an enemy of her father, and you'll regret it."

LEXIE SAUNTERED OUT to the waiting room. "Thanks for waiting."

"No problem." Lewis fell into step beside her.

"But it wasn't necessary," she said, leading the way out of the ER. "I could just as easily get a cab."

"In Laramie? At this time of night?" Lewis teased, as they walked through the automatic glass doors. "You have been away a long time."

Lexie came to a halt on the sidewalk beneath the portico. "There are still only two cabs in town?"

Lewis put his hand beneath her elbow. "And neither of them run past midnight without prior appointment, unless it is an absolute emergency. And when there's a medical emergency, an ambulance is summoned."

Lexie sighed, her frustration evident. “This isn’t an emergency.”

“Maybe not to you.” He guided her toward the parking lot. “You managed to get everyone around you pretty upset.”

Lexie drew away from him as they approached his Yukon. “Including you?”

“I admit you had me worried.”

Lewis held the door for her, then circled around to climb behind the steering wheel. The only thing he regretted about this mission was the short distance to her stepmother’s building on Main Street.

Jenna Lockhart Designs had been a mere storefront—albeit a highly exclusive one—when Lewis moved to Laramie at age eleven. Now, some twenty years later, the famous Texas boutique took up an entire block on Laramie’s Main Street. Women came from all over the country to purchase the one-of-a kind evening gowns and wedding dresses Jenna designed in her shop. Her off-the-rack creations, which carried a much more reasonable price tag, were made in a factory at the edge of town, and sold in department stores everywhere. “Your dad and stepmother, too,” Lewis continued.

Her lips took on a mutinous tilt. “I told them not to worry.”

Lewis drove as slowly as possible. “What happened in London anyway?” He stopped at a traffic light.

Lexie shrugged. “The usual. First I had to deal with my mother.”

When the light turned green, Lewis continued on down the street. “She still lives in Europe, right?”

“Italy. Right.”

“She married some Italian count, didn’t she?” Lewis kept the conversation going as he parked in front of the boutique.

“Riccardo della Gheradesca.” Lexie got a pinched look on her face. She vaulted from the truck, and waited for Lewis to get his keys out of the ignition and catch up with her.

"Anyway, after—" Lexie broke off, then tried again. "I was in Italy, seeing my mother and going to the funeral and all that..."

Lewis blinked. "Funeral?"

"Riccardo died last month."

"I'm sorry. I didn't know."

Lexie shrugged, her expression more numb than grief-stricken. "I barely knew him. The Count had no interest in children and, truthfully, neither does my mother. But the funeral was a pretty big deal, and she wanted me there, so I had to go."

"Your mom must be really upset."

Lexie nodded and looked even more distressed. "Anyway, from Naples I went to Japan for a major film festival there—"

Lewis waited while she punched in the security code that would let her in the building. "That sounds like fun."

She led the way through a dimly lit interior hallway to the stairs. "It was a nightmare. I had four clients all needing my help, all the time, all trying to elbow each other aside."

He chuckled at the low note of exasperation in her voice. "No wonder you had acid reflux."

"Anyway, from there I went on to London," Lexie continued, apparently unaware just how sexily her stylish jeans cupped her lower half. "One of my clients was simultaneously trying to change her image and making her debut on the London stage. She couldn't articulate what it was she wanted for her publicity appearances on British television, and I tried every look imaginable. Nothing was pleasing her. The next thing I knew I'd fainted dead away in Knightsbridge, and they'd rushed me to the hospital. My father came right over on his private jet and whisked me back to Texas."

Lewis studied her in puzzlement. "The doctors there didn't diagnose your reflux?"

Lexie shrugged, punched in another security code and then opened the door to the apartment. She hit the lights and led the way inside to what looked to be a two-room apartment, with living room and kitchenette in front, bedroom and bath in back. It was professionally decorated in the same shades of pale pink and cream as the boutique downstairs. "I didn't tell them about my symptoms."

Lewis watched her saunter over to the fridge. "Lexie!"

She brought out two plastic bottles of blackberry-flavored water and tossed him one. He caught it with one hand.

"It didn't seem to have anything to do with my passing out. I was jet-lagged and exhausted." Lexie frowned as she struggled unsuccessfully with the cap of her bottle. "I hadn't been eating right since I was still recovering from the nonstop bout of 'indigestion' I'd had in Cannes. They concluded that I needed a few days of rest."

Lewis took the top off his and did a trade with her. "If that's the case, I don't get why you and your father are quarreling."

"Because," Lexie enunciated clearly, "my father doesn't respect me or what I do for a living. Bottom line, he wants me to quit working as a celebrity stylist and come home to Laramie to stay."

LEXIE COULD SEE THAT Lewis did not think that was such a formidable offense.

"He was probably just upset."

Lexie stalked over to one of the cream-colored sofas and sank down onto it. "Gee. You think?"

Lewis followed, looking very handsome and very much at home in the soft lighting of the small but luxuriantly appointed apartment. "As soon as you get better—"

Lexie watched as he sat down next to her. "My father's still going to want me to leave Tinseltown for good."

Lewis took a long draught of flavored water, then let the bottle rest on his muscular thigh. "What do you want?"

That, Lexie thought, was the dilemma. She didn't really know.

"You do like your career, don't you?" he persisted.

She looked into his lively blue-gray eyes. "I did."

"Until...?" Lewis asked.

Lexie tried not to think what he would look like without the sexy wire-rimmed glasses. She swallowed hard. "A few months ago."

He stretched out his long, jean-clad legs. "What happened?"

She sighed, relieved to finally be able to bare her soul to someone impartial. "Nothing out of the ordinary, really. There was no great epiphany or anything like that."

The way Lewis was looking at her, as if he really wanted to understand her, prompted her to continue. "I just got tired of always being on a plane, always being at the whim of a client—a hundred clients, actually. I stopped waking up every morning wanting to go to work and meet the challenges ahead. Instead, I had to pull myself out of bed."

Tenderness radiated from his slight smile. "Maybe you just need a rest."

And maybe, Lexie thought wearily, pushing both hands through her hair, she needed a new life. Although what she would do, besides being a celebrity stylist, she didn't know. Thanks to the fact she had dropped out of college to follow Constantine Romeo to Hollywood, she wasn't prepared to do anything else. Besides, who gave up a lucrative six-figure career and professional acclaim to find themselves? She was remarkably successful for a twenty-seven-year-old. She'd be considered a fool for even trying to find something else to do for a living.

Lewis drained his bottle and put it aside. "Have you said any of this to Jenna or your dad?"

"No." Lexie traced the condensation on the outside of her water bottle with the tip of her index finger.

He touched the back of her hand with the back of his. "How do you think he would react?"

She luxuriated in the warmth of skin to skin. "He'd be relieved."

"Because he doesn't want you tending to celebrities," Lewis guessed.

Lexie bit her lip. "It's not that."

"Then what is it?" He turned toward her slightly, to better see her face.

Lexie began to pace the carpeted room. "My father thinks my profession is a joke, that in helping celebrities develop an individual style and image that I'm perpetuating at best a myth, and at worst, fraud."

"Ouch!" Lewis tugged facetiously at the frayed neckline of his band-collared shirt as if it were choking him.

Happy to have someone understand how outrageous her father's views were, Lexie stopped trying to contain her emotions. "He's basically said if a person doesn't know what to wear, or how to present themselves, then they have more problems than I can solve for them."

Lewis winced. "When did he say this?"

She shrugged. "Five years ago, when my business really started taking off."

Lewis got to his feet. "Because of the work you did for Constantine Romeo?" he asked, coming toward her.

Lexie nodded and headed back to the kitchen, this time to the cabinets next to the stove. She rummaged through them, until she found a box of saltines on the uppermost shelf. When she couldn't quite snag it, Lewis reached up and got it for her. "That's another sore subject between us," she allowed, their fingertips brushing as he handed her the box.

He lounged against the cabinets, watching her open a

wax packet and withdraw several crackers. "They didn't get along?"

She offered him some, too. "My dad never forgave Constantine for taking me to Hollywood with him. Or me, for running off with him." As always, the bland flavor of the cracker comforted her finicky tummy.

"You were just nineteen at the time."

Lexie hunted in the fridge to see if there was any cheddar cheese. To her disappointment, there wasn't. She got the peanut butter out instead. "Believe me, I know."

"Regrets?" Lewis asked softly.

"More than you can count," she admitted as she spread peanut butter on several crackers.

He smiled. "But that's how we learn, right? By our mistakes."

"You betcha."

They both ate six or seven crackers. The silence between them was at once companionable, and fraught with a new tension that Lexie preferred not to identify. "How are you feeling?" Lewis asked finally.

She took a long drink, then shared what was left of her water with him. "The truth?"

He nodded, holding her eyes.

"Sleepy."

He pushed away from the counter reluctantly. "Then I should be going."

For some reason, Lexie did not want him to leave. Not yet. "What time is it?" she asked.

Lewis glanced at his watch. "Nearly four."

"You must be tired, too," she commiserated.

He shrugged.

"Want to stay and sack out on the couch?" The words were out before she could stop them.

Lewis paused.

Letting him know this was a strictly platonic move on her part, she teased, "I'd offer you the bed if I thought you'd take it."

Desire lit up his blue-gray eyes. "Only if you're in it, too."

Lexie gasped. "Lewis!" she chided as heat filled her face.

He looked her square in the eye. "I may be a computer geek up here—" he pointed to his head "—but I'm a man down here." He indicated the rest of him.

As if she hadn't already secretly noticed how well he filled his jeans. Wishing he didn't look so damn sexy Lexie looked away. "I'm beginning to realize that," she said drolly.

"And you've already had one rough couple of days." Lewis reached up to gently touch her face. His thoughts undoubtedly amorous, he looked down at her tenderly and caressed her cheekbone with the pad of his thumb.

Doing her best to slow her racing heart, she bantered back carelessly, "So you're not offering to seduce me?" And why did she suddenly wish he were? Just because she had been totally in awe of him in their youth, did not mean they were right for each other.

"Not tonight." Lewis bent his head, kissed her gently—and far too briefly. Not that this lessened the impact of his caress in any way. The feel of his lips brushing ever so sweetly over hers inundated Lexie with a longing unlike anything she had ever felt or imagined she could feel. An explosion of pleasure and need went off inside her, and she looked at him. *What was happening here?* Lexie wondered, struggling not to go up on tiptoe and kiss him back. She couldn't be attracted to Lewis McCabe, could she? He wasn't even her type. She fell for the smooth ones. The ones with all the lines. Not the ones who were so challenged in the wardrobe and personal style department it would take her professional guidance to get him straightened out; and even longer to make him into the complete babe magnet she knew he already was. At least to her. She privately admitted she didn't want every other woman in his orbit feeling the same way.

Lexie caught herself up short. Aware she had already veered into dangerous territory, she said, "On second thought, maybe I shouldn't be the one consulting with you on your new look." It was too close to what she had done before. Taking on a man, making him her personal project. Helping him become everything he could be, only to have him leave her in the end. She did not want to go through that again. And she especially did not want to do that here in Laramie, Texas, under the watchful eyes of both their families.

Lewis grinned with a distinctly male satisfaction. "Too late," he declared, cheerful as ever. "We already made a deal. I'm holding you to it."

Lexie caught her breath, even as she wished he would kiss her again. Really kiss her this time. Not just tease her with the hope of what could possibly be.

"I'll sack out on the sofa." Lewis stepped back, ever the gentleman again. "That way, if you need anything, all you have to do is call," he promised her softly. "I'll be right here."

Lewis McCabe had no idea how good that sounded to her.

Chapter Three

Lewis spent a good hour and a half thinking about the incredibly sweet and sensual kiss he'd shared with Lexie. He fell asleep dreaming about her and awakened to sunlight pouring in through the windows and someone pounding on the apartment door. Fearing all the ruckus was going to wake Lexie, he grabbed his shirt off the back of the sofa and struggled to his feet. Thrusting his arms in the sleeves, he rushed to open the apartment door.

Standing on the other side of the portal was a haughty-looking fiftysomething blonde in an expensive designer suit and high heels. Everything about her, from her immaculately coiffed hair to the heavy jewels adorning her body, bespoke tremendous wealth.

"I am Contessa Melinda della Gheradesca from Italy."

Lexie's mother.

Her glance drifted over his open shirt, bare chest and shoeless feet. Disdain coating every word, the Contessa demanded, "Who are you?"

Before he could answer, an equally disheveled Lexie stepped out.

It was Lexie's worst nightmare come true, and then some. "Mother." She trod closer, aware how the situation must look, since she was clad in another of her stepmother's ethereal creations.

Melinda's eyebrows arched even higher as she took in the plunging neckline of the black lace negligee Lexie was wearing. Lewis couldn't seem to take his eyes off her, either. Trying hard not to blush, Lexie pulled the equally revealing black lace robe over her chest and folded her arms in front of her to keep it there. Steadfastly ignoring the flare of desire in Lewis's eyes, she whirled back to the woman who had given birth to her, but never really nurtured her. "Mother. What are you doing here?"

Melinda touched a bejeweled hand to her immaculately coiffed hair. "Your father told me you were ill—I came as soon as I heard."

That was a first, Lexie thought. Melinda hadn't done more than telephone Lexie—albeit reluctantly—when she'd been hospitalized with pneumonia in the sixth grade. Nor had she ever tended to her personally if Lexie became ill when visiting. Instead, Melinda left her with a nurse until Lexie's sniffles or tummy ailment cleared. Melinda was about as emotionally uninvolved a mother as could be, which made her appearance here now all the more strange. "When did he call you?" she asked.

"When he was en route with you from London. And I talked to him again two hours ago when my jet landed in Dallas. I must say, he did not mention anything about you—your new— Have you gone mad, taking a lover here in Laramie? Alexandra, for heaven's sake! You can do so much better than this!"

Lexie flashed a deliberately cheerful smile. "Might want to be careful who you're insulting, Mother," she warned pleasantly. "This is Lewis McCabe, owner of McCabe Computer Games."

Not a flicker of recognition, Lexie noted in frustration. "It's the fastest growing computer game company in the country right now." Melinda remained unmoved. Lexie took a deep breath and tried again to impress upon her mother why she should not denigrate Lewis further. "Or in other words, Lewis is a very wealthy and successful man, and destined to become even more so in the very near future."

"Thanks for the stellar introduction," Lewis said dryly, giving her a quelling look.

Lexie shrugged. Bringing up the cash value of anything was the quickest way to get her mother's attention.

"I don't understand," Melinda said, as contemptuous as ever with someone she considered an underling. "Why is he here, Alexandra? Why are you both dressed—or maybe I should say undressed—like this? Your father never mentioned a boyfriend."

"He's not my boyfriend," Lexie interrupted quickly.

To her chagrin, Melinda sighed in obvious relief.

A uniformed chauffeur appeared behind Melinda, his arms full of luggage. "Where should I put these, madam?"

Melinda gestured to the middle of the room. "You can set my things here."

Lexie gaped. "You're staying with me?"

Her mother huffed. "Well, I can hardly bunk at your father's ranch with him and Jezebel. And the lodgings in the area leave something to be desired. Actually, the whole town leaves something to be desired. I'll never understand why your father left Dallas. When we were married, we had such a lovely home there."

Here we go again. Lexie was aware that her mother blamed all of Lexie's shortcomings on the fact that she'd been raised in Texas.

"And speaking of home, I better mosey on back to mine," Lewis said tactfully, graciously closing the distance between them. His eyes met hers. He seemed to know she was as unnerved by her mother's sudden appearance on her doorstep as he was. "Lexie—"

She nodded, letting him know his decision to depart was the right one. Glad he seemed to understand that she had no control whatsoever over her mercurial mother, she squeezed his hand and looked him in the eye. "I'll call you," she promised.

Just as soon as I find out what my mother is really doing here.

FORTUNATELY, ONCE LEWIS got to the office, he finally managed to shake off the unsettling encounter with the Contessa. He was able to strike a deal that would get his line of computer games shelved in yet another retail chain. The prototypes of two games showed substantial improvement, and the talented graphics designer he had been trying to hire to work exclusively for his company finally accepted his offer.

At four-thirty, his assistant, Maxine Cossman, stuck her head in the door. A whiz at organization, the stout fifty-year-old with the curly red hair and thick glasses kept him on track. "Lexie Remington is here to see you," she remarked briskly. "I told her you had a prior engagement this evening. She hoped you would see her without an appointment anyway."

Lewis rocked all the way back in his chair. This was a pleasant, albeit somewhat inconvenient, surprise. "Send her in. And Maxine, you can go on to your yoga class if you want."

"Thanks."

Maxine disappeared and a few moments later Lexie sauntered in. She was wearing a pair of slim black jeans, a long-sleeved white T-shirt, a cropped red corduroy jacket and boots. She looked amazing. "You're supposed to be resting," Lewis chided as she neared, enveloping him in a drift of exotic perfume.

"Been there, done that," Lexie said sassily, perching on the front of his desk, just to his left.

Lewis tried to ignore the proximity of her long, sexy thigh next to his hand. Ignoring the jump of his pulse, he tilted his head at her and continued to regard her with lazy insouciance. "You're aware that if you don't follow doctor's orders, I'll be blamed."

She crossed her legs at the knee. "What's Riley going to do? Twist your arm?"

Lewis grinned at her soft, teasing tone. "Worse. He'll give me a guilt trip."

Lexie wrinkled her nose at him. "You look like you can handle a little remorse, provided it's balanced by a good time."

No kidding. It was all he could do to keep himself from dragging her down onto his lap and kissing her the way he had wanted to kiss her the night before, with no time limits and attempts at gentlemanly behavior. He didn't want to be gallant. He wanted to give in to temptation. But he knew pushing her too hard, too fast, would be a huge mistake on his part, so he held back.

"Is that what you're planning to give me?" He regarded her flirtatiously. "A good time?"

Flushing self-consciously, Lexie pushed away from his desk and bounded onto the floor. "Maybe we should just get down to business." Her gaze drifted over him, his body heating with each lingering visual caress.

Lewis tensed, aware his feelings were anything but transactional. Maybe his brothers and sister-in-law were right. Now was the time to level with Lexie, while boundaries were still being set. "About that style makeover..." he started carefully.

Lexie stripped off her jacket and regarded him purposefully. "I want to get started tonight," she stated, already pushing up the sleeves on her knit shirt. "Got a problem with that?"

"No sirree, I do not," he quipped, deciding to see where this makeover stuff took him, after all. He'd tell her about the misunderstanding later. "What about your mom? Are you just going to leave the Countess alone, during her first evening in Laramie?"

"She's sleeping. The jet lag and seven-hour time difference finally caught up with her."

"So for her it's midnight," Lewis guessed, glad Lexie had sought refuge with him, even if it was for work-related reasons.

"Right." Lexie lounged with her back to a metal file cabinet.

He strolled closer. "Does that mean she'll be awake when you get home at midnight?"

She made a face that would have been comical if not for the sudden vulnerability in her pretty turquoise eyes. "Doubtful. The Contessa usually sleeps until noon at home. She reserves her afternoons for shopping or hair appointments, her evenings for social events."

"Ah." Lewis watched Lexie walk over to inspect the half-dozen umbrellas. He could always remember to bring an umbrella. He could just never remember to take it home. What that meant, he wasn't sure he wanted to know.

Lexie picked up one emblazoned with the Stanford University logo. She inspected it, end to end. "The Contessa leads an exceptionally busy life, you know. She's a very important and socially well-connected person."

Lewis followed her over to the stand. He sensed she needed to vent, and he was only too happy to listen. "You don't have much respect for your mother, do you?" he asked in a low voice.

Lexie dropped the umbrella into the large, galvanized metal milk can. She picked up another he had picked up on one of his business trips. It was an unfortunate color of purple, but had been the only one available during the unexpected deluge he'd found himself in.

"No," she said, "I don't."

The lack of apology in her expressive turquoise eyes was interesting to say the least. As was the career path she had chosen. Why had Lexie chosen a profession that had her constantly catering to the whims of people much like her snobbish, self-involved mother? "Ever thought of having that kind of life yourself?" he asked, playing devil's advocate. She could have easily gone the pampered dilettante route, instead of working herself half to death.

She dropped the purple umbrella back into the can with a clang. "No, of course not. I'd be bored silly if all I did was go to parties."

The lusciousness of her full lips had his gaze returning to her face again. "Is that why you can't seem to slow down?"

Lexie mocked him with a look. "I *am* slowing down," she declared emphatically. "I spent the whole day in bed, pretending to sleep."

"Or avoiding your mother?"

She wrinkled her pretty nose at him, even as she inspected a small, rainbow-striped umbrella he'd also picked up on the run. "You are psychic," she said playfully.

He shook his head, watching Lexie close the child-sized umbrella and put it back in the can, quietly this time. Lewis would give anything if he could spend time with his own mother again. But it wasn't going to happen. They'd lost her to cancer when he was ten. "You ought to spend time with your mom while you have the chance," he advised soberly.

Silence fell as Lexie stuck her hands in her pockets and said nothing, which made Lewis wonder if Jake Remington weren't the only parent Lexie was fighting with. "How is your mom doing, by the way?" he asked gently, deciding to try a different tact.

She rocked forward and studied the scuffed toes of her red leather boots. "You saw the Contessa this morning."

Wishing he knew Lexie well enough to haul her into his arms and hold her there until the hurting stopped, Lewis edged close enough to inhale the fragrant softness of her skin and hair. "Physically, your mom looked great. But she just lost her husband. That can't be easy."

"Yeah." Tension tightened the delicate features of her face. "She'd never admit it, but I think she's finding widowhood a little tougher to navigate than she imagined."

Lewis heard the sympathy beneath the defiance in Lexie's low tone. "Which is maybe why she came over to visit you," he theorized.

The troubled look was back in Lexie's pretty eyes. "Maybe, but my mother never does anything without an agenda."

Lewis walked back over to his desk and shut down the e-mail and instant messaging system on his computer. "What agenda could she have here?" he asked. "Except to be close to you?"

"That's just it. I don't know." Lexie's teeth worried her lower lip as she inspected the mismatched furniture and state-of-the-art electronics in his office. "Financially, she's fine." She dropped down onto the black leather sofa in the corner. "Count Riccardo's lawyers read the will when I was over there. He had no other family left so Mother got everything—all the family jewelry, tons of money, the villa in Naples, the country house in Florence."

Lewis closed the distance between them and sat down next to her. "Well, that's good, isn't it?"

"You'd think so." She stretched her slender legs out in front of her. "But…"

"What?" he prodded.

"She seems so edgy. Restless."

Giving in to the need to comfort her, Lewis reached over and took her hand in his. "Isn't that to be expected?" he asked gently. "She just lost her companion of the last twenty years."

Lexie shook her head and left her hand clasped warmly in his. She ran the fingers of her free hand over the back of his. "They didn't really have that kind of marriage."

Trying not to get distracted by the heat of her caress, Lewis shifted his weight toward her. "What kind did they have?"

"Passionate, volatile." She swallowed hard. "They were both very old-world European in their outlook."

Lewis studied the veiled pain in her eyes. He tightened his hand protectively over hers. "I don't get what you're trying to say."

Lexie's voice took on an unhappy tone. "They both had lovers, lots of them, and they were okay with that."

Lewis could only envision how hard that must have been for Lexie, who would have been exposed to that from the tender age of six. Bad enough to have your parents divorced and remarried, living on different continents. To have one set openly cheating… "Kind of the opposite of your dad and Jenna," Lewis surmised compassionately.

"Yeah, those two are really devoted to each other." Lexie smiled reflectively. "Kind of like your Dad and Kate."

Lewis knew his own life would have been a lot harder had Kate Marten not stepped in to help him and the rest of his family deal with the loss of his mother. Kate's love and understanding had healed his family and brought love and laughter to their lives again. "We both lucked out in the stepmother department, didn't we?"

Lexie nodded. "So, are you ready to get to work?" she asked. Energetic as ever, she perched on the edge of the sofa.

Lewis kept a grip on her palm, wishing the situation were different. "Not quite yet," he said.

Lexie looked frustrated. "What's stopping you?"

Lewis frowned. "My previous plans for the evening."

"YOU'VE GOT A DATE." She didn't know why, but just the thought of him seeing someone else was very disheartening.

"With about sixteen people."

Now he had lost her.

"I'm hosting the monthly Laramie High School computer club get-together," Lewis explained. "The kids will be here at six." Noting the time, he said, "I've got to get the testing lab ready." An inviting smile curved his lips. "You can tag along if you like."

She regarded him in amazement. "You do this yourself?"

He shrugged his broad shoulders. "Why wouldn't I?"

Used to being around people who lorded their wealth and power over others at every opportunity, Lexie shook her head in bemusement. "You own an entire company."

"It doesn't mean I'm above getting out some game prototypes and ordering pizza and soft drinks." Lewis returned to his desk and typed in something on his computer screen. The menu for Mac Callahan's restaurant popped up. He gestured her over. "Anything here look good to you?"

Lexie moved behind his desk chair. She curved her hands over the back of it, as she bent down to scan the offerings from Laramie's favorite pizza place. "The hot wings," she said quickly.

Lewis turned to shoot her a glance, the side of his face lightly brushing the side of hers. "Not quite on your diet," he chided.

Refusing to acknowledge how sexy she found the brush of his evening beard against the softness of her skin, she shrugged.

Lewis turned back to the menu, clearly a man on a mission. "How about a white pizza?" he asked, after a moment. "Crust, olive oil, fresh mozzarella. Nothing there to get your acid reflux going, especially if we ask them to go easy on the basil and garlic."

Lexie appreciated the way he was taking care of her. No one—except her dad and Jenna—had done that for a very long time. "Sounds good," she said, surprised by the sudden huskiness of her voice. Aware the backs of her hands were still brushing the hard musculature of his shoulders, she stepped back and cleared her throat. "What is everyone else going to eat?"

"A little of everything," Lewis said, typing in the appropriate choices on his computer and then sending the delivery order via the Internet.

Doing her best to calm her racing heart, Lexie roamed the spacious office, which did as little to reflect Lewis's personality as his ridiculously out-of-fashion clothing. Both were things she could fix. In that way, she realized, she'd be taking care of him, too. Lexie paused to study one of the many awards hanging on the wall. "It's been a long time since I had Mac Callahan's pizza," she said in the most casual tone she could manage. "Mac still works there?"

"Along with his daughter, Casey," Lewis confirmed with a smile. He rose and crossed to her side.

"Funny how some things never change," Lexie continued awkwardly, acutely aware of how arousing she found Lewis's formidable size and masculine strength.

Oblivious to the ardent nature of her thoughts, he led the way out of the office and down the hall to a testing laboratory.

"This is where the kids are going to meet?" Lexie asked, wondering if he wanted to kiss her—really kiss her—as much as she wanted to kiss him.

He winked at her. "Since you're the one who's got me running behind schedule, make yourself useful." Lewis handed her a box of computer games with the McCabe logo. "And put one of these at every station, please."

Glad for the distraction from her thoughts, Lexie complied.

"How did you get involved in this?" she asked after a moment.

"The kids asked me to sponsor a monthly event. I know

what a great group it is—I was president of the computer club when I was at Laramie High School—so of course I said yes."

"That's really nice of you," she said sincerely.

Shrugging off the compliment, he moved to the other side of the room, dropping a game CD at every station. "It's the least I could do," he told her. "I know how hard it is to be a computer nerd amidst all the athletes and popular kids."

Lexie hadn't ever really fit in, either. "And yet look at where you are today." They met again, in the center of the room.

"Right here." Lewis wrapped both arms around her waist and drew her against him. Without warning, every secret fantasy she had ever had about him turned real. His voice turned husky. "With you."

Lexie trembled at the feel of his hard body, pressed up against her. His fingers brushed down her face, stroked along her jaw. Her skin heated and the pulse at the base of her neck fluttered wildly. Determined to keep some connection with reality, she batted her eyelids and teased, "Why, Lewis McCabe." She affected her best Texas belle drawl. "Are you hitting on me?"

Sifting both his hands through her hair, he lowered his head and tilted his face slightly to the right. He moved in even closer, all sexy, determined male. His eyes darkened to a smoky blue-gray. "What if I am?"

Lexie moaned as his lips captured hers and he invaded her mouth with his tongue. If the caress the night before had been full of promise and yet restrained, this one was so deliberately sensual it took her breath away. No one had ever kissed her like this, as if he had waited his entire life for her. No one had ever made her feel like this, she realized—so warm and wanted and feminine. His lips made a slow, mesmerizing exploration of hers. Swept up in the embrace, Lexie forgot she was supposed to be forging a strictly professional relationship with him. He kissed her until she moaned softly and clung to him, until every inch of her was tingling with need. Lexie hadn't meant for anything like this to happen but she was powerless to resist. Lewis's seduction left her vulnerable, and aching for more. It left her wanting to see where this would lead. Had it not been for the sudden, jarring sound of a phone ringing on the wall just behind them, and the collection of youthful voices coming ever closer, who knew what would have happened next.

The awareness they were no longer alone forced them to draw apart. To her surprise—and yes, pleasure—Lewis looked as completely affected as she felt, even as the guilt that she shouldn't be getting involved with a "client" filtered through her. She had done that to disastrous results once before. Did she really want to do it again? Mold a man into every woman's fantasy only to have him leave her behind, once he had gotten what he wanted…?

Her emotions in turmoil, she turned away from Lewis and spotted a group of high school kids coming down the hall, then filtering into the computer testing lab. It seemed to be about half guys and half girls, Lexie noted. All were dressed in jeans and gaming T-shirts. Name tags were plastered to their chests. Most of the kids, like Lewis, were somewhat challenged in the personal style department. But all were very happy to see him. He was obviously a hero to them, and Lexie could see why. Not many men as successful as Lewis would take the time to mentor a group of high school kids.

"What game are we trying out tonight?" Percy McNamara asked eagerly.

Lewis moved to the center of the group. "It's called 'The Deal Maker.' It's a game that puts the player in mythical business situations. The goal is to win each task without losing your moral compass or compromising your ethics."

A young girl with frizzy hair and glasses teased, "Are you trying to educate us, Mr. McCabe?"

Lewis winked. "Or teach you all how to become self-made millionaires without landing in jail."

Guffaws all around. The room reverberated with excitement. Lexie enjoyed seeing Lewis in his element. It gave her a sense of what kind of father he would be one day. "You've got ninety minutes until the pizza arrives," Lewis said, directing the eager group to their stations. He returned to Lexie's side and eased her toward a gaming station, too.

"THANKS FOR HOSTING this event, as always," the club sponsor, Josephine Holdsworth, told Lewis as the three of them walked toward the lobby. The computer science teacher at LHS was pretty and single and—if Lexie's instincts were correct—as romantically interested in the school organization's most famous benefactor as she was.

"My pleasure," Lewis replied, showing no evidence that he knew the pert redhead had a giant-sized crush on him.

"And thank you for attending our meeting, too," Josephine continued, regarding Lexie warmly. Josephine paused to shrug on her coat, before stepping out into the brisk autumn air. "I don't think the students know what you do for a living, but I certainly do. The spread they did on your clients in *In-Fashion Magazine* last year was downright amazing."

"Thanks," Lexie said.

"I'd heard from some of the other faculty who grew up here, too, that you were from this area." Josephine's expression faltered slightly. She swallowed and completed her fact-finding mission. "But I had no idea you were *dating* Lewis."

Lexie blushed, aware that if she let this misconception stand it would be all over Laramie in no time. "No. We're not. I would never..." she stammered, wishing she had never agreed to let him employ her as his stylist. Then this wouldn't be such a dilemma. She could let the rumors fly and just see where their obvious attraction to one another led. But she had a professional reputation to protect. Lexie gulped and forced herself to continue, "Lewis is a cl—"

"Friend," Lewis interrupted, before she could finish the word. He stepped slightly in front of her. "Lexie and I are *friends,* Josephine."

Josephine beamed. "Oh." She fished in her handbag for her car keys. "Well, in that case, perhaps Lexie would consider making an appearance at the LHS Career Night on Tuesday evening, too? The students would love to hear about your profession."

Lexie smiled. "I'd be glad to participate."

"Great! We'll see you both then," she announced cheerfully.

Lewis watched as Josephine exited, then turned back to Lexie. "Sorry I had to cut you off like that."

Lexie studied the guilty expression on his handsome face. She planted her boots firmly on the marble lobby floor. "Why did you?"

He moved toward her, not stopping until they stood toe to toe. "I didn't want word getting out that I had hired you to help me."

She propped her hands on her hips and lifted her chin. "Don't you think they're going to figure it out when you start looking a whole lot different after spending concentrated time with me?"

Lewis's probing glance made a leisurely tour of her body before returning to her eyes. "Well, maybe not so much if people thought we were dating," he offered in an offhand tone.

"Right," Lexie said dryly, savvy enough to realize when someone was embarrassed by what she did for a living. "Then they would just think you were whipped. That'd be sooo much better."

Lewis caught her by the arms and turned her to face him. "If word got out we were dating, would that be so bad?"

She ignored the warmth of his fingers that penetrated the

layers of her clothing. "Yes. You're a client," she reminded him, delicately extricating herself from his grip.

"But people here don't know that," he insisted.

"But I do," Lexie retorted stubbornly. "And I don't date clients, Lewis."

He paused to come up with a new strategy. "Then we'll just have to tell people we're spending time together because we're friends."

"You'd rather do that than let word get out you hired a stylist to help you change your image?" she asked in disbelief.

"Yes." Lewis's jaw was set.

Her heart pounding, Lexie fell silent as she studied the half-hidden apology in his eyes. "You're that ashamed of what I'm trying to do for you?" she asked, even as she struggled to ignore her reaction to his nearness.

Lewis released a frustrated breath. "Is that a trick question?" He peered at her from behind his lenses.

Temper flaring, Lexie rummaged through her shoulder bag for her keys. Thank heavens her stepmother and father had loaned her a ranch pickup to drive while she was in town, so she didn't have to rely on Lewis McCabe for her transportation home. "It's an honest inquiry," she replied in a voice laced with steel. She paused to look up at him and let their glances mesh, sorry now she had kissed him at all. "And yours was an honest answer." She held the keys so tight they pinched her palm. Chin held high, she marched past him, toward the exit.

Lewis fixed her with an exasperated look. "Where are you going?"

She barreled past. "None of your concern."

"Lexie. Come on."

She ignored the entreaty in his tone and tossed him a withering look over her shoulder as she sped through the double glass doors. Bad enough she had doubts about her chosen vocation—she didn't need to hear them from him! "Find yourself another stylist to help you, Lewis," she snapped. "I'm out of here."

Chapter Four

"Please, Mrs. R., you've got to help me," Lewis said.

Jenna Remington shook her head at Lewis. "To tell you the truth, Lewis, after what you said to Lexie last night, I think it's hopeless."

"I didn't mean to insult her." Lewis followed Jenna around the stylish dress boutique.

With a shrug of her slender shoulders, Jenna glided past rows of couture wedding dresses bearing the Jenna Lockhart Remington label, to a rack of equally dazzling evening dresses. "But you did insult her profession and hurt her feelings, Lewis. So maybe it's best you just let Lexie be."

Lewis ignored the lanky teenage girl who paraded out of the dressing room area in a bright blue beaded evening gown. "I can't leave things the way they are between us."

"Just a minute, hon," Jenna told Lewis. She swept over to the customer and helped her onto the pedestal in front of the three-way mirror. "What do you think of this one, Sydney?"

"I don't know. It looks so...adult," Sydney said, turning this way and that in the beautiful gown. She lifted her gazellelike neck. "I look like I'm twenty-three or something."

"Not the look you're going for," Jenna surmised thoughtfully while Lewis waited impatiently for them to finish so he could get back to finding a way to get back in Lexie's good graces.

Sydney flung her waist-length copper hair over her shoulder. "No! Looking older than you are can really date an actress!" She lifted her hair off the nape of her neck experimentally.

"What age would you like to appear?" Jenna asked seriously.

"Seventeen. The same age I'm going to be in the movie I just did," Sydney replied, studying how she looked with her hair twisted in a knot on top of her head.

The door to the boutique jangled. Swearing inwardly at the additional interruption, Lewis turned in the direction of the sound and saw Lexie and her mother walk in.

As always, the sight of Lexie took his breath away. His spirits sank as he took in the arctic chill in her turquoise blue eyes when their gazes met.

He had really, really screwed up.

Before he had a chance to say anything, Sydney clapped a hand to her chest. Completely ignoring the Contessa, who was dripping in jewels and some sort of fur stole, Sydney gasped in excitement. She hopped off the pedestal and rushed toward Lexie. "I can't believe it! Lexie Remington, in the flesh! Me, in the same room with the hottest stylist in Hollywood!"

Lexie shot Lewis a brief, withering glare, as if to say, "See? Some people do appreciate me," then turned back to Sydney with a smile. She extended a gracious hand. "Hi. And you're...?"

"Sydney Mazero. Hottest new thing in Hollywood." The young girl blushed self-consciously. "I hope, anyway."

"Sydney's movie—*Calamity Sue*—premieres in Austin at the end of the week," Jenna explained.

Sydney's head bobbed up and down. "And I'm still trying to find something to wear that—sorry, Jenna—doesn't look I'm dressing up in my mother's clothes!"

Jenna smiled, patient as ever. "No offense taken. My designs are for the older set."

"Could you help me find something, Lexie? Please?" Sydney clasped her hands in front of her in mute supplication.

"Lexie's on vacation," Jenna interrupted.

"Alexandra," the Contessa interrupted, even more preemptively, "is going to Dallas with me."

Lexie tensed. "No, I'm not, Mother."

"Alexandra," the Contessa corrected, "I thought we had agreed a few days of shopping and staying in a five-star hotel would do wonders for you."

"Shopping isn't fun to me, Mother. It's work. And as Jenna said, I'm on vacation." Lexie glared at Lewis again, letting him know she was sorry she had ever agreed to forget that and help him.

Sydney looked crestfallen. "I understand," she said softly. "I'm sorry I put you on the spot by asking. I know you only take the A-list actors now. It's just the way the business works."

"Actually," Lexie said, pausing to give Lewis another telling glare, "I'd be glad to help you pull together an ensemble for the premiere, Sydney. But first I have to tend to a few things, so if you could…just wait…"

"I'll be in the dressing room." Sydney picked up her skirt and dashed off.

"That was really nice of you," Lewis said.

"Wow," Lexie replied sweetly, "how nice of you to approve."

Ouch.

The phone rang behind the counter and a saleswoman picked it up. "Just a moment," she said, putting the caller on hold. "Lexie, Constantine Romeo's assistant is on the phone. Apparently, Constantine wants you to help him create a look for the European tour of his new movie."

The Contessa's eyes lit with interest. "Isn't that the young man who…?"

"Yes, Mother, it is." Lexie looked at the salesperson, who was still holding the phone. "Tell him thanks but no thanks. And if his assistant calls again, just do us both a favor and don't tell me about it."

"Okay. Sorry, Lexie."

"No problem."

Looking out the window, Lewis saw a limo pull up at the curb and a uniformed driver get out. "Alexandra," the Contessa implored, "I really want you to come with me."

"I really don't want to go."

The Contessa glanced at her watch. "Fine," she snapped. "I'll go alone. But when I get back you and I are going to spend time together."

Lexie merely nodded. The tension in the room lessened markedly as the limo pulled away with Melinda inside.

"I think I'll go see if Sydney needs anything," Jenna murmured. She and the saleswoman ducked into the back, leaving Lewis and Lexie to square off with each other.

"For the record, I think you should forgive me," Lewis began.

"For the record, I think you're an idiot."

Lewis shrugged. "No argument there."

She snorted in a most unladylike fashion. "Why did you even hire me if you didn't believe in what I do?"

He edged closer. "That's complicated."

She glared at him, her breasts rising and falling with every infuriated breath she took. "I'm still listening."

Lewis continued. "I've been hearing for a long time from everyone in my family just how bad my taste in clothes is."

Lexie's gaze swept over his orange, brown and white-striped bellbottom pants, brown Nehru jacket and scuffed leather boots. "No kidding," she said curtly.

"So I know I need help, but I'm also a guy, Lexie." He waited until she angled her chin up at him before continuing. "And the fact is real men don't need any help picking out their clothes or deciding how to get their hair cut or whatever. Real men do just fine on their own."

Without warning, Lexie began to laugh.

He scowled. "It's not that funny."

"Yes," she countered, refusing to let him take himself too seriously, "it is."

"All right." Lewis rubbed his jaw ruefully. "Maybe it is. All I know is that I need help in the wardrobe department. I just don't want to need help. I want to be as skilled at picking out the right clothes as I am at designing a software game, and I'm just not."

"I get that." She glided nearer, a mixture of interest and compassion filling her turquoise eyes. "I don't get how you got stuck in the Eighties." She looked him over again. "Where do you even *find* those clothes?"

Somehow, Lewis managed not to look too embarrassed. "Vintage clothing shops, near Stanford University. I've got a standing account at a couple of places and they just send me things in my size every three months."

"And charge you an arm and a leg to boot, I bet."

Once again, she'd hit the nail on the head. "Clothes like this aren't that easy to find."

Lexie sighed. "I can only imagine."

"It's a look that worked well for me for the past ten years. As long as I was wearing vintage, I was a trendsetter. The clothes just enhanced my rep as an eccentric genius."

"So why change?"

"Because despite all my business success, I'm starting to feel like a geek again."

"But at the same time you're afraid to change."

"What if the clothes I select make me the kind of joke I

was in high school?" His jaw tightened. "Or don't you remember?" he asked.

She reached over and gently touched his arm. "Unfortunately, I do. The polyester pants, the bowling shirts with your name on the chest and a lightning bolt on the back." She withdrew her hand and shook her head.

"Yeah, well, what can I say?" Lewis shrugged and settled on one of the sofas in the center of the dress salon. "Einstein probably didn't know how to dress, either."

Lexie plopped down beside him. She stretched out her long, black-suede-clad legs. "At least you put yourself in good company."

Lewis studied the toes of her black leather boots. "You know what I mean."

"Yes," Lexie said, favoring him with a sexy half smile that made him want to take her in his arms and kiss her again, "I do."

Silence fell between them, more companionable this time. "I still want to hire you."

Lexie bounded to her feet. "Even though it embarrasses the hell out of you."

Lewis stood and moved close enough to drink in the sweet, clean fragrance of her skin and hair. "I'll get over it," he vowed.

To his chagrin, she looked unconvinced.

"Please, Lexie, you're the only one I trust to help me."

She stared up at him thoughtfully. "If I agree to do this—and it's still a big *if,* Lewis McCabe—then you have to promise me you won't back out on me, that you'll be honest and forthright with me every step of the way and, most important of all, you'll let everyone in town know that you have hired me to give you a new look and aren't the least bit embarrassed about that."

Damn, she drove a hard bargain. Lewis rubbed at the tense muscles in the back of his neck. "I respect what you do for a living, Lexie. And I respect the heck out of you. So you've got yourself a deal."

He just prayed she never found out about the comic mix-up that occurred the first night he landed on her doorstep, hoping to ask for a date, instead of professional help. Because after what had just happened between them, Lewis knew Lexie would not take news like that well.

"SO HOW DID YOUR CONSULTATION with Sydney Mazero go?" Lewis asked Lexie when she joined him for a business lunch at the Wagon Wheel restaurant on Main Street.

"Good." Lexie sipped her iced tea. "I'm going to help her pull something together for the *Calamity Sue* premiere in Austin on Saturday evening."

Lewis paused to study her, then fished the sprig of mint out of his glass and set it aside. "That was really nice of you to help her out," he said, his low voice and tender glance reminding her of the kiss they had shared two nights before.

As their gazes locked, there was a moment of sizzling awareness. Forcing back her emotions, Lexie said, "It's not as selfless as it sounds. I'm always happier when I'm busy." *And don't have time to think about the obvious deficiencies of my personal life.* She forced a smile. "Clothing design is a hobby of mine. And I really enjoy helping people on the way up who are still living a more-or-less ordinary life. Besides, Sydney's a sweet kid."

"And you're a sweet lady," he said, a glint of approval in his eyes.

Lexie tensed. "Don't do that," she said, even as she felt herself leaning toward him.

He rubbed the pad of his thumb across the top of hers, making her feel gloriously alive for the first time in months. "Do what?" he demanded playfully.

Lexie set her menu down, her frustration with the situation building. "Don't hit on me." *Don't seduce me into making another mistake....*

Lewis's blue-gray eyes filled with unrepentant mischief, even as he released his hand and sat back. He crossed his arms, the muscles of his chest bunching beneath the thick cotton of his knit shirt. "You think that was hitting on you?"

Obviously not. Which begged the question, how would she react if he really made a play for her? Lexie's shoulders stiffened as she felt heat rise from her chest, into her neck and face. "I think it was preliminary—a warm-up to more kisses." She looked him in the eye, marshalling all her defenses. "They're not going to happen, Lewis. I make it a policy not to mix pleasure with business."

He frowned. "You did with Constantine Romeo. At least that's the story, although I never actually saw you photographed with him at any premieres or awards ceremonies or anything, when you guys were supposedly together."

Lexie felt her flush deepen. The romance had been a well-known fact in Laramie, because she had left Texas with the budding movie star over her family's objections. Then she had lived with Romeo until he began to get really famous, at which point she had stayed on in the apartment the two of them had been renting, and he had moved onward and upward. "That's because he never took me to premieres." She pretended she wasn't embarrassed about that.

Lewis accepted the basket of crispy golden-brown onion rings the waitress set on the table. He added a couple to a small white plate, passed it over to Lexie, and then helped himself to a few, too. "Why not?" he frowned in disapproval. "If the two of you were dating..."

She added salt to her onion rings, then cut into one with a fork. "Romeo didn't want his relationship with me to interfere with his image of a big-time Hollywood bachelor." She paused. "His publicist told him it would make him more of a heartthrob if women thought he was available."

Lewis poured a circle of ketchup on his plate. "And you went along with it?"

Lexie let the delicious blend of sweet Texas onion and crispy coating melt on her tongue as she took a bite. Damn, that was good, she thought. She was glad Lewis had ordered the popular appetizer ahead of her arrival. "At the time I was as invested in Romeo's career success as he was. I thought he needed me to help him refine his look and build his public persona as a heartthrob." Funny, how dispassionate she could sound about that, in retrospect. In some ways, it was as if it had happened to a whole different person. In other ways, the hurt and humiliation she had suffered were still all too present.

Lewis piled more onion rings on both their plates. "Obviously, you were successful at that," he told her admiringly. "Romeo's one of the hottest leading men on the movie scene today."

Lexie nodded, wondering if Lewis secretly wanted her to make him into a ladies' man. She didn't know why but she didn't like the idea of Lewis with other women, period.

He added more ketchup to his plate. "Do you think Constantine Romeo wants you to get back together with him? Is that why he had his assistant calling you today?"

Lexie shook her head. "His assistant's been calling me ever since Constantine and I broke up two years ago, every time he has something big coming up. Seems he can't find a stylist who 'gets' him the way I did, when we were together."

Lewis probed her face, his expression unreadable. "But you're not interested," he guessed.

Lexie frowned, "No, I learned my lesson about guys who say one thing and feel another."

Lewis tensed, and in that instant, could not have seemed

farther away from her intellectually—which would be good, given that she was trying to stay emotionally uninvolved with him. However, it was not helpful, in the professional sense. "Um…before we actually get started on your makeover—"

"Do you have to call it that?" he asked, scowling.

Lexie chuckled, pulling her notepad and pen from her shoulder bag. "What would you prefer I call it?"

Lewis thought a moment. "Retooling?"

She chuckled, already scribbling notes. "You need help in that area, too?"

"Oh, man." He released a long frustrated breath. "I can't seem to stop putting my foot in my mouth around you."

Feeling good and in command, Lexie tossed him a reassuring smile. "Relax, genius, I'm just yanking your chain a bit." Gathering her thoughts, Lexie studied the notepad in front of her. "Okay, first and foremost, I need to know what prompted your desire for a 'retooling.' Is there someone else involved that you are trying to please?"

Briefly, Lewis looked like a deer caught in the headlights. Then his expression became hooded and mysterious once again. "Like who?" he asked cautiously.

"Like a woman." She kept her tone purposefully flip.

A guilty flush moved up his neck and into his face.

"I thought so." She took a moment to contemplate, so she could be as professional as she needed to be. "I need to know who she is," Lexie stated bluntly, telling herself all the while that the fact Lewis lusted after someone else was of no concern to her, since they were not—repeat, not—getting romantically involved with each other.

"I'd rather not say," Lewis said stiffly.

Lexie leaned closer. "You have to tell me."

"Why?"

Lexie sat back and regarded him skeptically. "Because I

can't help you unless I know who you want to impress." Because I want you to tell me the truth!

"Why can't we just go for an all-around good look?"

Lexie clamped her lips together. "Because different women respond to different types of guys and I need to know what type of woman you are trying to impress. So who it is?" Lexie insisted doggedly. "Is it Josephine Holdsworth, the computer science teacher at LHS?"

"Absolutely not." Lewis leaned back as plates of piping hot chicken-fried steak were set in front of them.

Lexie dragged a fork through her mashed potatoes and gravy. "Josephine has a crush on you, you know." She looked at him through her lashes to gauge his reaction. It wasn't good.

"No, I didn't know," Lewis said, his expression implacable. "And for the record, I don't think of her that way."

Lexie savored the peppery cream gravy and crispy fried steak. "Then who do you think of that way?" she asked.

Once again, he was silent.

Frustration bubbled up inside Lexie. She set down her fork with a thud. "You either tell me or I leave," she said before she could stop herself.

"Okay, okay. It's....it's...." Lewis looked around the restaurant, seemingly in a panic. He focused on a golden-haired young woman in overalls and a flannel work shirt, standing at the cash register with a takeout bag. "It's Susie Carrigan," he said.

Lexie blinked. "My cousin by marriage, Susie? The landscape architect?"

Lewis averted her gaze. "She owns her own nursery and garden store, too."

"Yes, I know." Susie was as wild about perennials and annuals as Lewis was about computer software. "But... Susie has never mentioned you in that way."

Lewis shrugged, still not looking Lexie in the eye. "Like you said, she barely knows I'm alive," he muttered, taking a long gulp of iced tea. "So maybe it's not a good thing that I aim to please her. Maybe I should go for a more general approach."

Keeping her feelings to herself, Lexie promised sweetly, "If it is Susie's attention you want to get, then obviously we can do that."

He paused long enough for her to draw even more conclusions. "Why do you look angry?"

Why, indeed. "Because," Lexie snapped, losing momentary control. She leaned forward urgently and dropped her voice to a low hiss. "I thought—" *or was it hoped* "—you had more depth! I thought this whole makeover thing was for the sake of your business, because you wanted to impress some investment bankers so you could get the money to expand or something."

Lewis shrugged, looking taken aback by her sudden outburst. "Well, that, too." He began to eat his green beans.

Lexie's own lunch suddenly went from delicious to distasteful. "Hugo Boss or Armani will impress investment bankers." Lexie looked over at Susie, who smiled at them. Susie ambled over, take-out bag in hand.

"That's not likely to work on a woman who spends her days kneeling in the dirt."

"Hi, Lexie." Susie leaned down to kiss Lexie's cheek and give her a hug, which she returned. It wasn't Susie's fault Lewis McCabe was a slug!

"Hi, Susie." Lexie gestured politely at her luncheon companion. "You of course know Lewis McCabe."

"Sure." Susie couldn't have looked less interested. She smiled and greeted Lewis, too, albeit very briefly. "Listen, I'd love to stay and chat but I've got to take lunch back to the rest of the crew. Catch you later, Lexie?"

"You can count on it," Lexie murmured, knowing it would be soon since Lexie's stepmother, Jenna, and Susie's stepmother, Meg, were both Lockhart sisters. All four of the fabulously beautiful and accomplished women resided in Laramie with their families. Get-togethers were held weekly.

Susie waved and strode off.

"Forget I ever said I was interested in Susie," Lewis said, as soon as she was out of earshot.

Lexie set her jaw. She had never stolen a man from another woman, and she wasn't about to start now. "Nope."

"It's obviously not going to work between her and me." Lewis tugged at his collar as if it were choking him, which was ridiculous since the first button was completely undone.

Despite her unexpected personal interest in the situation, Lexie forced herself to concentrate on the task ahead. "It's my job to see that it will."

He studied her openly. "I'd rather concentrate on the retooling of my image."

Lexie, too. But she couldn't divert Lewis's attention away from her cousin, and turn it to herself instead. It wouldn't be right, even if that was exactly what her heart wanted her to do.

Chapter Five

Dark clouds threatened the horizon as Lewis passed a slow-moving pickup loaded with hay and resumed the stated speed limit. "Your father would kill me if he knew we were driving to Dallas today."

Lexie glanced at the flat, barren landscape on either side of the interstate highway. After miles of little but sage brush, cattle and oil fields, civilization loomed up ahead. "We're not driving. You are."

Lewis grinned. It felt so good to be spending time with Lexie this way. "You know what I mean. You're supposed to be at home, in bed, resting." The fact she didn't seem at all inclined to do so did little to mitigate his guilt.

Lexie replied in her usual carefree manner, "Two hours in the car never killed anyone."

Lewis had to admit that the color was back in her cheeks, and the smudges beneath her eyes—while still there—were fading slightly. Nevertheless, he felt compelled to be protective. "I doubt that is what your doctor would say."

"Oh, pshaw. The reflux is calmed down considerably, thanks to the meds your brother prescribed two days ago. And as for the exhaustion, well—" Lexie paused and stretched languidly, lifting her arms above her head "—I just spent the last two hours sleeping." She stifled another yawn.

Lewis directed his glance from the luscious curves of her breasts. He struggled to keep his attention on the growing traffic up ahead. "Which makes me feel only slightly less guilty," he said.

A fat raindrop appeared on his windshield, then another. Lexie squinted at the charcoal-gray sky. "You need to lighten up," she said, as the rain began to come down in earnest. "You know that?"

He switched on his wiper blades. "And you need to get serious about taking care of yourself," he returned as the blades swished back and forth.

She favored him with a mock salute. "Yes, sir."

Trying not to imagine how easily it would be for her to wrap him around her little finger, Lewis asked, "Where are we going first?"

Lexie scowled at the lightning flashing in the distance. "Galleria Mall. You have a hair appointment at a salon there."

Lewis tensed. He had agreed to new clothes. Nothing more. "What's wrong with my hair?" he demanded, turning his SUV onto the Dallas Parkway. He could see the three-story mall up ahead, sandwiched by three skyscrapers, multiple parking garages and luxury hotels.

"Let me count the ways," Lexie said as he drove slowly into the concrete parking garage. "For starters, it's all one length."

Lewis frowned and continued prowling the aisles until he found a space. "Well, I told them to cut it that way." He eased his SUV into the space, then cut the ignition.

Lexie shrugged as she got out of the car. "If you're going to spike it like that," Lexie continued after they got out of the car, "then your hair should be varied lengths that better conform to your head." She eyed him thoughtfully, then reached up to run a few strands of his hair between her fingertips.

A cool, wet wind blew through the garage. It was, Lewis found, exactly what he needed to lower his quickly heating body temperature. "If you say so." He shoved his hands in the pockets of his jacket and fell into step beside her.

The rain outside poured off the roof of the garage and onto the streets and sidewalk like a waterfall coming over a cliff. "I know so." Lexie paused in front of the elevators that would take them directly to the interior of the glass-roofed mall.

After the doors slid open, Lewis followed her inside. He leaned against one rail, she leaned against the other. Sexual electricity surged between them. Aware all he really wanted to do was take Lexie in his arms and kiss her again, he forced himself to concentrate on this makeover business. "I'm not going to look stupid, am I?"

Lexie rolled her eyes and crossed one boot-clad ankle over the other. "More than you already do?" she retorted, jumping lazily to attention as the elevator doors slid open once again. "I don't see how that's possible."

Lewis followed her out into the glass-roofed mall. "You have a smart mouth."

She cocked her head at him. "And you need more faith in me. Have any of the celebrities I've helped ever looked foolish?"

He shrugged, aware he was the last person on earth, as style-challenged as he was, to assess that. "I don't even know who most of your clients are," he told her, pausing next to her as she studied the mall directory for the exact location of the salon, "and even if I did, I doubt I'd be the one to try and figure out if they were in style or out."

She touched her finger to the map. "Well, they haven't! They're constantly being touted in fashion magazines as having the Look."

Lexie glanced at the store signs overhead to figure out where they were, then grabbed his sleeve and headed off like an explorer on an expedition. "I'm going to do the same for you."

Imagining how his brothers would razz him for this, Lewis kept pace with her. "Turn me into a babe magnet," he said dryly.

For some reason he didn't understand, his description irritated her.

She pressed her lips together. "You bet."

For the heck of it, Lewis decided to keep going, offering the smug prediction, "I'll be so damned sexy I'll have to beat the women off with a stick."

This time she glared at him. "Absolutely," she snapped back.

Lewis caught her by the elbow before she could stomp her way into the hoity-toity salon. He swung her back around to face him, so fast and hard she slammed up against his chest. She caught her breath. So did he. It was all he could do not to wrap his arms around her and deliver a kiss unlike either one of them had experienced, other shoppers or not.

But the sense that she would not appreciate him putting the moves on her during business hours kept him from following through. Reluctantly, he released his hold on her and stepped back. "Now who is full of it?" he asked, knowing that a simple haircut would not make a guy like him into the next World's Sexiest Man.

Lexie smiled slowly. "Oh, ye of little faith."

LEWIS SLIPPED HIS wire-rimmed glasses back on and stared at his reflection in the mirror. He seemed hardly able to comprehend the difference thirty minutes in the right barber's chair had made. He whistled softly. "Wow."

Lexie smiled, thrilled at the way the haircut had turned out. Jean-Paul had cut Lewis's thick, light brown hair so it perfectly framed the masculine shape of his head and face. He looked sexy and handsome in a breezy, casual, guy-next-door way. "Like it, huh?" She studied the short, thick, rumpled layers.

Lewis shook his head. "I look…"

Lexie turned so she was facing him, her back to the mirror. "Amazing," she answered for him.

Lewis chuckled, obviously embarrassed, not just by the attention he was getting from Lexie and Jean-Paul, but other patrons in the salon. People couldn't seem to stop looking at him in admiration and awe. "I wouldn't go that far," he muttered.

"I would." She stepped back, giving him wide berth, as Lewis got out of the chair. "Wait until we get some new clothes on you and substitute contact lenses for glasses," she promised as the two of them headed for the reception desk to pay.

"No way." Lewis glanced down at her and chided, "The glasses stay."

Lexie cocked her head. "You'd look really cute without them," she predicted.

Lewis paused at the front desk and handed over his credit card. "Yeah, but then my face would be naked."

"Got a problem exposing yourself to scrutiny, huh?" she goaded, as they headed out of the salon, amidst many admiring glances.

"To the general public, yes." Lewis took her elbow and steered her out of the path of ten excited teenagers.

Feeling her blood sugar slip a little—another indication she wasn't quite as rejuvenated as she'd like—Lexie headed straight for the ice-cream shop she'd noted on the mall directory. "How bad is your vision?" she asked as she followed the smell of freshly baked waffle cones.

"Let's just say if I were to take off my glasses and look at your face it would be like looking at it through a soft-focus lens."

That might have its advantages, Lexie thought. At least for her…er, the woman in Lewis's life. She was *not* the woman in Lewis McCabe's life. She had to remember that. He was just a friend, and a client. "Ever thought of getting laser surgery?" Lexie studied the menu hanging on the wall.

"Nope." Lewis paused next to her.

Unable to decide between the double dark chocolate and the mocha, Lexie slanted him a glance. "Or having people call you L.J. instead of Lewis?"

He shrugged his broad shoulders carelessly and moved over to view the substantial list of fruit, candy and nut mix-ins. "As much as I revere having my grandfather's moniker for my middle name, and loathe the fact my parents gave me a nerdy name like Lewis…"

"Yes, with a name like that, how could you help but turn out to be a wealthy genius?"

Lewis studied her with mock gravity as the line of customers inched forward. "Are you making fun of me?"

Lexie knew, from their youth, how much Lewis had hated his first name. As a kid, he had complained—and been teased—about it constantly. "I'm making fun of the people who've made fun of you." Plus, she liked yanking his chain, and more importantly still, he seemed to like it when she gave him a bit of a hard time.

They placed their orders and the concoctions were mixed on the cold marble slab and piled into freshly baked waffle cones.

After they'd paid, they settled at a table in the corner.

Lexie licked some of the ice cream that dripped down the side of the cone. "The point is," she said, picking up the conversation where they'd left off, "a name can convey 'cool' before a person ever sets eyes on you."

Lewis bit the top off his cone. "Which is why I have McCabe for a last name," he told her smugly.

"I get your point about that." Lexie took pains to deliberately misunderstand. "You do have some fine-looking, über-successful sibs."

Lewis's eyes lit up, his love of his family evident. "And we're all different," he added thoughtfully. "Kevin's law and order. Will's the adventurer. Brad's a cowboy. Riley's a healer. Laurel's the rescuer."

The only one not described aptly was him, Lexie thought. "And you're the shy one who knows how to conjure up fun, in the way of highly entertaining computer games."

He leaned toward her with a slow, sexy smile. Lexie noted she seemed to have hit the nail on the head.

"I'm not restricted to just those, you know." His free hand covered hers, transmitting a warmth that went from the top of her head to her toes. "There are all kinds of games, Lexie."

Reluctantly, she forced herself to return to the business at hand. "Back to the issue of your switching over to contacts." She cleared her throat. "Some of my clients…"

His seductive smile faded. "Let's get something straight, Lexie. I'm not most of your clients. I don't care if people like seeing me with eyeglasses or not. I like wearing them. End of conversation."

She smiled and went back to eating ice cream, and could feel her blood sugar spike.

"Now what?" he demanded.

Lexie shrugged and pretended to do a little people-watching over his shoulder. Although the truth was she could have cared less what anyone else in the mall was doing. Slowly, she turned back to him. "You're kind of tough when you get riled up."

Lewis sat back. "And you like that?"

She swallowed another delicious mouthful of premium chocolate ice cream. "It's a new side of you," she allowed matter-of-factly. "One I'd like to see more of."

He demolished the rest of his cone in two bites, rubbed a

paper napkin across his lips. "You're only saying that because you haven't seen me lose my temper."

Lexie lifted an eyebrow. "You have a temper?"

Lewis shrugged. "Doesn't everyone?"

Lexie decided not to go there. "What do you do when you lose your temper?"

"Depends."

"On?" She regarded him demurely.

"Where I am, who I'm with."

"Suppose you're with your brothers." Lexie finished her ice cream, too. "What would happen if you lost your composure?"

"Depends on what started it, but most likely there would be some foul language and hurling things, and if I'm really ticked off I might throw a punch at something inanimate."

So, he was as passionate as she suspected, deep down. Lexie wondered how that aspect of his personality would translate.

Oblivious to the random direction of her thoughts, Lewis leaned closer. "What do you do when you lose your temper?"

"Oh, I never lose mine," she claimed airily.

"Hah!"

"Okay, once a year," she allowed, annoyed at the ease with which he took the barriers around her heart down.

"And when you do, you…?" He gazed at her with an expression that brought to mind long kisses and hotter caresses.

Lexie flushed, her vivid imagination taking root. "When I get really mad I burst into tears. I know, I know—" she lifted both hands in surrender, then slowly put them down "—it's ridiculous but I can't help it."

"Well, I hope I never make you cry, Lexie Remington," Lewis said gently, touching her face.

Lexie hoped so, too, because she was beginning to like this guy way too much.

TWO HOURS LATER, Lewis had been fitted for three suits, three pairs of dress shoes and half a dozen coordinating shirts and ties. "So where to next?" he asked as he slipped his wallet back into his pants pocket.

"Actually, I—" Lexie's skin turned ashen and she stopped speaking.

Heart pounding, Lewis put his arm around her. Experience had shown him exactly how she looked when she was about to faint. Alarmed, he guided her back into the padded armchair opposite the register and forced her head down between her knees. The salesclerk—a stuffy, older man—looked as upset as Lewis felt by the washed out color of Lexie's skin. Lewis snapped abruptly, "Could we have some juice or water please?"

"Certainly." The salesclerk rushed off.

Lewis knelt in front of her, so their faces were level. "I'm going to have to start carrying smelling salts."

"Don't be ridiculous." Her voice was muffled against her knees.

He smiled at the characteristic feistiness in her voice. If she were this irritated with him, she couldn't be that ill. That didn't stop him from feeling guilty as hell about this latest predicament in which they found themselves. He eased a hand beneath the silky curtain of strawberry-blond hair and gently massaged the back of her neck. "I could kick myself for letting you do this today."

Lexie shook her head in disagreement. "If it's one thing I've demonstrated lately, it's an ability to faint just about anywhere."

The clerk was back, a glass of orange juice in his hand. "Low blood sugar?" he inquired.

"Yes." Lexie sat up carefully, some of the color coming back into her face. "I'll be fine." Steadfastly ignoring the concerned glances of both men, she sipped the juice slowly. "I just need a minute."

"I'm taking you to the emergency room again."

"Why? We already know what's wrong with me. The doc is just going to tell me what your brother Riley did—that I need rest."

She needed more than that, Lewis thought, as he took charge.

"Then we're checking into a hotel. Now."

She peered up at him. "Don't you think you're overreacting?"

"Not unless you're faking it."

Lexie moaned.

Lewis made the calls, and by the time Lexie had finished her juice, they had a room at a luxury hotel that adjoined the Galleria Mall.

"I think we should call security and get a cart to transport you," Lewis said.

She looked at him with weary eyes. "This isn't an airport."

"She's right. We don't have those here," the salesclerk said.

Lewis knew this was all his fault—for pushing her too hard, too fast, for wanting her all to himself—for wanting her, period. He swallowed around the sudden ache in his throat. He couldn't bear it if anything happened to her. He sure as hell didn't want her to end up in the hospital again.

His arm encircling her waist, Lewis walked Lexie the short distance to the hotel entrance. Thanks to the calls he had made, the concierge was waiting with their keys.

Lewis rushed her upstairs and into the suite he had reserved for her. "You need to lie down," he told her.

Looking a little shaky again, she lay back on the pillows. "Turn on the TV, would you? I want to see if *General Hospital* is on."

"What channel?"

She peered at him through a fringe of thick lashes. "You don't know much, do you?"

"About soaps set in hospitals?" he quipped back and saw her eyes darken in something akin to respect. "Apparently not."

He turned the TV on and handed her the remote. She found the show she wanted, and began watching it as if he weren't even in the room. Lewis set her up with a glass of ice, then headed for the minibar. "What kind of soda would you like?"

"Whatever has plenty of sugar and no caffeine."

He came back with a can of lemon-lime soda, popped it open and poured it over ice. "Anyone ever tell you that you have a future as a busboy?" she asked dryly.

He put the glass down beside her, reached across her for extra pillows and slid them behind her head. "Not lately."

"But in the past." She studied him cheerfully.

"My sibs have told me I had a future in a lot of things."

"Such as?"

"You don't want to know."

"I bet."

Only because he was trying hard to be gallant did he resist the impulse to stroke a hand through her hair. "You going to be okay if I leave for a few minutes?" he asked, noting she looked pretty good again, now that she was resting.

"You going to be okay, period?"

He grinned. Anyone with the strength to be that sarcastic was not going to expire in the next ten minutes.

"I'll be back."

She turned her gaze to the couple making out on TV. "Lucky me."

With a last, lingering glance at her, Lewis slipped out and headed to his own room to make the call experience told him Lexie would resist.

"What is it with you and this woman?" Riley asked as soon as Lewis had finished explaining the situation. "You go your whole life without getting a gal into trouble, and then boom, you meet up with Lexie Remington and can't seem to stay out of it."

"Don't remind me," Lewis groaned, pacing the hotel room as they talked. "What should I do for her?"

"See if you can get her to go to bed—for that much-needed rest I advised."

Check, Lewis thought.

"Keep her comfortable. See she has everything she needs."

Check, check.

"And most important, make sure she gets something decent to eat this evening, and takes her meds. Does she have them with her?"

"In her shoulder bag," Lewis confirmed.

"Then you should be all set," Riley said. "Meantime, if you have any problems, call me."

Lewis relaxed, glad the overall situation wasn't as dire as he had initially feared. "Thanks, Riley."

"And, Lewis—good luck."

Lewis paused, knowing from Riley's tone there was more of a punch line coming. "With what?" he demanded.

Riley chuckled. "That woman you're after."

"OKAY," LEXIE COMPLAINED five hours later as she opened her hotel room door for the sixth time since they had checked in to separate rooms on separate floors. "We really have to stop meeting like this."

Lewis knew he was going overboard with the attentiveness. He couldn't help it. Keeping a careful eye on her was the only way he could assuage his guilt.

Casting an eye out the hotel window, he saw it was still raining hard. In the distance, lightning flashed. "I realized you didn't have any pajamas." Trying not to notice how sexy she looked, he eyed the fluffy white hotel robe she had put on after her bath. He strode past her, inhaling soap and shampoo and her scintillating womanly scent. "I guess you realized that, too."

"Yep. Although I was prepared to make do."

Lewis didn't want to know how. The thought of Lexie, sliding naked beneath those crisp white sheets, was almost more than he could bear.

She shut the door to the hall and surveyed the department-store bag in his hand. "What do you have there?"

Telling himself to put a hold on the not-so-chivalrous thoughts, Lewis handed it over. "I thought you might need some pajamas and stuff so I went to the lingerie department and asked a very proper older lady to help me."

She pulled out the blue flannel pajamas. "What size?"

"The saleswoman said medium." Lewis tried not to behave like a man who had seduction in mind.

She peered up at him from beneath her lashes, eying his freshly shaven jaw. "The saleswoman has never seen me."

"I sort of gestured how big you were." Lewis strolled the length of the room, pretending to be a lot more adept at this relationship business than he actually was. He paused at the window, watching the rain come down in big thick sheets. "Is medium the right size?"

"Yes, actually, it is." Turquoise eyes alight with interest, Lexie pulled out a pair of matching slippers. And beneath that, a tissue-wrapped package.

Happy Lexie seemed to like what he had brought her thus far, Lewis said, "She also suggested you might need some…"

Lexie regarded him with mock seriousness. "Undies?"

Grinning, he set the other bag he had been carrying on the bureau, next to the TV. Lexie frowned. "What?" Lewis asked, anxious to discover what he had obviously done wrong.

"Slightly miniscule for my hips," Lexie decided, holding them up in the air.

He followed her flummoxed gaze to the French-cut panties. They were the most modest of the bunch the saleswoman had shown him—stopping just short of granny panties, that was. And even a moron knew enough not to get Lexie those.

Feeling more out of his depth than ever—what did he know about ladies' underwear?—Lewis gestured aimlessly, then shoved both hands in the pockets of his vintage jeans. "I didn't think they were that risqué." Although the thought of Lexie wearing them had him very turned on.

She rolled her eyes in obvious exasperation. "I meant small in size." She rummaged through the bag and brought out a matching cotton brassiere.

Lewis squinted at her expression. "Wrong size?"

Lexie's turquoise eyes sparkled with appreciation despite the miscue. "There are worse things than guessing too big on the bra and too small on the hips," she said humorously.

Lewis noted she had already washed the sexy lingerie she'd been wearing that day—an incredibly sexy red-lace thong and matching semi-sheer bra. Both were hanging over the bathroom towel rack to dry. Boy, had he guessed wrong, in trying to figure out what the still-tomboyish Lexie had on beneath her clothes.

She followed his gaze. "If you had brought me something like that, I probably would have been ticked off."

Lewis nodded sagely. "Good to know."

"Isn't it?"

"Not that I'll ever understand women."

She chuckled, looking pretty much fully recovered from her fainting spell that afternoon. "What's in the other bag you brought?"

Confident he had scored better on this one, he handed it over. She opened it up, the aroma of freshly baked oatmeal-raisin and peanut-butter cookies filling the room. "Milk, too," she noted, impressed. She bounded away from him. "Why don't you set us both up a glass—put ice in mine—while I get a little more comfortable."

She disappeared into the bathroom.

When she returned, she was wearing the light blue flannel pajamas and slippers beneath the thick and fluffy white robe. And she was still the sexiest thing he had ever seen.

She glided over to join him on the love seat beneath the window overlooking the city. Lewis tried not to let the romantic atmosphere get the better of him. It was damn near impossible, given the way she looked and the fact that night had fallen. Stars twinkled above the city lights, and the lights of the passing vehicles shone through the gently falling rain, illuminating the darkness. It was the perfect night for a tryst in a luxury hotel. And he had promised himself he would be a gentleman.

With effort, Lewis turned his attention away from the alluring woman next to him and looked down at the leather folder on his lap. "What's all this?" he asked, looking at the pieces of hotel stationary with sketches of dresses on the front.

Lexie tucked her leg up under her and settled next to him. She studied the sketch of what looked to be a very pretty three-quarter-length dress. "It's the outfit I'm going to ask Jenna's seamstress to make for Sydney Mazero's premiere—if Sydney approves the design tomorrow and selects a fabric."

Lewis closed the top of the binder and set it on the table next to him. "Can you get a dress made that fast?" He picked up her glass of milk and handed it over to her. He followed that with the bag of cookies.

Lexie rummaged around for an oatmeal-raisin cookie. "I have clout with the seamstresses at Jenna's boutique. Actually, in a pinch I could sew it up myself, but I imagine Jenna will veto that as too taxing and want one of the seamstresses who works for her to do it."

"That's right." Trying not to be too aware of the soft side of her breast pressed up against his arm, Lewis munched on a peanut-butter cookie. "You used to work for her when you were a kid."

Lexie nodded and continued to curl against him. "I loved being able to dream up designs and then sew them for myself."

He stretched his legs out in front of him, so his thigh was pressed up against her bent knee. "Why didn't you go into dress design?"

"That was the plan," Lexie acknowledged as she dunked what was left of her cookie into her milk, "until I dropped out of college and ran off with Constantine, started helping him with his various ensembles. Before I knew it, I was a stylist and my success more than paid the bills, so…"

Lewis drained the rest of his milk and set his glass aside. "You could do it now."

Lexie helped herself to another cookie. "I have the most sought after client roster of stars in all Hollywood."

"Yeah," he teased lightly, "but are you enjoying it?"

"Tonight isn't the night to ask me that," Lexie said as her cell phone went off again.

Sighing, she got up, fetched her phone from the bed and looked at the caller ID. The phone kept right on ringing.

"Are you going to answer that?" Lewis asked.

"Nope." Silence fell as she punched in instructions on the keypad to turn off the ringer.

"Good for you," he said, as she strolled back to help herself to another cookie. "You should take your vacation!"

She rolled her eyes, not above pointing out the hypocrisy of that statement, and waved a peanut-butter cookie in his face. "Says the person who just hired me to help him."

Lewis watched her dunk again and lose half her cookie in the milk. "That's different."

"How?" Lexie fished the fallen confection out of the glass. "Because you won't fire me the first time I refuse to take your call?"

Lewis blinked. "Someone fired you?"

Lexie brought the soggy cookie to her mouth. "Three people today. Apparently, taking time off for my health is not acceptable behavior for a celebrity stylist." She demolished what was left of the cookie.

Lewis watched her lick the milk off her fingers. "Why didn't you tell me?"

"Because I had my phone off," she said, draining the rest of her milk, "and I didn't know about it until after we checked in here and I listened to my messages."

"I'm sorry." Lewis studied her deliberately impassive expression. "Is there anything I can do?"

"You can pass me another oatmeal cookie."

Lewis obliged.

"And tell me what you hope to accomplish tomorrow."

"How about what I hope to accomplish tonight?" Lewis replenished her glass of milk, too.

"What would that be?"

Not what I want, that's for certain. "Getting you into bed ASAP for a good night's sleep," Lewis stated firmly.

She made a face and, finished with the milk and cookies, put her glass aside. "It's eight-thirty—an awfully early bedtime for anyone over twelve."

She was certainly all grown up, Lewis noted wistfully. Those full, round breasts, long curvaceous legs and sleek thighs definitely belonged to a woman—which was why he had to get out of here, and fast. Before he did something they'd both regret. He moved away from her deliberately. "I don't care whether it's impossibly early or not. You need to go to bed."

She smiled, all playful waywardness. She rubbed a strand

of her still damp hair between her fingers. "I really don't think I could fall asleep."

Viewing her flirtatious glance, it was all he could do not to groan out loud. Rising, he tugged her to her feet, too. "Give it a try, anyway." Hand on her arm, he steered her resolutely toward the bed.

She dug in her heels, effectively, slowing their progress. "Actually, I was thinking about watching a pay-per-view movie—with you."

"Fine." Lewis's voice was strangled as he peeled back the bedspread, sheet and blankets on her bed. "I'll watch it with you—if you climb beneath the covers."

Lexie sighed. "If I didn't know better—"

Which, Lewis noted, she clearly did.

"—I'd think you were trying to seduce me."

"If I didn't know better, I *would* be trying to seduce you," Lewis agreed, grabbing a couple of the pillows and propping them against the headboard. Of all the times to realize he'd been brought up right! "But right now all I want is to take care of you and make up for running you ragged today."

Looking annoyed rather than impressed by his chivalry, Lexie sat down obediently on the mattress. Keeping her feet firmly on the floor, she perched on the very edge of the bed. She lifted her eyes to his, serious now. "You didn't run me ragged."

Like hell he hadn't. He still recalled the look on her face, the way she had started to sway, when she had damn near fainted. Guilt flooded Lewis, once again taking precedence over his desire. "That's not what your Laramie, Texas, doc says," he countered roughly.

Lexie paused. "You talked to Riley about me?"

With every muscle in his body taut with barely suppressed longing, Lewis nodded. He ignored the arousal pressing against the front of his jeans. "A little while ago, after we got back to the hotel. Riley told me to make sure you had everything you needcd," hc rclayed, tucking the covers around her hips and thighs.

"Really." Lexie put her hand on the back of his neck and brought his face close to hers. Mischief sparkled in her lively turquoise eyes. "Did he tell you I needed this?"

Chapter Six

Lexie wasn't sure what had come over her…wasn't sure she wanted to know. Maybe it was the increasing intimacy of the situation, or the fact she had been without contact of this kind for such a long time. All she knew was that when Lewis was ever so gently but determinedly propelling her toward the bed and tucking her beneath the sheets, wrapping her arms around his shoulders and pulling him close seemed so natural. And once his lips were that close to hers, she couldn't think of any reason why they shouldn't kiss.

How was it, she wondered, as his lips parted hers and his tongue swept inside to deepen the kiss, that someone so challenged in the personal attire department could be so completely talented in the making love department. And as he took her face in his hands and continued to sweetly explore the edges of her tongue with his, she thought that was exactly what they were doing right now. Seducing each other. Tempting. Seeking. Learning. To the point she wanted so much more and would have pursued it, if only one tiny little thing hadn't been standing in their way.

Lewis wasn't making the changes in his life in order to impress her, Lexie reminded herself firmly—he was doing it to attract Susie Carrigan. And as much as Lexie wanted to hold on to the loving kindness Lewis had shown her from the very first, as much as she wanted to learn everything she possibly could about him, she couldn't—in good conscience—steal his attention away from her cousin. Especially when she knew that Susie needed a good man in her life as much as Lexie did.

"Okay!" Lexie pushed him away and made a vain attempt to catch her breath as she muttered the first excuse that came to mind. "This lesson is over!"

Lewis blinked and obediently moved back.

She noted he was sitting on the bed beside her. When had that happened? And how had the second and third buttons on her pajama top gotten undone? Heavens, the man was more skilled in the art of passion than she had imagined!

"Lesson?" Lewis repeated in a completely befuddled voice.

"Kissing lesson." Lexie rebuttoned her top with trembling fingers, pretending this "practice session" in sexual sophistication was what she had intended all along. "I thought you might enjoy one." As soon as the lame words were out of her mouth, she wished she could take them back. Too late.

"Ah. Yes," he said, the passion in his eyes dimming. He raised a palm in a gesture of accommodation. "Since you seem fine now—"

"I certainly am." Lexie looked down and saw she had rebuttoned her top crookedly. Rather than redo it she placed her palm over the mismatched edges, pressing the fabric to her chest.

"I think I better be going."

Heat shimmered off him and enveloped her. "I think so, too." Lexie flashed a businesslike smile, wondering how in the world she had ever gotten herself in this mess. Certainly, she knew better than to take on a man she was this attracted to as a client.

He picked up the empty cookie bag and tossed it in the trash can. "What time in the morning?"

She watched him carry the glasses to the sink, rinse them out and set them on the counter. "Oh, let's make it eight. I've made appointments with personal sales consultants at several of the casual clothing stores in the Galleria. I'd like to get you fully outfitted and on our way back to Laramie before the stores even open to the general public at ten."

Frowning, Lewis came back to stand beside her bed. "When did you do that?"

Trying not to think how much she wanted to kiss him again, Lexie shrugged her shoulders carelessly. "When you were out on one of your many errands."

He consulted his watch. "All right then. I'll see you tomorrow morning."

Lexie nodded and watched him slip out her hotel room door.

THE NEXT MORNING, Lewis was still trying to figure out what had happened between them. Lexie grabbing him and kissing him that way had been a surprise, but a wonderful one. However, her pushing him away with the same cool and sexy deliberation that she had captured him, and declaring the embrace a lesson, had left him stunned. Had she really set out to teach him how to kiss, he wondered? And if so, what did that mean? That his technique left something to be desired? For some reason, the notion that she'd been romanced by suave Hollywood types, and considered him "lacking" in the art of kissing, left him with a sour taste in his mouth.

Even more importantly, it left him behind in the race to win Lexie's heart. And he did want to win her affections. He was more sure of that than ever, after the sweet, evocative way she had kissed him and let him kiss her back.

Which meant, Lewis thought grimly, that he had some

studying to do. And fast, since she was only going to be here a matter of days, and he wasn't going to let her go without going all-out to earn her love.

Later, showered and dressed, Lewis found Lexie in the hotel dining room, where they'd agreed to meet for breakfast. Her head was bent over the Dallas newspaper. She looked anything but pleased.

Lewis caught a glimpse of the headline on the Lifestyle section. *Italian Royalty Visits The Big D.* Beneath it was a photo of Lexie's mother, the Contessa della Gheradesca, at some gala. She was dripping with diamonds, as per usual, and talking to the local bigwigs. "What's the matter?" Lewis asked, taking in the pale color of Lexie's face.

She waved away his concern. "It's nothing."

Like hell it was. He sat down next to her. "Tell me."

Lexie pointed to the photo. "See this woman standing just behind my mother and the mayor?"

Lewis shifted to get a better look. "Yes."

"That's Raven Walker."

Lewis drank in the fragrant scent of Lexie's hair and skin. "I have no idea who that is."

Lexie's face lost a little more color. "Raven is Constantine Romeo's second assistant."

"Second?" Lewis repeated.

"He has three." Lexie sat up ramrod straight. "The first one, Jasmine Rhodes, travels with Constantine, and takes care of everything moment to moment. The third one, Jimmy Lebrun, stays back in L.A., and makes sure everything is running fine on the home front."

Lewis pushed away the jealousy he felt whenever he heard Constantine Romeo's name in connection with Lexie. "What does Raven Walker do?" Lewis asked matter-of-factly, sipping his coffee.

Lexie's eyes clouded. "She's his advance person. She travels ahead of Constantine by a day or two or three, and makes sure everything is set up wherever he is planning to go next."

Lewis swore inwardly. "What does that have to do with your mother?"

"Exactly what I'd like to know," she muttered, running her finger down the stem of the silverware next to her plate. "Constantine Romeo doesn't do charity unless it is part of some promotion for an upcoming film. This benefit last night was for the new women's health center in Dallas. So there was no reason for Raven to be there, since the big fund-raiser with the all the attendant publicity happened last night."

Lewis tried not to read anything sinister into Constantine Romeo's actions, or the advance work being done by his second assistant. "Could he be supporting it to connect with his female fans?"

"Not a chance. And even if he were trying to do that, he would have been at the gala last night, not sent in his assistant to make a donation on his behalf and come in a couple of days after the opportunity for major publicity had passed. No, the fact that Raven Walker is standing just behind my mother—" Lexie pointed to the photo again "—tells me my mother is up to something with Constantine. And I don't like it," Lexie said grimly. "I don't like it at all."

LEXIE KEPT HER ATTITUDE strictly business the rest of the morning. Lewis did the same. Exhausted from the morning's activities, she fell asleep on the drive back to Laramie and woke only when Lewis dropped her back at Jenna's.

Congratulating herself on her success at wedging distance between them once again, Lexie took the Remington ranch pickup she'd been cruising around while in Texas and drove out to her cousin's garden and landscaping center on the edge of town. Immediately after arriving, she tracked down Susie. Then she set about unearthing as much information as she could while simultaneously getting a thank-you present for her stepmother, for letting her bunk in the apartment above the boutique.

"Why all the questions about Lewis McCabe?" Susie asked as she potted a beautiful African violet in a decorative urn that matched the décor of Jenna's sunlit office.

"I don't know." Lexie lounged against the worktable. She studied her cousin's fair, freckled face. "Don't you think he's cute?"

Susie rolled her eyes. "Are you kidding me?"

Lexie tried not to be cheered by her cousin's reaction. "I'm dead serious." She watched Susie carefully for any signs of suppressed attraction for Lewis.

Susie smirked and shook her head. "He's not my type," she said, blunt as ever. "If I were going to date again, and I have no plans to do so in this century, then it wouldn't be with a computer-game guru."

Lexie knew Susie'd had a hard time getting over the death of her husband. They had only been married three months. "Sure about that?"

Susie smiled. "As sure as I am that this African violet is perfect for Aunt Jenna." She wrapped it up and handed it over.

"Thanks, Susie." Lexie gave Susie her credit card.

Susie walked to the register out front. "I heard you're going to do an information booth in the Laramie High School career fair."

Lexie nodded. "The comp-sci teacher talked me into it." Then, seeing a way to glean even more information, she asked, "What do you know about her and Lewis, by the way?"

"Nothing except the fact Josephine Holdsworth's got a gigantic crush on Lewis, and he doesn't seem to think she is anything but casual friend material."

"So you don't think that relationship is going anywhere."

"Not in this lifetime." Susie paused. "You're asking an

awful lot of questions about Lewis McCabe, all of a sudden." She offered up a slow, insinuating smile. "Is he hitting on you or something?"

Actually, Lexie thought, remembering the way she had kissed him the night before, it was the other way around. She swallowed around the sudden dryness in her throat and attempted an airy tone. "He's a client, Susie."

Susie shrugged, and handed over the receipt and a pen. "And you're a single gal and he's a single guy."

Lexie scrawled her signature at the bottom. "He's a client, that's all," she fibbed.

Susie slid her hands in the pockets of her coveralls and walked Lexie to the door. "Are you this interested in all your clients love lives?" she queried as she held the door for Lexie.

Lexie shot Susie a quelling look. "Matchmaking does not come with my service."

"Good." Susie grinned, as amused as she was curious. "Because you'd be lousy at it."

No kidding, Lexie thought as she got back in her pickup truck, plant in tow, and drove down Main Street. Arriving at her stepmother's shop, Lexie brought in the blooming flower and handed it to Jenna. "For you." Lexie kissed her cheek.

Jenna looked surprised but pleased. "What did I do?"

"Many things over many years." Lexie gave her a full-on hug, which was promptly returned. She swallowed around the sudden ache in her throat, knowing there was no way to express how truly grateful she was to have Jenna in her life, but she figured she'd try anyway. "Have I ever told you how much I appreciated the way you stepped in to mother me, many, many moons ago?"

Lexie's flip tone brought affection to Jenna's clear blue eyes. "Many times." Jenna smiled as they slowly drew apart. Maternal affection softened her lips. "What's going on, Lexie?" she ventured.

Lexie made a great show of slipping off her jacket. "What do you mean?"

Jenna followed Lexie back to the break room. "You don't usually bring me flowers, except on Mother's Day."

"I should, though." Lexie filled a cup and set it in the microwave.

Jenna lounged against the counter, arms folded in front of her. As always, she was stunningly dressed—today in a fitted teal blue suit, of her own design. "What you should do is tell me what you were doing with Lewis McCabe in Dallas last night."

Lexie wished her stepmother did not know her quite so well. She searched through the basket of specialty teas and plucked out a decaffeinated black-raspberry blend. "It was a business trip."

Jenna looked unconvinced. "Uh-huh."

"Seriously." At least, Lexie amended silently, that was what it was supposed to be.

Jenna watched as Lexie ripped open the packet and dunked it into her mug of steaming liquid. "I don't recall you mentioning that to me in your note when you left here yesterday morning."

Lexie shrugged and searched for the sugar. "I had hoped to get it all done in one marathon eight-hour shopping session—"

Jenna frowned. "Lexie, you're supposed to be resting!"

"Exactly what my body said when it refused to go the distance—which is why we had to spend the night in the Big D—so I could go get forty winks and finish up this morning," Lexie acknowledged ruefully.

Jenna went to the fridge and brought out a plate of delicate tea sandwiches. "I assume Lewis was the perfect gentleman."

Lexie smiled and, as was her custom when her stepmother or anyone else went fishing into her private life, did not reply.

"Is something going on between the two of you?" Jenna asked.

"I wish people would stop asking me that." Lexie sighed, helping herself to a chicken salad triangle, and another that looked like cream cheese and cucumber.

"So there is!" Jenna mused, looking happier than Lexie would have expected about the possible love match.

There could be, now that she was nearly done helping him come up with a new style, Lexie thought.

Because once he was no longer her client, there wouldn't be any ethical reasons keeping them apart.

The question was, how would he react when their professional association ended? Would he thank her and send her on her way? Would he pursue her cousin Susie? Or a whole host of interested women? Or would he—as she secretly hoped—turn his sights on her?

"YOU'RE HOME EARLY," Brad's wife, Lainey, said to Lewis as he walked into the ranch house kitchen that afternoon.

She was browning a roast on the stove, and the aroma of sizzling beef filled the house. Her laptop computer was set up on the kitchen table. Lewis could see from the stacks of notes around it that Lainey was working on another freelance writing assignment.

"Josh and Julie napping?" he asked, referring to her preschoolers.

"Yes. Knock wood." Lainey smiled.

"Petey still at school?"

"Yes. Again. So what's up? It's not like you to knock off work in the middle of the afternoon," Lainey said.

Lewis shrugged. "I figure the company can get along without me for a day or two."

"Good for you. About time you took some vacation." Lainey turned the sizzling meat, wiped her hands on the dishtowel on the counter, then walked into the adjacent laundry room. She came back with a large shopping bag bearing the logo of the nation's biggest bookstore in hand. "By the way, these were messengered for you a little while ago. I signed for them. The person who delivered them said it was an urgent request." Lainey's cheeks pinkened.

Too late, Lewis realized he should have asked the store to put the books in a box or plain paper wrapping. Instead, they were lined up in the bottom of the shopping bag, their titles clearly visible.

"Oh, man."

Lainey held up a hand, blushing all the harder. "I don't even want to know."

Lewis sighed with relief when his sister-in-law discreetly disappeared around the corner. He prayed she wouldn't reveal the contents of his package to his brother, Brad. If she did, he'd never live this down.

Five hours later, he had skimmed his way through *The Bachelor's Guide to Sex: How To Make Love Like You Mean It.* He was just picking up the next tome when he heard the pickup truck in the driveway. Frowning, he set the book aside, got off the bed and padded down the short hall, past the kitchen, and through the living room. Expecting it to be eleven-year-old Petey, there to call him to the ranch house for dinner, he opened the front door.

Lexie was standing on the other side of the portal, professional-sized clothing steamer by her side. She wore a pair of snug-fitting black jeans, and a black turtleneck sweater. Square-toed western boots—in a cherry-red—peeked out from beneath the slightly flared boot-cut hem of her pants. She'd caught the length of her wavy strawberry-blond hair in a messy knot at the nape of her neck.

"I thought we were going to get out the new stuff and

organize my closet tomorrow morning," Lewis said, his pulse picking up at the sight of her.

She swept inside, her expression an intriguing mix of feisty determination and Hollywood cool. She turned her attention to the stacks of books on Texas history circa 1886 on his coffee table. "Tomorrow morning I'm going to be busy with the actress I told you about—Sydney Mazero."

Lewis followed her glance. "History is one of my hobbies." He pointed to the glass case of Alamo artifacts on the wall. "And I thought you'd already designed Sydney's dress for the premiere."

"I did. She approved it and the fabric this afternoon. The seamstress is already sewing it. But we've sort of expanded what I'm going to be doing for her. She also wants me to help her put together the clothes she'll wear on the publicity junket for *Calamity Sue.* So we're doing that tomorrow. Anyway, I thought we'd go ahead and finish what I'm doing for you this evening, and then we'd be done."

Nothing could have sounded worse to Lewis. He tried to think of a way to stall her. "I, uh—"

She cocked her head, suspicion in her pretty turquoise eyes. "You didn't have a date, did you?"

Lewis tried to decide if that was jealousy in her soft, low tone, or simply impatience. "No."

"Good. Then would you mind getting the bags in the front seat of the pickup and bringing them in?" she asked. "It's a lot."

"No problem," he said cheerfully, heading on out into the balmy autumn evening. Only when he was walking back inside the guest cottage did he recall another stack of books—the ones he'd left on his bed.

He went back inside but Lexie was nowhere in sight.

Lewis swore softly. Heart racing, he headed quickly down the hall to the master bedroom.

To his chagrin, she was standing next to the bed, staring at the stack of titles he'd been avidly perusing when she arrived. She turned to him with a lift of her brow. "A little light reading?"

Chapter Seven

To Lexie's amazement, Lewis maintained his cool. He set the bags down next to the door and sauntered toward her, hands thrust in the pockets of his hopelessly worn jeans. "I am a scientist, you know."

"Computer scientist," Lexie corrected.

"That's the thing about us inquisitive types. We don't limit our explorations to any one topic."

Lexie's b.s. detector went off, full blast. "Especially now that you're about to have this new look going for you," she countered, her heart beginning to race.

Lewis went very still. "What does that have to do with sex?" he asked, confused.

She shrugged and moved away from him. "According to my clients—everything. A rich, successful guy is one thing. A rich, successful, handsome guy another."

"You think I'm good-looking?"

Oh, yeah, Lexie sighed inwardly. But not about to give his ego any more fuel than it already had, she let his question pass without comment, and continued on her tirade. "But when you add extremely well-put-together to the mix, well, it seems the ladies can't help themselves. They're all over the newly made-over guy in droves. Kind of like houses."

"Really?" Amusement twinkled in his blue-gray eyes.

"Yep." Lexie nodded, reminding herself they were talking about sex here, not love. "A fixer-upper attracts a certain clientele."

Lewis regarded her carefully, a calculating expression on his face. "Someone with vision," he guessed finally.

"Like me." She reassured herself that she did not want him, not at all. With a smile, Lexie forced herself to continue her lesson on the aftermath of a style makeover. "But a house that's already in move-in shape, well, those tend to go quickly. So you're probably right to get yourself ready for the onslaught."

His lips took on a cynical tilt. "You really shouldn't tease me about something like that."

Was it possible, Lexie wondered, *Lewis didn't have a clue how truly "hot" he was? Makeover or no?* She knew he still carried some baggage from his "nerdy" childhood. But then they all did. She was still struggling with the fact her mother had never really loved her. Not the unconditional way a parent should, anyway.

Aware he was still waiting for her answer, Lexie shrugged. "I think you're man enough to take it." She just wasn't sure she was woman enough to handle seeing a host of women climbing all over him. "Besides," Lexie said, forcing herself to continue with deceptive casualness, "it's the truth. As soon as we can get rid of all this vintage stuff—and I do mean all of it, Lewis…it has all got to go!—and get you into your new duds, I guarantee every single woman in Laramie is going to be chasing you to the altar."

Lewis braced both his hands on his waist. "Who said I wanted to get married?"

Lexie began taking the vintage clothes out of his closet, and putting them in donation bags she had brought with her. "I just figured a guy like you would."

Lewis walked in to the closet to help her. "Because I'm a nerd."

"No." Lexie tried not to think how intimate it felt to be working with him in such a small space. "Because you're a nice guy. You're not a player. Not yet, anyway."

"Thanks. I think." Lewis carried two of the filled bags out of the bedroom and returned with two more empty ones. Grinning wolfishly, he asked, "Would it bother you if I were to become a player?"

Her shoulder nudged his as she slipped several more shirts off the hangers. "Yes."

He stuffed a pile of slacks, hangers and all, into two more bags. "How come?"

He was testing her. "Because I'd probably feel I had a hand in the ego transformation. And I don't particularly want that on my conscience. Bad enough I've helped countless actors and actresses make that leap into shallowness." Where they cared more about how they looked and who they were seen with, than who they were on the inside, she thought.

"Owww. You are brutal tonight."

"Sorry." Pushing away her guilt at having contributed, in some small way, to the superficialization of current society, she hurried to empty out the rack of horrid ties and belts…and promptly tripped over a filled bag next to the doorway.

He caught her before she fell and righted her gently.

Her skin tingled warmly where he touched her. Lexie flushed. "I just want to get this done."

Lewis gave her an odd look. "So let's do it." He helped clear out the rest of the closet in no time. Once the clothes to take to charity were set out on the front porch and the clothing they had purchased in Dallas brought inside, Lexie instructed him to help cut the tags off the clothes, while she utilized the steamer. "One question," Lewis asked affably, while they worked, side by side.

"Fire away."

He regarded her intently. "How am I going to know what goes with what?"

"Look at the back of the tag on the clothes," Lexie advised in her most businesslike tone.

Lewis looked at her in confusion.

"I color-coded them before we got here." Lexie paused to show Lewis the back of a shirt tag she was working on. There was a slash of orange marker across the silk. "All you have to do is look for other oranges, purples, yellows or greens. If the item in question is white, it's not marked, because white goes with anything."

Lewis smiled, relieved. "That sounds simple enough."

Lexie handed him another pair of slacks to hang up. "I did the same with your dress shirts, suits and ties. So once we get this stuff all organized and hung up, you'll be all set."

Lewis walked back into his now extremely organized closet. "I can't believe you did all this in just two days. So now that we're through with all the makeover stuff, how about you help me out with something else?" he said cheerfully.

Lexie caught the unexpected glimmer of the legendary McCabe mischief in his gorgeous blue-gray eyes. "Like what?" she inquired cautiously.

Lewis nodded at the stack of books still strewn across one end of his bed. He answered casually, "How about telling me what you think sounds like it might work on a woman like you and what would totally turn you off."

LEXIE STARED AT HIM. "I'd laugh if I thought you were joking," she managed wryly, after a moment. "But you're not, are you?"

Lewis shrugged, suddenly uncertain.

"Why does it matter what I would like or not like in bed?"

He shrugged again, apparently having no good answer for that. "It's not what you think," he said, after a moment. "I wasn't trying to hit on you."

"Were you hitting on me last night—at the hotel—when you tucked me in?" she asked, fascinated by the inner workings of his mind.

He sighed. "Yes, but in my defense, Ms. Remington, you started that."

"True." Lexie tapped a finger against her lips in a parody of thoughtfulness. She still tingled, recalling the experience. "I did grab you and kiss you."

"And I kissed you back," Lewis murmured.

"Wholeheartedly, it seemed."

Lewis took her in his arms, "I'd still be kissing you now if you hadn't called a halt."

Lexie could not find the strength to move away. She tilted her head back, to better study his face. "Which is, I presume, somehow connected to why you were boning up on your sexual expertise?"

He took a lock of her hair that had fallen free of the knot at the nape of her neck and tucked it behind her ear. "It's a weakness," he confessed with mock gravity.

A thrill spiraled through her, lingered in her thighs. She adapted the same breezy tone. "Lusting after me?"

The twinkle left his eyes. "Not being able to translate my feelings into action that would compel you to look at me in a different light."

If only he knew, she thought, her heart aching for him. She stepped back. "Last night you were a client. Interested in dating my cousin, Susie," she said to remind herself as much as him.

He spread his hands wide. He looked tired of defending himself on that score. "Well, as we have established that is no longer the case, on either score. Our work here is finished. I'm not after Susie."

"Which is good." Lexie smiled, trying not to look too relieved because she didn't have to worry about her professional integrity or stealing a potential beau from her cousin. "Because Susie isn't the least bit interested in you, either."

Lewis slipped both hands around her waist. "The question is, are you?"

The evening was becoming so surreal. Lexie bit her lip. Her heart was pounding again. "I don't know how to answer that."

He flattened his palms over her back. "How about honestly?"

"It would never work," she said.

He brought her closer anyway. "That's not an answer," he chided softly.

"I have a job that has me on the road constantly."

He bent and pressed a kiss to the nape of her neck. "So get another one," he murmured against her skin. "You don't seem to be enjoying the one you have all that much."

She trembled at the sensation his touch invoked. "I can't just quit." She splayed both her hands across the hard, unyielding muscles of his chest.

"Why not?" He turned his attention to her left ear.

She caught her breath as he caught the lobe between his teeth and sucked lightly. "I can't quit my job in L.A. because I like someone back in Laramie, Texas." She voiced the words out loud to let him know how ridiculously juvenile they sounded. "Not when there are planes, trains and countless other ways to see each other."

He grinned and drew back so he could see her face again. "So you like me."

Lexie pretended to be a lot more jaded and sophisticated than she was. "And you like me, obviously, or we wouldn't be having this conversation. That doesn't change the fact that we're adults, with adult responsibilities." Just because she felt like a besotted teenager when she was with Lewis didn't mean she could act like one and drop everything to be with her new boyfriend.

He rubbed the pad of his thumb across the curve of her cheek. "Adults are still allowed to have fun."

She inclined her head at the how-to manuals still scattered across his bed. "I gather we're back to talking about the 'research' you have been doing."

Lewis nodded, suddenly as sober as a judge in court. "Here's the bottom line, Lexie. I know you're only going to be in town for another week and a half or so. I think we have something special developing between us and I'm willing to take a chance and see where it might lead. The question is—" he paused gravely "—are you?"

LEXIE DIDN'T KNOW the answer to that. She did know she couldn't continue this conversation while standing there, clasped in his arms, and so much as pretend to think rationally.

She moved away from him and began to disassemble the clothing steamer. "I haven't been involved with anyone in that way since Constantine Romeo dumped me two years ago." Conscious of his eyes on her, she removed the plastic compartment that held the water, carried it to the sink and poured the remaining liquid down the drain.

Lewis bent to wrap up the electric cord on the machine. "Then you're in good company cause I haven't been involved with anyone in that way since my fiancée left me a year and a half ago."

Lexie knelt next to Lewis, to snap the water compartment back into place. Aware her knees were already weak with need, she looked into his eyes. Swallowing around the parched feeling in her throat—and the fear he might turn out to be a player after all—she warned, "Even if we were to further explore whatever this is, it wouldn't be more than a casual flirtation." She wanted an easy out, should she need one.

He stood, offered her his hand. "All right."

Joy shot through Lexie, right along with the nerves. She rose to her full height on legs that felt about as substantial as jelly. Already her breasts were tightening in anticipation of his touch. "You're going to be my one-night stand?" she asked, wanting to make absolutely sure they were on the same page. They were doing this with their guards up.

Lewis's face split into a sexy grin. "Hopefully ten- or eleven-night minimum, but yeah, I'll sign on for that," he said huskily, taking her back into his arms. "With one stipulation." He pressed a kiss to her temple.

"And what is that?" Lexie asked, the unexpected reservation in his low tone making her tremble.

Lewis's eyes darkened to an intense blue-gray. Some of the laughter left his eyes but none of the desire. "That while we are doing whatever it is that we are doing, you put your whole heart and soul into it, just as I plan to do."

Lexie let out the breath she had been holding and nodded in agreement. She had always believed if you were going to do something you should do it all the way.

"Good." He sealed their agreement with a swift, hard kiss that ended all too soon.

Lexie rested her head against the solidness of his shoulder, loving his strength and warmth. "I can't believe you're talking me into this."

Lewis chuckled. "I can't believe I am, either." He tucked a hand beneath her chin and lifted her face to his. "But there's one more thing."

Uh-oh, Lexie thought, here it comes. The stipulation that would end up spoiling the deal. "And that is…"

Lewis grimaced and released her. He put the how-to guides in a canvas backpack and zipped it shut. "We have to go elsewhere to have our…fling."

No doubt about it, Lewis McCabe was the most complex

guy she had ever met. Reminded of the years she had spent hiding her real relationship with Constantine Romeo from everyone who knew them in the movie industry, she flushed. "Are you ashamed of me?" she asked, pretending that even if that were the case, that she did not care.

Lewis slanted her an insulted look that immediately put her worst fears at rest. "Man, you are tough on a guy. No. That is not it. House rules."

Aware her hair was falling out of the untidy knot at the nape of her neck, Lexie gave up, and just took it down. "That makes even less sense," she said as she shook her head. Her hair fell over her shoulders.

His eyes tracking the movement of her hair, Lewis handed Lexie her shoulder bag. He picked up the steamer, slung the bag of books over his shoulder and escorted her toward the door. "Lainey's son Petey is at an impressionable age. At eleven, he knows the basic science of what goes on between a man and a woman, but he is still trying to make sense of the rest."

Aren't we all, Lexie thought sagely.

"Or, in other words, he doesn't miss a trick these days and he asks *a lot* of questions."

"Oh." Lexie certainly didn't want that. Especially when she herself wouldn't have a clue how to answer them.

"He's also been known to forget to knock once in a while and just come barging in here to find me. I could lock the door but since I never do that when I'm home he's going to wonder why I've got it locked, and then if he sees you're here, well, you get the idea."

"Unfortunately, yes, I do," Lexie said, with real feeling.

Lewis exhaled ruefully and shoved a hand through the newly shorn layers of his hair. "Anyway, it won't be a problem once I get my own ranch house built on the other end of the property. Then I'll have all the privacy I need, but for right now, to ensure our evening goes the way we want it to go—" Lewis gave her a smile filled with an anticipation that matched her own "—you and I better cozy up elsewhere."

"OH, NO," LEXIE SAID as they drove up to her stepmother's old apartment on Main Street, and saw a limousine parked in front of it with the trunk open. Lights were being turned on in the apartment upstairs, one by one. No doubt, Lexie thought, by her mother.

Lewis kept right on driving down Main Street. He slanted her a glance and quipped, "Here we are with lust in our hearts and lovemaking on our mind and nowhere to go."

Lexie felt the heat of a blush moving from her neck to her face. "I haven't felt this ridiculous—" and sexually charged "—since I was a teenager." Not that she'd ever had much chance to experiment beyond a few simple kisses with the boys she'd dated. Her father had kept such a tight rein on her she'd rarely been without a chaperone of some sort.

"Kind of hard to get into trouble in a town this size," Lewis lamented.

"No kidding." Lexie sighed, thinking there might be something to that notion that it takes a village to raise a child. "With everybody keeping their eyes and ears peeled and watching out for you."

Lewis came to the end of Main Street. He paused at another traffic light. "Well, I guess we could just go to dinner." They were in full view of both the Wagon Wheel restaurant and the Lone Star Dance Hall.

Lexie was hungry all right, but not for food. She looked at Lewis in exasperation. "You're missing the big picture."

He steered his SUV over to the curb and shifted into Park. "Which is?"

Lexie tried hard not to notice how handsome he looked in the dim lights of the car. "If the Contessa is back in Laramie, it is not for the nonexistent social life. She wants to talk to me. Probably about Constantine."

"Want to go back to the apartment and get it over with?"

"No." Just the notion filled her with dread. Not because she didn't know how to stand her ground, but because she didn't know how to make her mother listen to her. And she was getting really tired of repeating herself.

"Well, I don't see how you're going to avoid the Contessa."

"Easy," Lexie replied, trying not to notice the familiar anxiety suddenly building up inside her, along with the feeling that she wasn't nearly woman enough to please a man as "scientifically adventurous" and professionally accomplished as Lewis McCabe. A man like him was probably used to acing whatever task he undertook. "I'll go back to my dad and Jenna's ranch to sleep tonight. They'll be delighted to see me. My mother won't bother me there." At least until morning, Lexie thought.

"Okay."

His eyes glimmered. She knew what he was thinking even if he didn't come right out and say it. "You look disappointed."

"I am." He furrowed his forehead in comic fashion. "Those how-to manuals are burning a hole in my knapsack back there."

Lexie was suddenly a little nervous. First-date nervous. Not that this was a date. "I'm sure you'll be able to use them sometime," she returned glibly.

His eyebrow lifted enthusiastically. "The evening is still young."

Heart racing, she turned away from the mixture of pleasure and anticipation in his lively blue-gray eyes. "Surely you're not suggesting we go to the local motel and check in together."

"Of course not," he teased in a soft, low voice that sent thrills coursing over her body. "That'd be like taking out a billboard on Main Street, saying Lexie and Lewis Are Getting It On."

She tried not to think how cozy it felt, sitting there with him, that way. Or how much she wanted to kiss him again. Really kiss him. Yet, she didn't see how—or even where—they would get the privacy they craved this evening.

Lewis took her hand, his fingers lingering warmly over hers. "There's always the lake."

Lexie's heart did a funny little flip-flop in her chest. "You want to go parking at the lake?"

He nodded, looking all the more determined. "It's a school night, nearly nine. If we grabbed a little dinner and then headed out there, chances of us running into anyone else we know would be nonexistent."

Lexie traced a hand down the seam of her black jeans. The evening was cool but she felt impossibly warm in her black cashmere turtleneck sweater. "One would hope so."

"It could be fun," he persisted.

Lexie raked her teeth across her lower lip. "I didn't even do that as a kid." On the rare occasions when it would have been possible, she'd been too afraid of being discovered and hauled into the local sheriff's department.

Lewis flashed a seductive smile. "Neither did I. That's what makes it so appealing. We'd be 'parking' virgins. It'd be a first for both of us."

"I CANNOT BELIEVE you talked me into this," Lexie said several hours later. She watched as Lewis parked his SUV in a secluded grove, overlooking Lake Laramie.

Lewis checked out the console between their bucket seats with a frown. Lexie had an idea what he was thinking—it was quite a barrier to physical closeness.

"We haven't done anything yet." Getting out of the vehicle, he circled around to her side, opened the rear passenger door, then hers.

"Yes," Lexie murmured, trying not to blush as he helped

her out of the front seat and steered her up onto the rear bench-style seat. She gulped as he slid in after her and shut the door.

"But you have that look in your eyes," she murmured, as the air left her lungs in one big whoosh. And the setting couldn't have been more romantic, with the air so crisp and cool. Stars filled the velvety Texas sky. Moonlight shimmered off the water. The only sound was the whisper of the brisk autumn wind through the trees and the even softer music he had left playing on the car stereo system.

"What look?" he mocked her innocently, pulling her into the curve of his arm, then shifting her legs around so they were across his lap.

"The same one you had last night in the hotel," Lexie declared breathlessly, feeling the strength of his arousal beneath her thighs. She wrapped her arms around his neck. "When you realized I was going to kiss you."

Lewis bent his head, letting her know with a glance that was exactly the mood he had been going for. For a second, they simply stared at each other with anticipation in the light of the full moon. And then his head came even closer, his lips touched hers and everything else fell away but the feel of his mouth moving insistently over hers. Taking possession. Showing her all the ways they had yet to explore. The feel of his strong, hard body wrapped around her was wildly sensual. It filled her with excitement. Murmuring her surrender, she tasted the sweetness that was Lewis, felt his untamed nature in the plundering, demanding sweep of his tongue. If the night before she had been the instigator, he was now the one in charge, showering her with hot, impatient kisses that made her tremble, and seducing her with slow, tender kisses that rocked her world all the more.

And yet he wasn't hurrying her. Not at all. And that, she found, as he lifted his head once again, was even sexier.

"What about now?" he asked her softly, lifting his head, waiting for her perusal with his usual "scientific" approach.

Lexie traced the curve of his lower lip with the pad of her thumb. "You have the look you had after I kissed you," she said, even more softly. The look that said he wanted her as much as she wanted him. The look that said he found her to be everything he had ever wanted in a woman. The look that said he wanted nothing more than to make her his.

Lewis slouched down on the seat, and shifted her around again, so she was straddling his lap, facing him. Her thighs rested on either side of his. She felt the rock-hard muscle and the heat transmitting through his jeans. And lower still, a mounting desire that matched her own.

An ardent look in his eyes, he tunneled both his hands in her hair and brought her face back down to his. Had she not known better, she would have thought—in that instant—that he was falling for her in a very major way. Just as she was beginning to feel something really special for him.

"Sounds promising," he murmured gruffly, kissing her again.

Lexie wondered why he ever thought they needed manuals. They were practically combusting, and all they had done was kiss. Afraid things were going to get out of hand before she had time to sort out her emotions, which were fast spiraling out of control, she drew back. "Lewis…"

He read her heart as readily as her mind. "Let's just kiss, Lexie. In every way we can think of, and if we run out of ideas, we'll consult our manuals and figure out even new and better ways to kiss." He kissed the back of her hand, the inside of her wrist…

Lexie inhaled a shaky breath. She wasn't used to a man putting her needs before his own. "You'd be content with that?" she asked, stunned.

His eyes softened, as did his touch. "I would be content

to just look at you and talk to you and be able to be with you. That alone, Lexie, is a dream come true."

It was feeling like a dream come true to her, too, which was why, an hour later, when they were so deep into kissing she no longer knew where his lips ended and hers began, the hard rapping on the driver-side window, accompanied by the sweeping arc of flashlight, felt like such a rude interruption.

LEWIS STRAIGHTENED, saw the flashing light of the sheriff's department cruiser behind them and groaned. "Let me handle this," he ordered gruffly.

"Believe me, I have no intention of defending this," she managed, blushing to the roots of her hair.

Recognizing the interloper, Lewis grimaced and rolled down the fogged-up window of his SUV. "Kevin."

Kevin McCabe grinned in obvious amusement. "Well, well, if it isn't my big brother, and Lexie Remington," he drawled. "Look at the two of you!"

Lexie restored order to her hair with her fingertips, muttering, "Let's not!"

Lewis could tell she was hideously embarrassed, even though they'd done nothing to be ashamed of. Nevertheless, he regretted putting her in this position, even inadvertently. Their highly satisfying—and romantic—encounter should have remained a private affair.

His face resuming an all-business look, Kevin set his flashlight on the clipboard in front of him. Lewis tensed, knowing his law-and-order brother would not fail to do his job, despite their familial connection. In fact, knowing Kevin, Lewis figured that he would be even more diligent about it because a relative was involved, lest he be accused of an ethical or moral lapse in his professional judgment.

"You know parking is illegal this time of night, especially for such purposes," Kevin lectured sternly.

"No. I wasn't aware of that," Lewis fibbed innocently. "But thanks for telling us." He started to put up his window. "We'll be sure not to make this mistake again."

Kevin sighed and motioned for Lewis to put the window back down. He poked the brim of his hat, pushing it away from his forehead. "Not that simple."

"Sure it is," Lewis replied levelly, sitting all the way back in his seat. He regarded Kevin with an uncompromising look. "Since you and I are family and you know that Lexie and I are consenting adults."

Kevin took his pen out of his shirt pocket. "I'm still going to have to give you a ticket."

"Why?" Lewis retorted furiously, getting out of the SUV to stand beside his brother. "You've made your point!"

Lexie climbed out of the vehicle, too, and came around to stand between Kevin and Lewis. Kevin nodded at her in polite acknowledgment and then continued his lecture in a low, implacable tone. "If I do a favor for you and look the other way, then I've got to excuse the next family member's speeding ticket, and someone else's expired license or violation of the noise ordinance. Before you know it I'm looking the other way all the time for my family and friends, and holding them to a different standard of the law than everyone else, and that's not fair and you know it. Not to mention the fact that if I start not enforcing the rules on everyone I *like* in this town, I'd be putting myself out of a job since I like darn near everyone who lives and passes through here, including you, Lexie Remington." Kevin paused and flashed Lexie a friendly smile. "You were always real sweet to me when we were in high school together."

"Thanks, Kev." Lexie grinned back at him. "I always liked you, too, even if you were a year behind me."

Kevin beamed, obviously pleased Lexie had recalled just

how much younger he was than she. Lewis scowled. "Can we stop the mutual admiration society and start talking about how we're going to deal with this?"

"I already told you," Kevin retorted in exasperation. "I can forgo the fine and ticket—this time—but I've got to give you both a written warning."

Lewis threw up his hands in frustration. "At least keep Lexie out of it," he requested.

Kevin continued to write. "Can't do that, either."

"Why not?" Lewis demanded, as Kevin ripped off the first page, handed it to him and then started up writing on a second.

"Because the law is the law and she's here with you. As much as I might like to look the other way for a pretty woman, I can't do that," Kevin explained patiently.

"You are so out of line here," Lewis muttered.

Kevin continued writing, unperturbed. "And you're out of line, parking here after hours, when the lake is closed to all except those who have purchased camping permits at the ranger station, which you haven't done. Have you?"

Lewis remained stubbornly silent as Kevin finished the paperwork and then radioed the results in, via the radio on his sleeve.

"What do you think the chances are it's going to get back to my folks?" Lexie asked as Kevin backed his sheriff's cruiser up, and waited, headlights glaring, for Lewis to drive off, too.

Lewis set his jaw. "Given the fact that Kevin just called our transgression into the Laramie's sheriff's station? Pretty high."

Lexie moaned and buried her face in her hands. How had a night that had been filled with such sweet promise turned into an utter catastrophe?

Chapter Eight

"Thanks for helping me, Lexie," Sydney Mazero said the next afternoon. She turned this way and that, examining her reflection in the three-way mirror. The bright blue ultra suede dress with the high collar, long sleeves, fitted bodice and calf-length prairie skirt looked great with the lace-up high-heeled boots. An eyelet lace petticoat peeked from beneath the hem of the full flaring skirt.

"You're welcome," Lexie replied graciously. She welcomed the distraction because it kept her from dwelling on the mortifying incident at the lake the night before—and the fallout with her father when she and Lewis gave a white-washed account of what had transpired.

Sydney flicked her long red hair from her shoulders and her blue eyes sparkled with delight. "I definitely feel like me in this outfit. And it's going to be great for promoting the movie, too. I mean I can't exactly show up at the premiere and hit the talk-show circuit dressed in belly-exposing jeans and a halter top and then expect people to want to see me as a frontier woman in Beau Chamberlain's new western. I have to make people believe I can carry it off before they ever set foot in the theaters. Otherwise, there is no way I'm going to carry this movie."

Lexie knew Sydney was under a great deal of pressure. It

was her first starring role. She had equal billing with three other name actors. If the movie tanked—which was unlikely, given the screenwriters and legendary director attached to the project—she'd have a hard time getting work in the business again. These days, an actor was only as good as their latest box office success. "My uncle Beau has enormous faith in you," Lexie soothed.

Sydney took a deep breath and let it out slowly. She stepped off the pedestal, and turned her back to Lexie so she could help her with the zipper. "I know we had settled on a trendy look for all my interviews but now that I see this…do you think you could pull together a wardrobe for my appearances on the talk shows?"

Lexie wasn't surprised Sydney had changed her mind. Her clients did it all the time. It was her job to be accommodating. "We could outfit you with a split skirt, blouse and vest. Something reminiscent of the Old West, yet fun. Innocent, yet sexy."

"Could I wear boots, too?"

"Sure. We could go with traditional cowgirl leather if you want. Or something more daring."

"Rattleskin? 'Cause I really loathe snakes and I have some funny stories about my encounters with reptiles while I was filming on location for the movie."

"Sure." Lexie continued making notes. She was well versed in the art of setting up talk-show chitchat, for star performances. "When do your TV appearances start?" she asked.

"Next Monday." Sydney bit her lip anxiously. "Is that enough time to come up with five outfits, so I'll have a different one to wear every day?"

Used to working under immense pressure, Lexie nodded. "Do you want all the outfits to follow the design of the clothes you wore in the movie?"

"Yes. But at the same time I want them to look up-to-the-minute. Not like an actual costume from the film. Can you handle that?"

"No problem. We'll need to do another fitting on Friday, before the Saturday premiere in Austin. Say nine a.m.?"

"I'll be here. Thanks, Lexie." Beaming, Sydney dashed off to change clothing.

Lexie turned to see her mother standing in the hallway that led to the apartment above the store. The Countess had still been sleeping when Lexie arrived at Jenna's boutique, after spending the night at her father's ranch, so she had put off talking to her mother. But now there was no escaping it, it seemed.

"Alexandra, I'd like a word with you upstairs."

Lexie did her best to suppress a sigh. Knowing she either had to comply with her mother's request or risk a scene in Jenna's boutique, she followed her mother to the privacy of the apartment upstairs. The twenty pieces of matched luggage took up much of the small but luxuriously outfitted living room. In the bedroom beyond, Lexie could see the rumpled covers on the bed, clothes and towels strewn about. In counterpoint to the disarray, Melinda looked perfectly put together in a Chanel suit, ruby necklace and earrings.

"Why do you bother waiting on those actors, hand and foot?" Melinda asked, with a shudder of disdain.

"I enjoy helping up-and-coming actors like Sydney," Lexie said. She especially enjoyed designing outfits, instead of just matching celebrities with other clothing designers.

Melinda examined her manicure. "You should be concentrating all your attention on your husband."

"One problem with that, Mother. I'm not married."

The Contessa dropped her hand and stared at Lexie intently. "But you could be, if you play your cards right, Alexandra."

Dread spiraled through Lexie. "What are you talking about?" Lexie asked cautiously.

Her mother checked out her reflection in the mirror. "Constantine Romeo. He knows what a mistake he made, leaving you behind."

"And you know this because..." Lexie asked dryly.

Melinda patted her coiffed hair. "I've talked to him numerous times in the past few days."

Which could only mean trouble. Lexie paced closer. "What are you planning?"

Melinda perched on the sofa and continued with a Cheshire cat smile. "He's coming here this evening, to see you."

"Why?" Lexie demanded.

"His new movie, *Collision,* debuts in New York City a week from Friday. As you know, he's already been promoting the picture in Europe, and it's made a big splash there, but he needs to do the same thing in the States, and he's interested in getting himself on the men's best-dressed lists again, as well. He realizes you are the only one who can help him do that."

Lexie scowled. "There are plenty of talented stylists out there."

"None of whom are the daughter of Italian royalty."

"By marriage," Lexie corrected. She wasn't really sure that counted since her mother had only become royalty herself when she married Riccardo della Gheradesca when Lexie was seven years old. Lexie had never actually lived as Italian royalty. She had been brought up on American soil.

"If Constantine marries you, I will personally see he has access to every palace in Europe."

Lexie felt the beginnings of a huge headache coming on. "Only one problem with that, Mother—I don't want to marry Constantine Romeo any more than he ever wanted to marry me."

The Contessa's eyes flashed with temper. "But you did want to marry him."

"When I was young and foolish! Before I realized he was totally incapable of ever being faithful to me, never mind actually loving me!"

Melinda looked even more aggrieved. "Fidelity is overrated, Alexandra."

"Not to me," Lexie countered stubbornly.

Melinda lifted her shoulder in an elegant little shrug. "So you'd take lovers, too, Alexandra. It's not the end of the world."

Lexie shook her head miserably. "It would be for me."

Melinda looked down her nose. "What counts is position in society. Connections. Luxury. Constantine can provide all of that for you and more. All you have to do is get him securely on the hook and reel him in."

Lexie rolled her eyes. "Love the fishing analogy, Mother."

"He's coming here tonight to propose you work for him again, exclusively. I expect you to appear tempted but put conditions on that. Tell him you expect him to marry you as soon as possible and that my attorneys will be negotiating the pre-nup for you."

Lexie scoffed. "You're not serious!"

The Contessa picked imaginary lint from her skirt. "Completely. I'll help you, of course. Constantine's second assistant is driving down as we speak, to help me set the stage for his arrival. Together we will see it is done up right. All you have to do is appear at the apartment at seven-thirty this evening and put our plan in motion."

Lexie lifted her hands to ward off any further advice. "Forget it, Mother."

"Alexandra," Melinda chided sternly.

"I am participating in the Career Fair at Laramie High School this evening, Mother. And that's final."

Melinda folded her arms in front of her. "Constantine Romeo expects to see you this evening, Alexandra."

Lexie gestured uncaringly. "Well, then, you might want to tell him to save himself a trip because no way am I going to be here to greet him."

"I AM GUESSING FROM THE LOOK on your face that your session with your mother did not go well," Lewis remarked as he met up with Lexie in the LHS parking lot. They each carried a poster-board display indicating who they were and what they did for a living, and headed for the brick building where they had both attended high school nearly a decade before. "Was she upset about the parking-at-the-lake citation?"

"Actually, she doesn't know about that yet unless my father or Jenna told her and I doubt that they did."

"Then what's wrong?" Lewis paused to open the glass lobby door.

Looking gorgeous as ever in a cropped pink cashmere blazer, white silk T-shirt, black skirt and sexy high heels, Lexie strode on in ahead of him. She had put her hair up in a clip and tendrils of hair framed her face and escaped down her neck. "She's been busy arranging a marriage for me."

Lewis still cringed at the memory of sitting down with Lexie's folks the night before to 'fess up about the incident at the lake. They'd had no choice but to spill all before Jenna and Jake heard it through the Laramie grapevine. Thankfully they'd bought their "innocent account," or at least pretended to believe their squeaky-clean version of the story. Still, to say they were displeased with the citation was an understatement. But at least Jake hadn't chased him off with a shotgun!

Lewis paused. "You're kidding." His jaw tightened when he saw her serious expression. "You're not kidding." He took her elbow and steered her down a hall, away from the gymnasium where everyone else was gathering. He backed her up against a wall of lockers. "With whom?" He searched her face, trying to determine how she really felt about this latest maneuver. "Some European count or something?"

"Worse." Lexie set her poster board down. Her laugh sounded hollow and she looked upset. "Constantine Romeo."

Lewis snorted in contempt, thinking once again that this

had to be a bad joke. He stopped when he saw Lexie's grim expression had not changed one iota. This was for real. "Besides the fact that your ex is handsome, internationally famous and successful," he intoned dryly, "why would the Contessa want to do that?"

"Exactly what I've been trying to figure out." Lexie sighed. She rested her shoulders against the metal behind her, but let her hips fall forward, just a bit. She placed her palms flat on either side of her. "Mother never does anything unless it benefits her directly."

Silence ticked between them. Lewis watched Lexie's delicate fingers trace the metal locker. "She has plenty of money, right?"

"And wealthy, titled friends," she confirmed with a sigh. "The only thing lacking in the Contessa's life, that I can see, is excitement."

Using his body to shield Lexie from view of people walking in, Lewis braced a shoulder against the wall. "And movie stars generate excitement."

"In droves." Lexie nodded. "Wherever they go. Whatever they do. Women practically pass out they get so excited when men like Constantine Romeo appear on the scene."

"You think she wants to grab some of that herself?" Lewis asked.

"I think she wants another husband. Someone in the film business would probably do nicely. I mean, think about it. If she married a successful director, she could attend premieres all over the world. It would open up her life to a whole different kind of power and excitement. If I were with Constantine and she was with us, she'd meet everyone there was to know because he goes to every hot event there is."

Lewis searched for a solution that would leave the path to Lexie's heart free and clear. "Maybe you could just work on matching your mother up with someone eligible you know, then."

She gave him a look. "Like I could do that in good conscience. Like I'd want to do it."

Aware this was the first time he had ever seen Lexie with her guard completely down, Lewis said, "So what are you going to do?"

Shrugging, Lexie picked up her poster again and headed across the lobby, toward the gymnasium. "Hope and pray that Constantine Romeo heard the message I left on his cell phone and decided not to helicopter into Laramie after all."

AS IF HE DIDN'T HAVE enough to worry about, Lewis mused as he headed to the storage locker at the other end of the gym, where all the cafeteria tables and chairs were kept. All four of his brothers were already over there, helping with the setup.

"Wow. Don't you look nice this evening," the LHS computer science teacher, Josephine Holdsworth said, waylaying Lewis in the center of the large room. "You look like a different person."

Lewis thought so, too.

For the first time since he could remember, his cowlicks weren't out of control. The khaki trousers, crewnecked sweater and wool blazer were comfortable. Sophisticated. And masculine. The combination of his new haircut and the clothes Lexie had helped him pick out left him feeling both confident and at ease. He felt as if he could hold his own with just about anyone and, most important of all, was no longer the most socially awkward person in the room.

Clothes might not make the man.

But appearances, it seemed, did count for something.

Except in his brother's eyes….

Kevin was the first to meet up with Lewis after he and Josephine parted company. Kevin was wearing his sheriff's department uniform and wore the smug look of a guy who felt he knew a whole heck of a lot more about women than Lewis ever would.

"I just saw Lexie Remington," Kevin reported, concerned. "She didn't look happy. Can't say I blame her."

Nor could Lewis, given the latest trouble Lexie's mother was giving her.

"What were you thinking, anyway, taking her parking at the lake last night?" Kevin continued disapprovingly. "Don't you realize that's one of the fastest ways to ruin a lady's reputation?"

"Me!" Lewis retorted hotly, resenting the advice. He jabbed a finger at his sibling's silver badge. "You're the one who had to go and report it!" he accused.

Kevin shot Lewis a scornful look. "I already explained I was just doing my job. Don't blame your bad decisions on me."

"And speaking of bad decisions," Lewis's brother Brad chimed in, "I heard about all the sex books you had delivered to the ranch yesterday. I'm not sure what you're planning in that regard. But it's not smart, either," he said with a disapproving frown. "Anything too scripted is not going to seem genuine."

As if he would let a how to manual, instead of his heart, guide him, Lewis thought, incensed.

When were his brothers going to realize he knew what he was doing?

"Brad and Kevin are right," Will added, doing his best to be helpful in that protective oldest brother way of his. Clad in a rugged leather aviator jacket and jeans, Will looked like the former Navy fighter pilot he was. "I know you don't have a lot of experience with really sophisticated women." He paused. "I hope you're not planning to use Lexie to hone your technique. There are better ways to learn how to be charming."

"I'm not using her as a learning tool!" Lewis insisted.

His brothers all regarded him skeptically. They knew he had

always been awkward around the fairer sex—until Lexie came into his life, that was. With her, everything felt right and natural.

Out of the corner of his eye, Lewis saw Susie Carrigan heading toward them.

Given the fact he had impulsively—and falsely—told Lexie that he was getting a style makeover to impress Susie, he hoped she would not talk to him tonight.

Lewis turned away from her and lifted another folding table out of the storage closet.

"Is it part of the joke you were playing on Lexie then?" Riley demanded, looking every bit the successful family doc in his white lab coat, with a stethoscope around his neck. "By pretending you wanted to hire her to give you the makeover you obviously had done. Because I have to tell you, I've perpetrated my fair share of practical jokes. And the one you've been playing on Lexie is going to put you on the road to hell and back."

"You don't know what you're talking about," Lewis muttered. "So maybe you all should just shut up."

"And maybe you should start acting like the gentleman you were raised to be..." Riley abruptly stopped talking as Susie entered their circle.

Susie smiled, and stuck her hands in the deep, slash pockets of her landscape gardener's coveralls. "I was sent over here to tell you fellas that the teachers want the tables arranged according to this chart. And Lewis, a word with you privately, please?"

Lewis headed off with Susie, wondering just how much she had overheard. Judging by the accusing look on her face as soon as they left his brothers, a fair amount.

"You want to tell me what you and your brothers are doing to my cousin Lexie?" Susie demanded sweetly.

Lewis swore silently. What was it they said about tangled webs? "My brothers don't have a thing to do with this."

Susie scoffed. "The guilty looks on their faces, and the way they were all huddled together, whispering with you just now, say otherwise." Susie sized Lewis up in grim silence. "Fine," she bit out when no confession was forthcoming. "I'll just go ask Lexie why you were *pretending* to hire her to give you a makeover. Not that you didn't need one. Obviously, you did."

"How do you know that?"

"Simple deduction. You've never cared whether your clothes were in fashion or not. You've always had your eye on Lexie. Suddenly, she's back. You want to spend a lot of time with her. Only she's not dating right now."

Desperate to keep Lexie from being hurt, Lewis moved to stop her. "Susie, wait."

She swung back around. He took her by the elbow and guided her toward the far corner of the stage. He bent his head low to whisper in Susie's ear. "You're right. I never meant to hire Lexie. It was all a misunderstanding and I couldn't figure out how to get out of it without hurting her feelings, so I went along with it."

"And while you were at it, you told your brothers," Susie accused.

"No," he corrected. "They figured it out."

"How?" she regarded him indignantly.

Lewis inhaled deeply and made every effort to divert her. "Because they knew I went to see Lexie the first night she was back to ask her for a date. I'll be honest—I didn't think Lexie'd go out with me, given the lah-de-dah crowd she'd been running with. But I was going to ask her anyway, and then everything got all messed up, and before I knew it I had agreed to a makeover. My brothers thought the mix-up was hilarious. How was she going to help a nerd like me look as sexy as the movie stars she usually outfits? They gave me a hard time, and they're still giving me the business, as you just witnessed. I told them to shut up about it, then and now. I don't want Lexie ever to know it was all a big misunderstanding."

Susie folded her arms in front of her. The restless tapping of her foot was the only indication of her indecision. "Your brothers agreed to keep quiet?"

"Yes."

Susie's eyes narrowed. "Then what was the McCabe family huddle about just now?"

Again, Lewis said nothing.

"That parking incident at the lake last night…?"

Lewis swore and ran a hand through his hair. "You know about that, too?" Usually Susie avoided gossip like the plague.

"Everyone in town knows about it," Susie declared. "Lexie is pretending it doesn't bother her." She angled a thumb at her sternum. "I know it does."

"Yeah, well, I'm sorry about that." He released a disgruntled breath. "I never figured we'd get caught last night, I swear." Even as he spoke the words, he knew how lame they sounded.

Lexie had deserved better.

"Just see that it doesn't happen again," Susie warned, "'cause I swear if you hurt Lexie, if you make her a laughingstock in any way, I'm going to tell her everything I know. And then I'm coming after you, Lewis McCabe, with everything I've got."

"WHAT WERE YOU AND Susie whispering about just now over by the stage?" Lexie said as she walked with Lewis through the parking lot, toward his SUV.

Lewis hit the Unlock button on his key chain, waited for the click, then lifted the hatch. He leaned in to gather up an armload of glossy information folders on job opportunities at McCabe Software Game Company. "She was giving me the business about the parking thing. Along with everyone else in town."

Wishing she had thought to create flyers of her own about her business, instead of the poster she had just set up, Lexie picked up an armload of promotional folders, too. "Hardly anyone's said a word to me about us getting caught making out." Although she was pretty sure everyone knew from some of the amused looks she had been getting thus far this evening.

Lewis smiled mischievously. "That's because you're the *female* involved. The man's always considered responsible for idiot stuff like that."

"Not always," Lexie bantered back. She moved away from the vehicle so he could shut and lock the hatch. "Sometimes people blame the woman for leading the man astray."

They headed companionably for the building once again. "When the truth is we both sort of led each other astray," Lewis said, the look in his eyes telling her he wanted to kiss her like that again.

"Or tried," Lexie said dryly, beginning to see the ridiculousness of the situation they found themselves in. They were as lust-driven as two teenagers.

"The question is, do we want to try again?" Lewis leaned down to whisper in her ear as they walked through the side door to the gymnasium, which was now teeming with local business people, teachers and the first trickle of parents and students.

"Heck, yes," Lexie teased right back with a grin.

Lewis looked down at her. Their eyes locked. She felt her heart skip a beat. Had they not been in public, she was pretty sure he would have hauled her into his arms again and really planted one on her.

Without warning, there was an uproar near the entrance to the gym. Lexie turned, saw the crowd part, and Constantine Romeo saunter into the Laramie High School gymnasium.

Lexie's spirits sank.

Lewis looked none too pleased, either. "I guess he either didn't get or ignored your message," Lewis said, keeping whatever else he was thinking or feeling well hidden from her.

"No surprise there," Lexie murmured back. A smile plastered on her face, she headed straight for Constantine. He looked ridiculously handsome—and out of place—in black leather pants, knee-high boots and a white poet's shirt, worn open to his sternum. His inky black hair swept nearly to his shoulders. His face was suntanned and stubbled with beard, his eyes—aided by colored contacts—were a strikingly brilliant turquoise blue.

"Hello, Lexie." He leaned forward with movie-star grandeur and brushed his lips across her temple.

Behind her, Lexie heard the sounds of professional cameras going off and noted her ex had brought a few paparazzi with him, which was again no surprise. Constantine never did anything to remotely benefit others without making sure he got the maximum publicity from it.

It bothered her to realize she had ever considered herself in love with this self-absorbed womanizer. Telling herself she'd been too young and foolish to know better, she said, "If you're looking for my mother—"

He flashed a megawatt smile. "I found what I'm looking for." He looked deep into her eyes in a way that would have knocked her off her feet, years ago. Now, it did absolutely nothing.

She ignored the way he was already undressing her with his eyes. "If you'll excuse me I've got to get back to my booth and begin setting up."

"That's fine." He lifted a hand and waved at someone behind Lexie. "I'm going to sign some autographs and drum up publicity for *Collision.* What do you say we meet back at the apartment around…ten o'clock?"

Aware Lewis was now at her side again, Lexie smiled and said, just as easily, "Sure. Why not? You and I need to make a few things clear with each other. Ten o'clock it is."

"So much for you not being interested in your ex," Lewis murmured as the man strolled away and was soon gathered up by the crowd.

Local TV crews were there to film for the evening news, as well as small town newspapers. Lexie also noted that cameras for several tabloid TV shows were swarming around Constantine.

"I meant what I said," Lexie murmured, taking Lewis's hand, and holding it firmly. She looked into his eyes. "I want to be very clear with Constantine Romeo where we stand. The question is…will you help me?"

"YOU'RE SURE THIS IS GOING to work?" Lewis asked warily as Lexie and he rushed up the stairs to the guest apartment where she had been staying. He normally had an aversion to being used as a means to an end, but in this case, cooperating with her hare-brained scheme was the only way he knew to simultaneously protect her and stake his claim.

"Absolutely," Lexie said with a grim sense of purpose Lewis found vaguely alarming. "If I know one thing about Constantine, it's the size of his ego. He can't stand not being number one."

"Wow." Lewis came to a dead stop as they swept into the living room. Flowers and candles and soft music filled the room. A lavish cold supper for two had been set out, complete with a bottle of chilling champagne. In the bedroom were more flowers, more champagne on ice and another gift basket filled with what looked to be perfumed oils and lotions.

Scowling, Lexie walked over to investigate. "I don't believe it," she muttered unhappily.

Wishing he could spare Lexie the pain of a mother who

clearly did not have her daughter's best interests at heart, Lewis kept his eyes on Lexie's. Noting how vulnerable she looked, he moved closer to her. "What?"

Lexie pivoted to face him in a drift of exotic perfume. She waved a small book in front of him like a bull confronting a red flag. "A copy of the *Kama Sutra.*"

Lewis took in her flushed cheeks and wind-tossed hair. Noting her hands were trembling, he took her all the way into his arms. "Who did this? Constantine or your mother?"

"Are you kidding me?" She rolled her eyes and continued indignantly, "My mother. That man doesn't have a romantic bone in his body. Publicly, he might be all about the grand gesture, but in private he never bothers to do anything except look at himself in the mirror." She tossed the *Kama Sutra* onto the nightstand.

"So how do you want to do this?" Lewis said, reminding himself it was all a ruse, no matter how much he wished the setup were real.

Lexie slipped off her blazer and shoes. "Well, we don't have much time." She raced around the bedroom, dimming the lights. "So I say we toss off our clothes an article at a time, then climb in to bed and wait. Leave the front door slightly ajar, of course. We want him to be able to walk right in and catch us *flagrante delicto.*"

Lewis walked back to do her bidding. By the time he had returned, Lexie had already shimmied out of her skirt and long-sleeved silk T-shirt. The sight of her in a pale pink décolleté bra edged with black lace, black thong and sheer black pantyhose had his mouth watering. "And that won't make him want to kill me?"

Lexie bent over to peel off her stockings, affording him a view of the uppermost curves of her breasts that had the blood roaring through his lower half. "The only thing it's going to hurt is his ego." She took both her hands and thoroughly rumpled her hair. "Seriously, don't worry about him hitting you or doing anything but telling me to go jump in a lake. He won't want to scratch up his hand or take a chance that his nose job will get messed up."

Aware he wanted her so badly he could barely stand it, Lewis dropped his wool blazer on the chair and tugged the crewneck sweater and cotton T-shirt over his head. Schooling himself to get a grip—and keep his intentions strictly admirable—Lewis kicked off his Italian loafers. "He had his nose done?"

"And his chin." Lexie raced to pour a couple of glasses of champagne, and quickly downed half of one, in the process giving him an equally tantalizing view of her backside. "You should see his high school yearbook picture."

Knowing he wasn't seeing much more than he'd see on the beach, if she were clad in an equally sexy swimsuit, Lewis took a long gulp from the glass she handed him. "Glad to know that," he said, struggling to keep his mind on the conversation at hand, instead of what he wanted to do with her—make love to her until they fell into a, deep exhausted sleep.

She climbed into bed and pulled the covers up to her chin. He watched as she wriggled out of her underthings out of view, and then carefully lifted a hand out to toss bra and thong, one at a time, before slipping her arm back beneath the covers once again. "Okay, you can join me," she ordered as matter-of-factly as if she did something this inane every day. "Just be careful not to lift the covers too far. I don't want to flash you."

Lewis knew the bedroom was cloaked in semidarkness. He still didn't know how he was going to take off his khaki trousers without her seeing just how aroused he was. The last thing he wanted to do was embarrass them both. "Close your eyes."

Lexie blinked, her expression a mixture of surprise and bemusement. "What?"

"Can't have you peeking," he teased.

He waited until she complied, then shucked his trousers, slipped off his boxers and slid beneath the sheets. He'd barely gotten situated when footsteps sounded on the stairs leading to the apartment.

"Now!" Lexie ordered, sweeping Lewis into her arms. She pressed her breasts against his chest. "Make it look good," she whispered. "Because if it's not authentic he won't buy it."

Lewis didn't have to be told twice. He pulled her against him, hearing her soft gasp as she felt the size and heat of him pressing against her, and then lowered his head to hers. Their lips met in a sizzling flame of awareness. She moaned and opened her mouth to his. He gave in to the desire that had been plaguing him since they entered the apartment. She responded, as hotly and wantonly as he had wanted her to. Had it not been for the sound of a quick intake of breath behind them, who knew what would have happened, Lewis thought.

Aware it was time to face their audience, and push Constantine Romeo out of Lexie's life for good, Lewis smugly lifted his head. Looking sexy and vampish, Lexie slowly pulled away from him, too. She studied him with one last lingering, smitten look that almost had Lewis believing she was falling head over heels in love with him, too.

"Show time," she murmured, so only he could hear.

Both of them turned in slow motion, expecting to see the black-haired, turquoise-eyed movie star in the tight leather pants and the billowy white poet's shirt.

They gasped in unison when they saw just who was standing at the foot of their bed.

Chapter Nine

"Oh my goodness," Lexie said.

"Oh my goodness is right!" her father replied, switching on a light.

"I didn't know the two of you were this involved!" Jenna gasped.

"We're not, exactly," Lexie said.

Lewis sent her a look. "We sort of are."

Jake's expression turned grim. "You two don't know if you are serious or not?"

Ever the family peacemaker, Jenna put a hand on her husband's arm and gently said, "Maybe they just haven't put a label on it yet, Jake."

"That's it, exactly," Lexie agreed in relief.

"Are you still his stylist?" Jake asked.

"No," Lexie replied.

Jake folded his arms in front of him. "I would say, 'Good!' but I think I prefer whatever it was to whatever it is."

"I know how this looks but I have the utmost respect for your daughter," Lewis interrupted staunchly.

"Really." Jake's gaze narrowed in silent warning. "Then suppose you explain how and why you happen to be in bed with her now."

Lewis was glad there were no shotguns in proximity. Otherwise, he was sure he would find himself at the wrong end of the barrel.

Jenna looked at Jake. "I don't think that's necessary. Lexie is an adult, free to make her own decisions, same as you and me." Jenna turned back to Lewis and Lexie. "We just came over to make sure you were okay. We saw Constantine Romeo come in to the career fair and speak to you before he was swallowed up by the crowd."

Jake Remington nodded grimly, further delineating his concern. "You slipped out of the gymnasium before I could check on you. Then we saw Constantine Romeo leave with your mother in the chopper—"

"Wait," Lexie interrupted, perplexed. "The Contessa left here with Constantine Romeo?"

"Just now, yes," Jenna replied in her usual soothing tone.

Jake shook his head. "They took off from the center of the football field if you can believe it. I don't have to tell you that caused quite a commotion."

Almost as much as the movie star's arrival, Lewis noted.

"I wanted to warn you the two of them are in cahoots about something," Jake said.

Lexie nodded. "I know what it is," she said wearily. She sat up against the headboard, primly holding the sheet against her bare breasts. "Mother wants us back together," Lexie continued with an exasperated sigh. "She wants me to marry Constantine."

"Over my dead body!" Jake Remington declared fervently.

"My feelings exactly," Lewis muttered back.

Lexie shot Lewis a sidelong glance, as if she were as grateful for his support as he was glad to give it. "Constantine was supposed to show up here at the apartment, after the career fair." She paused to regard her father and stepmother earnestly. "That's why Lewis and I were staging our liaison. We wanted him to catch us together. I figured it was the quickest way to get the egotistical jerk to leave me alone. I had no idea you and Jenna would be the ones to walk in on us!" she concluded.

Jake studied them. "So this isn't real?" He appeared to be very relieved.

Lewis could imagine how Jake felt. If Lexie were his daughter, he'd be ready to kick some Texas butt, too.

"It was just a ruse, Daddy. And since it's failed—" Lexie paused and bit her lower lip, the somewhat hopeful note coming back into her voice "—maybe you would excuse us?"

"Actually," Jenna intervened tactfully, linking her arm in Jake's, "I think we're going to head back to the ranch, Lexie. Now that we know you are okay, there's no reason for us to stay."

Jake glared at Lewis, sizing him up, still looking as if the protective part of him wanted to haul him out of that bed and punch his lights out. Whereas the rest of Jake seemed to know intuitively that Lewis was as honorable as the rest of the McCabes. Hence, he gave him grudging respect for trying to help Jake's daughter, even if Lewis had gone about it in the wrong way.

"We'll lock the door on the way out," Jenna promised, urging her husband along. They left the room and shut the door.

Silence fell between Lewis and Lexie as she dropped back onto the pillows. Moaning, she covered her face with her hands. "I can't believe they walked in on us when we were naked…kissing…in the bed!"

"Yeah. Not exactly in my game plan for winning your father over," Lewis assured with real feeling, aware his arousal was coming back, full force, now that he and Lexie were alone again. "I can only imagine what he would say if I were to ask for permission to…um…date you."

Lexie uncovered her eyes. She peered at him suspiciously. "Why would you want to do that?"

Because we have to start somewhere. "Well, because."

The corners of her lips curved up slightly. Her turquoise eyes glimmered in interest. "Keep going."

Deciding to test the waters, Lewis shrugged. "If we were to ever get serious, then it would help if I already had him on my side."

Lexie flushed, looking even prettier and more delectably sexy than she had when they'd just finished kissing. "You're not talking about…"

"Well." Trying not to fantasize what it would be like to actually make love with her, Lewis shrugged. "In the abstract. Sure. Purely hypothetically, if I were to ask for your hand in marriage," he drawled lazily, to cover the fast-growing ache inside him, "it would help if your father already liked and approved of me."

Lexie harrumphed and aimed a killer look at him. "You're assuming my father would get to decide that issue. He wouldn't."

He quirked a brow at her, liking it when she revealed herself to him this way. "You'd really marry someone he did not approve of?"

Exasperated color flowed into her cheeks. "I would hope when it comes to that, if it ever comes to that," she amended with droll humor, "that my dad would trust my judgment and be happy if I'm happy." She rolled toward him, the softness of her breasts brushing his biceps. "I mean, I understand why they used to do that, in the old days…."

He moved closer, liking the way her strawberry-blond hair tumbled around her shoulders.

"'Cause I was really young when I ran off with Constantine Romeo and really wasn't equipped to figure out what guys are trustworthy and who are not."

He didn't know why, but he enjoyed quizzing her like this. "So you trust your judgment now?"

Lexie hedged. For the first time since they'd come up to the apartment and climbed into bed together, she looked uncertain. "I think I have enough life experience to know the con artists from the ones who have only my best interests at heart."

A sharp sense of regret swept through Lewis as he thought about the misunderstanding about him hiring her, which he had yet to correct. Lewis had never felt the style makeover she'd given him was a joke. But his brothers had. And now Lexie's cousin, Susie, knew he had never intended to hire Lexie, too. He wished he could just tell her what had happened. But knowing how sensitive she was about her profession, how determined she was that the people close to her respect what she did for a living, the way her own mother and father did not, he wasn't sure she'd find humor in the situation. He did not want to risk alienating her. Not now, when he was finally getting his shot at winning her heart.

She studied his brooding expression. "You're upset that Jenna and my dad found us here together like this, aren't you?" she queried softly.

Lewis shifted restlessly, wishing that was all he had to feel guilty about. "Well, coming on the heels of us getting caught out parking together last night—you have to admit, Lexie, it doesn't look good."

She studied him from beneath the fringe of red-gold lashes. "You care that much about what people think?"

"I don't have a choice. And I haven't since we moved to Laramie when I was a kid. Living in a small town like this forces you to be accountable for your actions."

"Because everybody knows everything."

"It sure seems that way. Which is why…" He paused.

"What?" she prodded.

"Are you sorry that Constantine didn't come in here and catch us together?" he asked, studying her expression.

Still holding the sheet to her breasts, Lexie reached for the champagne glass on the nightstand. "Only in that I know him finding us together would have gotten him out of my life forever." She paused to take a sip. "Now, I still have to worry about whatever he is doing with my mother. Where they were going. What they are up to now."

Lewis let the sheet fall to his waist. He retrieved his glass, too. "You think she hasn't given up on her matchmaking?"

"The Contessa? Heavens, no! The worst is yet to come." She drained her glass and set it aside. The sheet covering her breasts dropped a precarious notch. "Which is why—" she turned to him once again, smiling in a way that had his lower body responding all the more "—as long as we've got the guilt, we may as well have the fun that goes along with it."

Lewis wanted to make love to Lexie more than he had ever imagined possible. However, he didn't want her on the rebound, which was what he suddenly feared this was. He shifted, so they were no longer touching, and put up both hands before he could be tempted by her sexy mouth and enticing body. "Whoa. Lexie."

Lexie stared at him in silence, as if trying to make sense of a puzzle whose pieces just didn't fit. She pivoted toward him, her bent knee touching the rock-hard muscles of his thigh. "You've got to be kidding! You're not going to try and put the moves on me? Even though you have the perfect opportunity to follow through on the deal we made with each other last night to help each other brush up on those bedroom skills neither of us seem to have?"

That was the sum of it, yes. "I don't want to take advantage."

The room grew unnaturally quiet. Hurt shimmered in her soft, turquoise eyes. She studied him suspiciously as she tilted her head slightly to one side. "You were willing to experiment with me last night."

Damn but it was hard being noble, Lewis thought on a disgruntled sigh. "Last night we were behaving recklessly," he countered, trying hard not to think about the sweet kisses they had shared, but the horrified look on her face when they'd been caught necking in his SUV. Never mind her expression when her dad and stepmother had walked in and caught them, buck naked and kissing in this very bed.

"So?" She looked perplexed.

Lewis wasn't sure why he had started this. He just knew someone had to shake up Lexie's cockeyed view of man-woman relationships and make her understand she deserved so much more from a guy than what she was apparently ready and willing to settle for. It looked like it was going to be him. "Every time we act impulsively we get ourselves in trouble," he explained.

Lexie shot Lewis a glance, letting him know she was as reckless and impulsive as ever, and proud of it. "So you're saying what? That you don't want me or that I'm not worth the risk?"

Lewis *knew* she had felt his arousal, pressed up against him the way she had been. He leaned back against the headboard, wishing like heck the two of them weren't naked beneath the sheets. "I'm saying," he corrected patiently, "that I'm beginning to want a lot more than a casual roll in the hay with you."

The words that should have reassured her did the opposite. "Like what?" She regarded him nervously.

Like a lifetime with you. Knowing that was too much too soon—to be saying out loud anyway—Lewis shrugged. "I don't know yet."

Her cheeks turned an even pinker hue. "I don't know, either."

"And yet…I can't get you out of my mind." Or my heart, he added silently. And that was something that wasn't going to change. Lexie was the woman he was supposed to be with—every day that passed, he was more sure of that than ever.

She ran a hand through her tousled hair, pushing it off her face. "So maybe we should experiment again, just a little," she insisted stubbornly. "Given the fact that we both admit we could use more expertise in that particular regard."

He had to hand it to her—she was persistent. And looking a little apprehensive beneath the feisty exterior, too. "I suppose you've got a point," Lewis said, mocking her too-casual tone to a T. "It is always good to know what you're doing."

She slid farther beneath the sheet, dropped back onto the pillows and rolled onto her side. She propped her head on her upraised hand. "So where do you want to start?"

Doing his best to ignore the lissome curves of her body beneath the soft cotton sheet, Lewis lifted the barrier of sheets still between them and stretched out beside her, almost—not quite—touching. He lifted a hand and brushed an errant strand of hair from her cheek, then cupped her chin in his hand. The silky heat of her skin warming him through and through, he answered her in the same cavalier tone, "How about with a few kisses?"

Lexie jerked in a breath and closed her eyes. "Sounds good."

Lewis brought his mouth to hers, half expecting her to stiffen with resistance, given the unromantic way they were approaching this practice session. Instead, she wreathed both arms about his neck, opened her mouth to the plundering pressure of his and let her body melt against his. His body ignited. And once he felt her surrender, there was no stopping with just one kiss. He stroked, he teased, he cajoled. Until she was kissing him back wildly, wantonly, passionately, and he knew he had to take yet another step closer to the fulfilling intimacy they both craved.

Reluctantly, he drew away, aware they were both breathing as if they had just completed a 6-K run. He dropped kisses at her temple, along her cheekbone, the delicate shell of her ear, the pulsing hollow of her throat. He brought his gaze back to hers, and the air between them vibrated with escalating excitement and desire. "How about touching?"

The sparkle of her eyes grew ever brighter. "Where?"

Lewis decided he liked the excited glitter in her eyes. He liked the rapid rise and fall of her chest with every breath even more. "Here." He swept the sheet downward, to her waist. He sighed with sheer masculine pleasure as his glance roved her breasts. They were soft and full and as beautiful as he had expected. Admiring her unabashedly, liking the fact she didn't insist the lights be off, he caressed the creamy skin and pouting pink nipples.

She reached for him.

He took her hand and put it back on his shoulder. "We'll get there," he murmured, in no hurry to rush this along. "Right now I want to taste you." He lowered his mouth to her breast, suckled gently. Her back arched. Her lower body shifted restlessly.

"Oh, Lewis," she gasped. "That feels…so…good."

Satisfaction poured through him as he noted the depth of her pleasure. He realized what had been eluding him in the lovemaking department had not been physical moves, but the requisite emotions. His blossoming feelings for her made every sensation so much more fulfilling and intense. He turned his attention to her other breast and lingered there until she gasped and trembled uncontrollably. Realizing they were finally where they belonged, he shifted her onto her back and pushed the sheet away entirely. Deliberately, he let his hand caress the flat plane of her abdomen, lower still, to the delta between her thighs. She shuddered at his touch. He liked her response so much he explored the delicate folds until she groaned. "What about this?" Not content with tactile exploration, he bent his head, circled the most sensitive part of her with his tongue, laved it gently.

She sighed contentedly, even as she shifted positions with a mixture of anticipation and desire. "That's nice, too."

"And this?" She moaned as his fingers found the slick, silken heat. She arched against his lips, her body pleading for a more intimate union. Aware, even as she moaned, that she was on the brink, he furthered his exploration, gently, tenderly, until she was gone, floating, free. Then he held her until the aftershocks subsided.

Slowly, he slid his way up her body, to cradle her against his chest. Still trembling, Lexie rested her head against his chest. Pulling her buttocks against him, Lewis began to think about his own needs.

As did she.

Her bare breasts brushed against his chest, she found his lips with hers, and kissed him, her mouth soft and warm and oh, so tempting. She ran her hands through the mat of hair on his chest, explored his flat male nipples until he groaned. Blood rushed to his groin, hardening him even more. Afraid he would explode in her hands, instead of deep inside her, where he desperately needed to be, Lewis schooled himself to slow down. It was a futile request as she rolled him onto his back, straddled his thighs and slid, slowly, evocatively, ever lower. Her lips touched his waist, lingered sweetly, tracing the line of hair leading to his groin. The closer she got to her destination, the more he throbbed.

Lexie knew it, reveled in it. With the expertise of a born seducer, she caressed and kissed him, in all the ways he had fantasized that she would. Enjoying it every bit as much as he. "Learning is always a two-way street," she murmured, her hair falling across his abdomen. She followed the swishing softness with her lips. "Seems to me we need to go down your avenue, too."

He arched as she closed around him. "Lexie…"

"Let me explore…." She continued kissing, touching. Her

fingertips made lazy explorations until he was writhing with desire. Not about to climax without her, Lewis pulled her up, toward him. He shifted her onto her back, stretched out over her, taking control once again. "I know it's old-fashioned..."

She opened her legs to accommodate him, the insides of her thighs rubbing against the outside of his. Her head fell back in an age-old gesture of feminine surrender that heightened the excitement between them even more. "As it happens," she gasped between subsequent kisses and caresses, "I've always had a fondness for missionary...." She wrapped her arms and legs around him and lifted her hips to his.

"Good." He penetrated her slowly, lifting her and filling her with the hot, throbbing length of him. "Because I have a primitive need to be the one on top right now."

And then they were one, kissing hotly, succumbing to a hunger and emotion neither one of them had known they possessed. No longer novices discovering what each of them wanted, needed, they were two equals, coming together in a blaze of innocence and passion, wonder and satisfaction, until there was only this exquisite moment in time. Thrills swept through them, one after another. Together, they moved toward a single goal, the passion so strong it didn't feel quite real. But it was, Lewis noted with a satisfaction deeper than anything he had ever felt, as she writhed beneath him and did what it took to make him relinquish control and join her at the edge of ecstasy and beyond.

THE PLAN HAD BEEN a good one, or so Lexie'd thought, when Lewis suggested they hook up as a way of relaxing, having fun and learning a lot about the possible pleasures of the physical interactions between a man and a woman. They'd been expected to make love to expand their bedroom knowledge and keep their emotions out of it.

Lexie'd learned a lot, all right, she realized as Lewis rolled onto his back and took her with him, keeping her clasped against his chest. She'd learned that for her, heart and body were inextricably linked. She closed her eyes and struggled to regain her composure and her breath.

She'd learned she wanted everything Lewis McCabe had to give—his tenderness and daring, kindness and patience. And with good reason, she mused wistfully. Lewis saw her as an equal worthy of his respect, not a stepping stone to his success, useful only as an ego-booster. Lewis protected her without reining her in, or constraining her. He celebrated her and their passionate attraction to each other unashamedly. She loved the way he matched her reckless move for move and the fact he "got her" the way no one else ever had. Too late, she saw Lewis McCabe was someone she could see herself building a future with.

And that, Lexie knew, had not been part of their initial deal.

Lewis hadn't proposed a long-distance relationship or continuing ties of any sort. Yet here she was, once again smitten by a man who might not ever feel for her all that she was beginning to feel for him. Realizing that, it was all Lexie could do not to bolt from the bedroom before he had a chance to say or do another thing.

Knowing, however, that behavior would engender more questions than she wanted to answer, Lexie forced herself to casually withdraw herself from Lewis's gently protective embrace and sit up, dragging her half of the sheet with her. She reached for the champagne bottle and her empty glass and refilled it.

Letting his sheet drape low across his hips, Lewis propped himself up on the pillows, too. Wordlessly studying her, he handed her his glass. Lexie had only to glimpse the expression on his face to know he had picked up on her abrup change in mood, and was as determined to know the reason why as she was to hide it.

"You know," Lewis said casually, sipping his champagne, "it's not the girls who are Trouble with a Capital T that I should be watching out for." He traced a fingertip from her shoulder, to her wrist. "It's the smart, sexy, sweet, funny ones."

Lexie frowned, aware they were headed into dangerous territory again. Once again, she couldn't stop tingling. She took another sip of her champagne, forced herself to keep her gaze turned away. Lexie slipped from the bed, and walked naked to the closet to retrieve her robe. "Is that what you think I am?" She slipped it on and knotted it in front of her, wishing it covered more than just to midcalf. She felt way too naked, yet knew the key to her emotional survival was feigning a lazy insouciance she couldn't begin to feel.

Smiling, Lewis rose, without benefit of cover of any kind, and strode over to her. He lounged against the bureau beside her. "You are the most captivating person I have ever met."

Cheeks pink, Lexie kept her gaze away from the magnificent view of his toned body and abundant manhood. "The same goes for you," she murmured, wishing she hadn't noticed he was already aroused again. As was she….

Lewis settled more comfortably beside her, flashed her a sexy, provoking grin. "Before or after my makeover?"

"The new clothes and hair did not change who or what you are."

He quaffed the rest of his champagne, set the empty flute aside. "Funny words coming from a professional stylist."

"But true, nonetheless," Lexie said softly, aware she had explained the same thing to clients many times. And it was something she knew from personal experience as well. The problem was, she'd spent so much time helping celebs mold their images into whatever they deemed would most help their careers, that she still didn't know who she really was, at heart, or what she really wanted out of this life. Except, she thought wistfully, more intimacy and more lovemaking with Lewis McCabe… And maybe someday, if she were really lucky, a home and family, too.

He took a lock of her hair, tucked it behind her ear. "And you didn't answer my question."

I was hoping to dodge it.

"Would we have ended up in bed together if you hadn't made me over?" he asked her.

Lexie fiddled with the knot of her belt. "That's a loaded question."

He lifted an eyebrow, persistent as ever. "Because?"

Lexie ignored the musky scent of lovemaking that clung to their skin. "Me working with you enabled us to spend a lot of time together, and it's why I caught you with all those how-to books and why we started talking about sex in the first place. Without any of that—" Lexie shrugged, fibbing madly now to keep up the pretense "—who knows what might or might not have happened?"

Casually, he reached for the belt on her robe, undid the knot and slipped both hands inside. Lexie knew, for the protection of her heart, she should resist, but the feel of those warm, caressing hands on her bare skin was so incredibly enticing and, as it happened, exactly what she secretly wanted from him….

"I need to know if the hair and clothes made the difference," he persisted, regarding her with utter concentration. "Are you more attracted to me now than you were before you worked your wizardy on me?"

She had only to look into the depths of his blue-gray eyes to know that her answer was vitally important. She splayed her hands across the hard, bare surface of his chest and angled her chin up at him. Before she could stop herself, the truth came pouring out. "Don't you know," she murmured softly, sweetly, "that I've *always* had a crush on you?"

He received the news with equal parts aggravation and pleasure. "Why didn't you let me know?" he whispered back, bending his head and delivering another long, soulful kiss that had her insides rioting.

Figuring it was safer to talk about what had happened in the past, than what was going on between them now, Lexie let him dance her toward the bathroom. "You were just so brilliant," she murmured.

He led her toward the shower stall and turned on the water, before divesting her of her robe and leaving it in a puddle at her feet.

"I was always afraid of making a fool of myself if I talked to you so I usually just…didn't," she said.

His sexy smile gentled even more. "Ah, Lexie, you should have talked to me."

"Maybe it's better I didn't." She stroked her fingers through the mat of hair on his pecs. Lexie knew she was vulnerable, knew that they were going to make love as voraciously and wantonly as before, damn the consequences. She was unable to feel even the tiniest bit of regret. She had waited a lifetime to experience such unadulterated pleasure and tenderness. A tryst this good might never happen again. She didn't want to look back, and think, if only she'd dared. She wanted to enjoy it while she still had the chance. And somehow find a way to protect her heart in the process. "Maybe if we had talked then we wouldn't be—" she gasped as he found her nipple and stroked it into a tight pearl of arousal "—doing this…now." Playing together as if they hadn't a care in the world.

"Doing this now—" Lewis responded humorously, as he dragged her beneath the warm, invigorating spray, shut the glass door behind them and caught her body against his own "—feels awfully damn good."

"And to think," Lexie said, between slow, leisurely kisses that incited her body and filled her heart with joy, "we haven't even consulted the books you bought yet."

Lewis poured liquid soap into his palm and lathered it slowly over her breasts, tummy, thighs. The air smelled like a field of wildflowers, just after a rain. "I'd like to say we aren't going to need them but…" He worked his way around to her the small of her back, lower still.

"Why not," Lexie gasped, as he pressed the tip of his sex against the widening juncture of her thighs, "have a little fun?"

"Exactly." Smiling in agreement to her proposal, Lewis locked one of her thighs around his waist and shifted her against the smooth tile wall.

Water sluiced down around them, over them. Her weight on one leg, she welcomed him even more, needing no additional foreplay as she lost herself in the slow, steady rocking and thorough joining. "Where are those books anyway?" she demanded breathlessly, resisting the notion that she just might be falling in love here. Her taut breasts swelled and pushed against the hard muscles of his chest as she told herself all she needed to think about was the incredible pleasure.

"They're locked inside my SUV." His voice was rough, filled with the longing for more as he continued to watch her in that unsettling way. He withdrew slowly, paused, then cupped her buttocks with both hands, spreading her, and penetrated her a little more.

Lexie gasped in reaction, the erotic reality of being one with Lewis almost more than she could bear. She let her head fall back against the shower wall. "For everyone to see?"

He peppered the exposed line of her throat with sweet, satisfying kisses. "Of course not," he murmured passionately, rubbing his thumb across her mouth, parting her lips, kissing her slowly, thoroughly, even as their bodies remained inexrably linked. "Although," he paused to look his fill, before eturning his gaze ever so slowly to her eyes and volunteer-ng mischievously, "if I *wanted* to proclaim to everyone in own that I have no shame in doing whatever it takes to make ou mine, leaving those how-to manuals in plain view would e one way to go."

Pleasure shot through Lexie as she thought about what it vould be like to be publicly declared his woman. "What else vould you do?" she murmured, feeling him grow ever harder, otter and more possessive.

"This." Lewis tunneled his hands through her hair and issed her again, slowly, thoroughly, until Lexie no longer new just who was arousing whom. She only knew that othing had ever felt this right, and that she felt connected o him, body and soul. "And this." His hands moved between hem, setting off another firestorm of tingles. "And this."

Lexie whimpered low in the back of her throat as he filled er to overflowing. Breathlessly, she admitted, "I think you're etting your point across."

"Am I?" He brought her other thigh up to wrap around his vaist, too, and embedded himself deeper yet. Hands cupping er breasts, he pinned her against the wall, the passion in his ow voice fueling her own. "Because I think I might need to e a little clearer."

"Oh, Lewis," she whispered, achingly aware of every hard nuscular inch of him, as he drove her relentlessly toward the dge. She could never have imagined he'd be so command-ng. Or that she, a person who had never really liked sex, ould be so completely enthralled.

"That's it." His hands caught her hips, dictating their slow, ensual rhythm, while she pulled him deeper still. "Say my ame. And I'll say yours," he promised as the two of them lipped slowly into oblivion, and floated softly, slowly back. 'Over and over and over again…."

THEY MADE LOVE twice more—once in the kitchen, another time sprawled crosswise on the bed. Too tired and sexually replete to do anything but live in the splendor of the moment, in the sensation that at least for now they belonged to each other, Lexie fell asleep wrapped in the comfort and security of Lewis's arms. She woke to the ringing of her cell phone. Groaning, she reached for it, and checked the caller ID.

Knowing her mother would not stop dialing until Lexie answered the insistent ringing, she flipped open the phone and put it to her ear. "Yes, Mother. What is it?"

"Turn on the television show *Rise and Shine, America!* right now!" Melinda demanded.

"Why?" Lexie rubbed the sleep from her eyes.

"Just do it, Lexie!" Melinda commanded irritably.

Sighing, Lexie reached for the remote beside the bed and punched in the appropriate channel numbers. Seconds later, Constantine Romeo's face filled the screen. He was seated opposite the perky blond co-host, Cynthia Hewitt. Lexie had only to look at her ex to know he was up to no good.

"So, rumor has it you have love on your mind," Cynthia prodded with a smile.

"It shows, hmm?" Constantine flashed his trademark movie-star grin.

Cynthia leaned in. "You want to tell us about this mystery woman?"

Constantine held his hands in front of him. "Now, Cynthia, you know I can't name names. But I can tell you this much," Constantine said, grinning broadly. "For the first time in my life I feel like I know what true love is all about!"

"Oh…my…goodness," Lexie muttered in dismay. Beside her, she felt the waking Lewis tense, even as he reached for his wire-rimmed glasses and put them on.

"So you're saying you have met someone?" Cynthia persisted, angling for a scoop.

"Actually," Constantine said, laying a hand across his heart dramatically, "I've known this woman forever. I just never realized how important she was to me."

"Oh, please. Peddle that fake sincerity somewhere else," Lexie muttered, sitting all the way up in bed.

Beside her, Lewis sat up, too.

"But now that I've seen her again, I realize this woman is 'The One' for me—she always has been."

"And I gather she feels the same way?" Cynthia smiled.

The star's brilliant turquoise blue eyes lit up as the TV cameras zoomed in for a close-up. "Would I be acting like a besotted fool if she didn't?" he queried slyly.

"Is marriage in the picture?" Cynthia consulted her notes.

Constantine winked. "You'll just have to wait and see. But I promise you this," he vowed emphatically, as the camera lingered on his face once again, "by Monday, the woman of my dreams is going to be wearing a ring on her finger."

"Well, there you have it, folks," Cynthia said, turning to the camera for her close-up. "The world's sexiest bachelor, according to this year's *Personalities!* magazine poll, is in love." Beaming at her exclusive, Cynthia turned back to Constantine. "You'll come back and see us again on Monday, won't you?" she persisted. "With your new love?"

He nodded at the TV journalist. "You bet."

Lexie switched off the television. And her cell phone. She lay back on the pillows with a groan.

"What was all that about?" Lewis asked.

She just shook her head in dismay. "Me. Obviously, my mother put him up to it."

"He's that sure you're coming back to him?"

She tugged the soft cashmere blanket free of the bed, stood and wrapped it around her multiple times. "He's that sure no woman can resist him."

Lewis grinned at her unabridged version of her thoughts. “Is it true?”

Lexie shrugged and walked over to the bureau to retrieve her hairbrush. “You’ll have to ask the many women he bedded before, during and after he was with me,” she murmured, dragging the bristles through the tangles.

Lewis stood, found his boxer shorts and pulled them on. Although the cloth covered the most male part of him, Lexie noted, it did nothing to hide the rest of his body, which was just as fit and toned and beautifully made.

He strolled masterfully closer. “And you knew this?”

Lexie sighed and dropped her brush on the bureau. She walked into the bathroom, being careful not to trip on the blanket hem, all too aware of the fact he was right behind her. “Of course not. What is it they say? The girlfriend is always the last to know.” She picked up her toothbrush, layered on the paste and continued her sad story. “Of course it wasn’t hard for him to fool around, given the highly illicit way we were conducting our relationship.”

Lewis eyed the toothpaste wistfully. “I don’t get it.”

Lexie reached into a drawer and tossed Lewis one of the plastic wrapped toothbrushes that Jenna kept on hand for guests. “Constantine’s manager and publicist at the time had decided he would go farther faster if he were ‘available’ in the mind of the female viewing audience. So we were never seen together in public in anything but a professional capacity. And when he went to events, he always went with some starlet or established star on his arm.”

While Lewis brushed his teeth, Lexie reached for the face soap and squirted a liberal amount in her palm. “Everything was focused on turning him into a huge celebrity as quickly as possible. Once he hit the big time, he decided he didn’t need a steady girlfriend after all, so he decided to stop seeing me.”

Lewis looked as if his heart went out to her.

Aware it felt cathartic to finally talk about it with someone who cared about her, Lexie forced herself to go on. "And I decided to dump him as a client. Because by then, I had plenty of work on my own. And that's when people we both knew started coming forward, telling me how relieved they were that I had cut the lying, conniving cheat loose. And I realized that everyone but me knew that he had been fooling around behind my back the entire time we'd been in Hollywood."

Lexie bent to rinse her face. "So why is he after you now?" Lewis asked, handing her a face towel.

She buried her face in the soft Egyptian cotton. "Because I'm not interested." She let the towel fall away and straightened once again. "And my apathy doesn't fit into Constantine Romeo's view of the world, or himself."

"So it's a conquest thing," he concluded, eying her with a depth of male speculation she found very disturbing.

Lexie nodded and swept back out of the bathroom. "That, and Constantine wants to be back on all the best-dressed lists."

"Couldn't he hire someone else?" Lewis asked, walking beside her.

She went to the kitchen and pulled a jug of orange juice out of the fridge. "He has. In the two years since we split up, he's had a half a dozen different stylists working for him. No one has been able to get him back on the lists."

"Why not?" he asked.

Lexie shrugged. "He's always dressed in Armani or Hugo Boss for his appearances at premieres. My guess is that it's his everyday apparel that is bringing him down."

"And a stylist can't fix that." Lewis took her by the hand and led her out to the sofa in the living room.

"A stylist could if she were with him twenty-four hours a day, like a wife or a mistress would be, and she could keep him from making spontaneous purchases on his own or going out the door in clothes that weren't flattering. But no one in their right mind is going to sign up for that after what happened to me. And if another stylist is foolish enough to be seduced by him and then he cheats on her, well, let's just say no top person is going to stay around long for that kind of treatment. So he's stuck. His image needs a boost. He has to keep himself out there as this bigger-than-life romantic if he wants to maintain his leading man status with all the ladies, and keep them pouring into the theaters for his films. Thanks in part to my mother's calculated intervention, he only sees one way to get that."

"Through marriage to you."

Lexie balanced her empty glass on her knee. "Right."

Lewis took both their glasses and put them aside. "How does that make you feel?"

Lexie didn't even want to think about it. "Disgusted by the efforts to manipulate me, but beyond that…nothing really."

"So you don't want Constantine Romeo back," Lewis observed, shifting her over onto his lap.

Lexie felt his arousal. Knowing Lewis would never lie to her, or mislead her in the way the way Romeo had, she slid into his arms and tilted her face up to his. "Why would I," she countered softly, pressing her lips to his, "when I've got everything I need right here with you?"

"THAT WAS SOMETHING this morning on the TV," Will McCabe opined as the five McCabe brothers began unloading the wooden cabinets from the back of two pickup trucks parked in Kevin McCabe's driveway.

"You saw the Constantine Romeo interview on *Rise and Shine, America!*" Lewis guessed, not sure whether he welcomed his four brothers' take on the situation, or not. Regardless, Romeo's latest move had set him on edge. Not because he thought he couldn't compete with a big star in the romance department, or that Lexie would set out to hurt him deliberately. He worried she might not be quite as "over" Mr. Romeo as she thought.

And that left him in a quandary. He was definitely committed to Lexie—their night together had shown him that. However, he was not sure what she felt for him, other than lust and friendship. And he wanted so much more. He wanted to make her as happy as she deserved to be.

Brad propped open the back door so they could carry the new cabinets in. "I didn't see the interview this morning when it aired, but I heard about it and saw it later—it's posted on the Internet."

Kevin speculated with a shrug, "Everyone here in Laramie thinks Constantine Romeo was talking about Lexie."

"So does she," Lewis admitted grimly as he hoisted a box to a comfortable carrying level.

"Does she want to get back together with Romeo?" Will asked.

"She says not," Lewis said, striding toward the house.

"But you have your doubts," Riley guessed, unloading one of the bigger boxes off a wheeled dolly and onto the center of the kitchen floor.

Lewis set down his load right next to it. "My gut is telling me to believe Lexie when she says it's over."

"But given what happened to you in the past…" Brad said gruffly.

Lewis's jaw tightened. He didn't even want to think about the humiliation and pain he had suffered when his engagement to Glory Bauer ended, and she went back to her previous lover. He turned the talk back to Lexie. "You all saw Lexie when Constantine Romeo showed up at the LHS career fair. She isn't acting as if she is the least bit interested in him."

"Still, you need to protect yourself," Kevin cautioned, ripping open a protective cardboard box.

Lewis wasn't surprised by the warning. They all knew Kevin was still smarting over his romantic involvement with a clever con artist, several years prior. The fact Kevin was in law enforcement had made his humiliation all the worse.

Kevin removed the cabinet, set it into place, then turned toward Lewis. "Look, I'm not saying Lexie Remington is doing it deliberately, but I think she might be using this whatever-it-is with you to make Constantine Romeo jealous."

Hearing someone else echo his suspicion stung. "You don't know what you're talking about," Lewis argued, as irked by his family's interference as he was by the Contessa's ruthless meddling.

"I know this much—" Kevin got out the level to make sure the cabinet was situated appropriately "—none of us can compete with Romeo's glamour. He's got the Hollywood lifestyle Lexie left here to get."

"Not that it's done her much good, given the state of her health," Riley observed dryly. "How is she doing by the way? From what I hear, she hasn't been getting much of the rest I prescribed."

"Jake and Jenna concur, which is why they insisted Lexie spend the evening at home tonight, relaxing at the Remington Ranch. They want her to get at least a solid twelve hours sleep, without worrying that the Contessa or Constantine Romeo is going to show up to harass her again." And Lewis couldn't help but think, Lexie had wanted to put herself in a position where she could sort out her feelings about what had happened between the two of them, without being tempted to sleep with him again. Putting herself under Jake Remington's roof was a great way to accomplish that.

Normally, he wouldn't have minded such a self-protective

move. But maybe now was the time to ask his brothers for help. "Riley's right. Despite all her outward success, Lexie hasn't exactly flourished living the jet-set life."

"Maybe because up to now she has been living it as a lackey, one of the hired help, instead of the wife of a movie star," Brad pointed out bluntly, nailing one of the upper cabinets into the wall. "If Constantine Romeo's now seeing what a mistake he made dumping Lexie the way he did, and he wants her for his wife, how are you going to compete with that?"

"I care about her," Lewis announced stubbornly, cutting yet another new cabinet out of its protective cardboard cover.

"We can all see that," Will said.

And Lewis was sure Lexie knew it, too.

Kevin gave Lewis a frank, pitying look. "She can still stomp all over your heart."

"You think I should give Romeo room to make his move, see what happens and then proceed?" Lewis asked.

Silence fell. "That's one way to approach it," Brad said with a halfhearted shrug.

"What would you do?" Lewis asked, figuring if anyone would know, it was the reformed bachelor, Brad.

"That's easy." Brad grinned and let his hammer fall to his side. "If I were you, I'd elbow that other guy aside and go after Lexie with everything I had."

Lewis turned to the oldest McCabe sibling. "Will?"

"No way am I letting any other guy move in on my territory," Will replied gruffly.

Riley sobered. "I don't see any way that man can be good for Lexie. I vote for doing everything we can—as a group—to protect her, and keep her from making another mistake."

Lewis turned to Kevin. "And you, little brother? What do you say?"

Kevin shrugged, for the moment shoving his misgivings aside. "Just tell us what you need," Kevin said finally. "We're family. We'll do anything we can to help you."

Chapter Ten

Lexie turned to find her stepmother regarding her with concern after she hung up the phone with a frown.

"Another client quit on you?" Jenna asked gently.

Lexie sat down on one of the tufted chairs just inside Jenna's personal workroom. She rubbed at the tension gathered in her temples. "That makes ten so far."

"I'm sure your roster will fill up quickly again when you return, if that's what you want," Jenna said quietly.

Lexie smiled ruefully. "And I thought Daddy was the only one who gave me the 'You're too talented to be simply chasing after celebrities and telling them what to wear' speech."

"I'm beginning to think he's right. The dress you designed for Sydney Mazero to wear to her premiere is sensational. As soon as people see her in it, they're going to want to know who designed it, and where they can get one for themselves. And when that happens you're going to have to make a choice."

For the first time in her life, Lexie felt confident enough to pursue another avenue of employment. Knowing Jenna—who'd started her own business on a shoestring—would understand both the risks and reservations, she nibbled at her lip, confessing, "I don't want to do anything high-end. My interest lies in more affordable pieces."

Jenna moved away from her drawing table. "So you have thought about it," she observed triumphantly, adding the sketch she had been working on to the bulletin board that covered one whole wall.

Lexie watched her stepmother select several samples from the bolts of fabric and pin them next to the sketch. "How could I not think about it, having grown up in this boutique, watching you design the most incredible evening wear and bridal gowns ever, and go from being a designer known only to those who could afford your gowns, to someone whose name is recognized by women everywhere?"

Finished, Jenna turned off the workroom lights, and swept out into the center of her boutique. "I have your father to thank for that. He's the one who convinced me to let Remington Industries open a manufacturing plant here in Laramie and expand into department stores."

The move had made Jenna a very wealthy woman in her own right. And yet, she was still the same loving, wonderful, down-to-earth woman she had always been. Lexie admired her tremendously. "You've been able to straddle couture and ready-to-wear very successfully."

"And you could, too, honey," Jenna encouraged with a smile. "All it would take is…"

A rap sounded on the glass door to the shop. Lexie and Jenna turned in the direction of the sound. At 7:00 p.m. the shop was closed for the day. Through the window, Lexie could see a white stretch limo at the curb. A uniformed driver stood just outside, a huge bouquet of pink roses in one hand, an envelope in the other.

"Is Daddy getting romantic again?" Lexie teased.

"I don't think so. That's not Jake's driver," Jenna replied, perplexed. She walked over to let the courier in.

"I'm here to pick up Ms. Alexandra Remington," the driver said.

A feeling of dread spiraled through Lexie. "Who sent you?" she demanded. As if she didn't know!

"I think that's supposed to be a surprise," the driver replied.

"I'll bet," Lexie muttered as she tore open the envelope, fully expecting to see some sort of demand from her mother and/or Constantine Romeo. Instead, inside was a handwritten note on McCabe Computer Game stationery.

Lexie,

Let's make this a night to remember. I'll be waiting for you at the Lone Star Dance Hall.

Sincerely,

Lewis.

Sincerely? Lexie thought. What the hell did that mean? And why was Lewis asking her out via an intermediary? None of this was at all like him.

"Well?" Jenna asked impatiently.

"I've been commissioned to drive you to dinner," the chauffer explained.

Lexie looked over at Jenna. Had it not been for the official stationary, and the chicken-scratch handwriting—which she recognized as Lewis's—she would have suspected this was some sort of trap, concocted to get her alone with Constantine. "It would appear I have a date with Lewis tonight," Lexie mused finally.

Deciding she was overreacting to what was in all likelihood a very genuine gesture of interest from Lewis, she responded a great deal more matter-of-factly than she felt. "Unfortunately, I'm not dressed to go out, and I don't have anything appropriate in the apartment upstairs, so I'm going to have to go back to the ranch and change." Lexie looked over at the driver. "Mind if we take a little detour?"

The driver smiled. "Not at all."

"EVERYTHING IS ALL SET and ready to go," Greta Wilson McCabe, the proprietress of the Lone Star Dance Hall, and Lewis's second cousin by marriage, said. In her mid-forties, the willowy businesswoman was still a dazzling beauty. Her curling pale blond hair formed a halo around her head, and her light blue eyes bore the wisdom of being married to Shane McCabe and mothering their very lively brood of three girls and three boys. "When do you think Lexie will be arriving?"

She should have been here half an hour ago, Lewis thought, trying not to sweat in the expensive Italian suit. Too late, he realized he should have gone in the limousine with the driver to pick Lexie up.

"She should be here any time now," Lewis said.

"Well, then, I'm going on home to make dinner for Shane and the kids at our ranch. If you need anything just tell the shift manager, and she'll pass the word along to whomever. And of course our DJ is here to please."

"Thanks, Greta."

Greta grinned and shook her head. "Look at you. So grown up. So sophisticated. Lexie has done an amazing job turning your image around."

Now if he could just get Lexie to see they had a future together, too, Lewis thought, life would be good indeed. Unfortunately, it took another twenty minutes before Lexie came sauntering in. Dressed in cowboy hat and yellow floral-print dress with a snug-fitting bodice and a skirt that stopped just above her knees, she looked like the kickin' all-Texas girl she had once been.

Her smiled faded as her gaze landed on him waiting at the bar in a brand-new Armani suit.

"I thought..." She broke off and looked around at the dance hall, which was empty except for the two of them and the staff. "Where is everybody?" she demanded with a perplexed frown. "This place is usually rocking, even on weeknights." She surveyed him head to toe, and looked around again. "It's not a surprise party, is it? Lewis, you know it's not my birthday."

And he'd thought his days of looking extremely foolish were over. Okay, so this wasn't going exactly the way he had planned. He could still do an admirable save. All he had to do was think about how passionately she had responded to his lovemaking the night before, anticipate another night of the same and everything would be fine.

He sauntered closer, too. "I rented the place out for us."

Lexie blinked. "The whole dance hall and restaurant?"

Lewis glanced around at the rustic décor, with the four raised dining areas and the centrally located oak dance floor. The whitewashed walls gleamed in the soft light. Gingham curtains and varnished wooden shades adorned the windows. Near the ceiling, a shelf held all sorts of Texas memorabilia—ancient signs, pottery, old-fashioned cooking and/or ranching tools. Hominess exuded from every angle of the large, deserted dance hall. "I wanted tonight to be special."

Lewis took her arm and ushered her to the table that had been set up, just for them. The DJ caught his nod, and began playing the first of the slow songs Lewis had selected. "I want you to have whatever you want," he told her solemnly. *I want you to be with me.*

THROUGHOUT DINNER, and the intimate conversation that followed, Lexie couldn't help but be caught up in the romance of the evening. The music, the ambiance…Lewis. He looked so handsome and sophisticated in the suit she had personally picked out for him.

No one had ever gone to so much trouble to try and please her.

No one had ever looked at her the way Lewis looked at

her—like she was the most wonderful woman on earth. No one had ever treated her with such kindness and consideration. No one had ever touched her with such tenderness, or made her feel so thoroughly a woman.

He respected what she did for a living.

He realized how much it had taken for her to get where she was, professionally. And he also understood why she was unhappy, doing what she was doing, yet scared about leaving it all behind and taking that next fateful step. "I had a talk with my stepmother before I came over here," she confessed finally, after both of them had caught up on each other's day.

Lewis nodded, listening.

"Jenna thinks I have what it takes to design my own clothing line." She hesitated. "She wants me to consider staying in Laramie, and setting up operations here. We could form a limited partnership and her company could absorb some of the start-up costs."

Lewis's expression gave nothing away. "Are you going to do it?"

Wondering at how much his approval meant to her, Lexie nodded. She held his gaze deliberately. "It's time I started going after what I want, the way you have with McCabe Computer Games."

"But you're scared," Lewis guessed gently, taking her hand in his.

"It's a big step," she admitted nervously as the waiter cleared away their dinner dishes and set down plates of homemade pumpkin and pecan pie, and mugs of steaming coffee.

He squeezed her palm. "You have the talent. Even I can see it, Lexie, and we both know—" he paused for comic affect "—I don't know anything about fashion."

The silence grew more intimate still.

"It would mean I'd be living here permanently," Lexie cautioned, curious to see what his reaction would be to that.

To her relief, he looked happy. Very happy, as a matter of fact. "I think I could adjust to that," he drawled. "Could you?"

"It depends." She wanted to ask where their relationship was going. Was this just a fling? Or was he beginning to feel as deeply enamored of her as she was of him?

"On what?" Lewis asked, serious again.

On whether or not you care about me as deeply as I'm beginning to care about you.

But try as she might, the words Lexie wanted to say would not come. She shrugged. They sat there in silence, watching each other, still measuring each other's reactions.

Finally, Lewis broke the silence. "Well, I think now is the time." Lewis reached into his coat pocket and brought out a small blue box with a white satin bow.

Recognizing the famous jewelry store logo, Lexie felt her pulse begin to race. It looked like a ring box. Surely Lewis wasn't going to ask her to marry him tonight. Was he? They hadn't even told each other they loved each other! "I have something important to ask you," Lewis said, looking deep into her eyes.

Trembling, Lexie placed a hand over her heart. He *was* going to ask her to marry him!

Lewis frowned and started again. "Well, let me back up a minute. First, I want to tell you how very grateful I am to you."

Lexie's spirits sank. This did not sound like a proposal. It sounded like a kiss-off. Lewis was inept when it came to romance, but he wouldn't be foolish enough to go to all this trouble just to say goodbye to her. Would he? On the other hand, when Constantine Romeo had finally dumped her, he had done it in a restaurant. Where she wouldn't make a scene. Lexie swallowed nervously, struggling for breath.

"All the time that we've spent together the last week has meant so much to me," Lewis said. "And I am so grateful to you for all the help you've given me with my clothes and hair."

Constantine Romeo had told her that, too, as part of his "goodbye and good luck" speech. Why hadn't she seen this coming? she wondered, stunned. Why had she thought this was all a method of furthering their romance instead of a polite ruse to end it?

"Which is why I want you to have this." Lewis pushed the box toward her.

Lexie sat there, unmoving, no longer so eager to open it.

"Because I want you to know how much you mean to me," Lewis continued soberly.

Okay, he was back to sounding like he was trying to propose to her again. Sort of. Or just extremely grateful she had made him look as hot and sexy as he was.

Feeling as if she were perched on the edge of a cliff, Lexie did her best to pull herself together.

Lewis waited, an expectant smile on his face that did not quite reach his eyes. He seemed as nervous and uncertain as she felt.

Swallowing, she undid the white satin bow, took the cover off the aqua blue box and lifted out the velvet jewelry case inside. Heart pounding, she flipped the lid and saw…the state of Texas?

"It's a money clip," he said.

A money clip! What the…blue blazes…was that supposed to imply? Lexie wondered, hurt and temper mingling to form a combustible substance deep inside her.

"I know." Lewis held up a hand, completely misreading her silence. "It's unconventional. But when I saw it I totally thought of you."

And wasn't that special.

Eyes stinging, face and neck hot as fire, she struggled to her feet.

"Lexie? What are you…"

She pretended not to hear.

Blindly, she rushed toward the exit.

A wooden chair clattered behind her. He raced to catch up with her, cutting her off most ungraciously. "Where are you going?"

"Home." Upset with herself for allowing herself to be so vulnerable, and determined not to cry—in front of him anyway—Lexie marched toward the door.

He grabbed her arm to slow her progress. She shook him off. "We haven't danced yet."

Hard to believe how truly clueless he was. "Maybe you can find someone else to do that with you."

He blinked. "And you didn't take your clip." He tried to push the jewelry box into her hand.

She pushed it right back at him, pivoted and continued on her path. "Gee," she forced the sarcastic words through her teeth, "I wonder why not."

He strode ahead of her and blocked her way out the front door. "You don't like my gift?"

Trying hard not to lose what little composure she had left and whack him a good one with her brown leather shoulder bag, she stared at him. "No."

"Why not?"

Lexie became aware of the entire restaurant staff staring at the two of them. Lovely, now it was going to be all over town they'd had a fight. She searched her brain for a scorching comeback but all she could come up with was a rather lame, "Are you really that dense?"

He regarded her stoically. "Apparently so." He paused, his gaze raking a slow, steady path over her body before returning to her eyes. "I went all out here, Lexie."

Heaven help her, she really was going to punch him in the nose. "Yes. You did. And now I want out. So if you'll excuse me, I'm going home. Alone."

She stormed through the swinging wooden doors. As soon as they hit the sidewalk outside, he grabbed her arm and swung her around to face him. "Wait! You can't leave. I have a jet on standby. It will take us anywhere in the world—even a deserted tropical island, where there are no phones, no one to bother us—if you want. I have to be back in the office on Tuesday, but—until then, anyway—you and I have all the time in the world."

"Tuesday," Lexie repeated, everything abruptly beginning to make sense, as she thought about what was supposed to happen on Monday morning on *Rise and Shine, America!*

He flashed her a winning smile. "Yes. I have to take some new distributors on a tour of the facility and put the final ink on the marketing deal, but after that, we could jet off again, if you want."

Sweetly, she summed up, "So if we left tonight, we'd be gone the rest of the week, and all weekend, too. No one would even know where we were or how to get in touch with us."

"Well," Lewis allowed reluctantly, "my brother Will would know. He's flying us wherever we want to go on one of his charter jets. But he wouldn't tell anyone."

Lexie hugged herself to ward off the evening chill. "So, for instance, my mother would not be able to get in touch with me."

"Right." His brow furrowed in satisfaction. He slipped off his suit jacket and draped it over her shoulders.

"I must congratulate you. Brilliant move on your part." Lewis had outmanuevered Constantine Romeo, one of the smoothest operators on the planet. Pretending she loathed—instead of craved—the warmth of her lover's body, she took hold of the jacket with two fingers and handed it back to him as if it were an odious piece of trash. "But no deal."

"You don't want to go?" His jaw took on a combative thrust. The glimmer of battle appeared in his eyes.

And be used again, by the man she had come to care about, albeit in a much different way?

"Not in this lifetime," Lexie replied, her voice dripping ice.

"WHERE'S LEXIE?" Will asked as Lewis walked into the airstrip hangar alone.

Lewis shrugged desultorily, reporting, "Home, so far as I know."

Will propped his feet on the battered metal desk and folded his hands behind his head. "Packing for the trip?"

"There is no trip," Lewis replied sourly. He walked over to inspect the coffee sitting on the warmer. It smelled like diesel fuel and appeared thick as molasses. No telling how long it had been there.

Will got up to pour more coffee into his navy mug. "Date went that well, hmm?"

Too restless and keyed up to sit, Lewis stuck his hands in the pockets of his trousers and slouched against the wall. "I thought it was going great. At least until I gave her the eighteen-carat-gold money clip in the shape of Texas."

Will spewed coffee onto the papers on his desk. "You did what?" he demanded, frantically mopping the spreading stain with a stack of old take-out napkins.

Briefly, Lewis explained how, when and why he had chosen that particular gift.

"Okay, that makes sense—in a convoluted way," Will said finally, tossing the soggy napkins in the trash.

Frowning, Lewis resumed pacing the gray cement floor. "Well, Lexie didn't think so! She didn't even take it with her when she stormed out of there."

Will tilted his head to one side. "And you explained you thinking to her the way you just explained it to me?"

Lewis tensed. "She didn't give me a chance."

Will shrugged. "Then you can't blame her for jumping t the wrong conclusions about what such a gift meant."

"Which would be what exactly?" Lewis demanded.

Will responded dryly, "I think the answer to that quer would best come from her."

Lewis scowled and looked out at the twinkling runwa lights. "Well, I'm not likely to get it since Lexie has apparentl stopped speaking to me. She wouldn't even let me ride in th limo when it drove her back to the apartment above the boutique."

Will set his coffee mug down with a thud. "You want m advice?"

Lewis wished he didn't need it. "Obviously, that's why I' here," Lewis muttered bad-temperedly. He hadn't come jus to be insulted, as per usual, about his lack of expertise regarding the fairer sex.

"Tell her she's got no right to be ticked off at you."

Back to the he-man approach. Once again, Lewi wondered if his brothers knew as much about women as the all thought they did. "I don't think Lexie is going to agre with that position." In fact, given the expression she'd had o her face the last time he had seen her, she would probabl punch his lights out if he so much as tried to offer it up. An all because he had tried to give her an evening to remembe

Will rubbed his jaw with the flat of his hand. "Then you'v got a real problem," he said. "Don't you?"

Chapter Eleven

Lexie had just washed her face and put on her pajamas, when she heard the knock at the door. A glance through the viewer showed Lewis McCabe standing on the other side, holding the velvet jewelry box in his hand. He was still dressed in the suit, but the first two buttons of his shirt were undone, and his tie was askew, as if he'd jerked the knot loose and left it that way. Otherwise, he was as gorgeous as he had always been, even before his style makeover.

Temper spiking once again, she swung open the door, not sure whether she wanted to kick his butt all the way to Oklahoma or invite him in and give him a real piece of her mind this time. She had never been so furious with a man in her entire life. She folded her arms in front of her. "Haven't you done enough damage to our relationship for one night?" she queried sweetly.

He regarded her stoically from behind the lenses of his glasses. "So you admit we have a relationship."

She hated his implacable tone almost as much as his temerity in showing up there, knowing full well how she felt about him now. "Yes. A very bad one." She made a great dramatic show of shooing him away from the door. "Now be on your merry way."

He propped his hands on his hips and made a great dramatic show back. "You'd like that, wouldn't you?"

"Yes." She annihilated him with her eyes, aware her traitorous heart had already accelerated its beat. "As a matter of fact, I would."

He barged right in and closed the door behind him. "Well, it's not going to happen until I have my say."

Lexie picked up a copy of *Women's Wear Daily* and pretended to peruse it lazily. "I don't know what you could add to what you said earlier in the evening that would make me loathe you any less."

He plucked the magazine from her hands and tossed it aside. "Look, I'm not the sharpest tack in the bunch when it comes to women."

Annoyed at the way he continued invading her space, she lifted her head. "Gee. You think?"

He angled a thumb at his chest. "But I know my heart was in the right place tonight!" He tossed off his suit jacket and threw it aside, too.

Pretending she didn't feel ill at ease, standing there clad in a pair of pink-and-white pin-striped pajamas, she pressed her lips into a taunting smile meant to get under his skin in the same way his presence was annoying her.

"Don't you mean your competitive juices?"

He blinked. "Excuse me?"

"Don't even try and pretend this isn't all about Constantine Romeo and what he said on TV this morning!"

"About asking someone to marry him," Lewis gathered finally.

She hated the too-real confusion on his face. It indicated his actions weren't as diabolical as they first seemed. "Yes," she snapped, wishing that he would do something to vindicate himself. She hated thinking he was so obviously manipulative and competitive.

He moved nearer, still studying her closely. "You think the only reason that I arranged a special evening for us is because

Constantine Romeo obviously has designs on you again?" He slouched against the wall and studied her with critical eyes. "Is that why you think I gave you jewelry, too?"

Lexie wasn't sure a money clip qualified as jewelry. "I have no idea why you gave me that gift," she countered stiffly, wishing she didn't care so very much about what happened next between the two of them.

Oozing testosterone, he prowled closer. "I gave it to you because it was the only thing they had in the shape of Texas."

Lexie blinked.

"I was looking for something sentimental that would tell you how I felt about you."

"So you got me a money clip," Lexie observed wryly, shaking her head.

"No," Lewis corrected, "I got you 'Texas' because I wanted you to know how very glad I am that you came home to Texas. And that we…hooked up…in Texas. And because Texas is where I first got to see you, and admire you, even if it was only from a distance. And because we first made love in Texas. And I love Texas. And I—" He broke off, clearly at a loss how to explain any further.

She could see his intentions about the gift were sincere. His thinking was pure Lewis McCabe.

"Believe me," Lewis continued, softly, sincerely, taking her wrist in hand. He rubbed her skin with the pad of his thumb. "If they'd had a Texas necklace in stock, or Texas earrings, I would have purchased those, but they didn't, so I went with the money clip. I'm sorry it upset you. I don't have a lot of experience getting gifts for women."

"No kidding, genius." Heat and sensation, engendered by his tender evocative touch, swept through her.

He regarded her with bemusement. "Now, can we kiss and make up and go on our trip?"

"No!" Lexie withdrew her hand and put the barrier around her heart right back up.

Lewis smiled, enthusiastic as ever, at getting things done quickly and efficiently. "Why not?"

Because if I kiss you again, I'll be lost and I know it. Because I realized tonight—when I erroneously thought you might be about to propose to me—that what's going on between us isn't just a fling. For me, it's always been about love. But the rules haven't changed for you, and it is unfair of me to expect them to do so.

Unable to say all this to Lewis without making herself susceptible to being hurt all over again, Lexie scowled. "Because I have no intention of letting you make me the prize in your competition with Constantine Romeo."

"Meaning what?" Lewis countered. "You want to be around when he comes after you again?"

Trying not to think how good it felt to be alone with Lewis again, Lexie shook her head. "He's not going to come after me."

Lewis dropped onto the sofa and stretched his long legs out in front of him. He took off his tie, tossed it onto the coffee table and unfastened another button on his shirt. "Now who's not dealing with reality?" he asked.

Determined to show Lewis's appearance did not unnerve her, Lexie dropped onto the sofa, too, and propped her legs on the coffee table, too. "And even if he does," Lexie continued stubbornly, "it won't make a difference because I don't want anything to do with him. Which means he's going to have to find someone else to propose to by Monday morning so he can make the announcement on TV as promised."

"I think you're underestimating your allure," Lewis retorted. "He's not going to give up any more than I am."

Lexie's heart gave a nervous kick against her ribs. "So you admit you want to ace out Constantine Romeo in the competition for my heart?" she asked.

"Heck, yeah." Lewis looked at her as if she should relish—not resent—being fought over that way. "He doesn't deserve you. I do. Which is what I was trying to show you tonight by giving you a dream date," he continued in a low, determined voice. "I may not be as rich or as famous, but I can still give you a pretty darn exciting life, if you give me half a chance."

She sighed. "You think those things mean anything to me?" she asked, doing her best to remain imperious.

Lewis shrugged.

"I grew up with money. Both my parents are wealthy. I've been to Europe and Asia and Australia more times than I can count. I've stayed in five-star hotels, eaten in the best restaurants, worn haute couture—mainly because when I'm with her, my mother won't let me wear anything else. None of that made me happy, Lewis."

"Then what has?" he asked her gently.

You.

But she couldn't say that, either, not without giving her heart away.

"Lexie, I know I screwed up tonight," Lewis said amiably, reassuring her with a glance. "I'd like to tell you it will never happen again, but that's just not true." The corners of his lips crooked up ruefully. "If there is one thing you can count on with me, it's me doing the exact wrong thing in any deeply personal situation with you. But that doesn't mean you should write me off entirely, just because I haven't got all the mushy stuff down pat." He reached over and took her hand, clasping it in his. "You and I have something really special here, Lexie." Able to see she still wasn't completely convinced, he struggled to explain, "It's sort of like computer games."

Lexie sighed in bewilderment. "You had me. And then you lost me."

Lewis stood, as if making an important business presentation to a group.

Lexie sighed, aware she had always had a thing for absent-minded professor types.

"Well, you know how when we design a game and then put it into production and get it on the shelves, each one of them is identical?" Lewis asked.

The look in his eyes told Lexie that he would soon be speaking over head. "Okaaay."

"And yet every person who actually plays the game has a completely different experience."

Lexie figured that was true.

"There are so many variations of what can happen that even if you play the game yourself over and over it will never be an exactly identical experience—even if you win every time. Or lose…it doesn't matter." He gestured as if to wipe the slate clean. "It's always going to be a little bit different every time you play."

Lexie nodded slowly.

"Well, that's how you and I are," Lewis declared triumphantly.

She released an exasperated breath. "Now you lost me again," she told him in frustration. This was the genius part of him that seemed way way out of her lexicon.

He knelt down in front of her, like a knight bowing before his queen. "I've met hundreds of women in the course of my life. I dare say you've met hundreds of men. But my synapses have never fired as potently as when I'm with you. All I have to do is be with you, look at you, think about you and I'm completely mesmerized and enthralled." He took both her hands in his, clasped them possessively. "What you and I have is so unique, Lexie." He looked deep into her eyes. His voice dropped another sexy, persuasive notch. "Now that we've found each other, in the way we were always meant to find each other, can you really blame me for doing everything I can to make sure that no one else comes along and spoils it?"

WHEN LEXIE HAD first opened her apartment door, Lewis thought he didn't have a chance of making her understand how much he was beginning to care about her. But he'd followed his gut and poured his heart out to her, anyway—to great result. "Tell me you're feeling something here, too, Lexie," he whispered, moving up onto the sofa beside her, taking her all the way into his arms. Something that would never be duplicated, no matter how far and wide they looked.

She slid over onto his lap, tipped her face up to his. The happiness and wonder he had wanted to see shimmered in her eyes. "I'm feeling something, too," she whispered, wrapping her arms about his neck.

Her lips touched his in a tender kiss. He took what she offered, what he had dreamed of his entire life. Kissed her back in the same all-encompassing way, then buried his face in the fragrant softness of her hair. "We can't let it go."

She looked at him, her turquoise eyes filled with longing as she kissed him back thoroughly. "You're right. We shouldn't."

Determined to give her the kind of complete and thorough lovemaking she deserved, he swept his hands down her body, kissed her until he felt her tremble, until their bodies melded in boneless pleasure. "We have to see where the passion takes us."

Her cheeks flushed and her eyes sparkled as she finished unbuttoning his shirt, and pulled the ends from the waistband of his trousers. "Into the bedroom, it would seem," she teased.

He stood, scooped her up into his arms and took her where they both wanted to be….

He set her down gently beside the bed. "First things first," he whispered.

She unbuckled his belt.

He made short work of her pajama top and pants.

Satisfaction flowing through him in waves, he cupped the

full weight of her breasts with his hands, flicking the nipples with his thumbs before bending to pay homage with his lips and tongue. Lexie drew in a quick, urgent breath and dove her fingers through his hair. He suckled gently. She arched again.

Feeling empowered by her response, intoxicated by her nearness, Lewis kept up the sexual exploration, sliding back up to kiss her thoroughly, taking her mouth in a slow, hot, mating dance, palming her breasts and capturing the silky globes in his hands. Her palms slid around his back, massaging the hard-muscled contours on either side of his spine, dropping lower still, pulling him against her, all the while kissing him again and again and again, to the point he was afraid he wasn't going to be able to pace himself with the utter control and tender expertise Lexie deserved.

He danced her backward, guided her slowly down onto the bed. Her strawberry-blond hair spread across the pillows in glorious waves, looking exactly as he recalled, all soft and tousled and touchable. He lay down beside her, then draped her with his length, planting an arm on either side of her. "I want tonight to be everything you've ever dreamed," he told her huskily.

She brought his head back down to hers, kissed him with a passion so hot it sizzled. "It already is."

"It will be," Lewis promised. He stroked her tongue with his, circled it, and flicked it across the edges of her teeth before dipping deep. She responded with equal fervor, the softness of her body giving new heat to his.

Lewis rubbed his chest across her bare breasts, savoring the feel of her budding nipples against his. Triumphing in the sweet soap-and-flowers fragrance of her skin, he moved lower to her abdomen, dipped his tongue into her navel, lingered. Reveling in the warmth of her skin, he lifted his head. "Do you think this is too pedestrian?"

She whimpered as he traced a hand down her body, to the

velvety red-blond curls. "Believe me," she moaned, as he quickly made her gloriously aroused, "there is nothing dull about what you…are…doing…to…me…now."

Relishing the strength of her response to him, Lewis kept loving her with his hands and mouth and tongue. "Because I could get out one of the books."

She surged against him, falling apart in his arms. "Maybe later," she allowed when her shuddering had finally stopped. "First, I have to pleasure you…." She rolled him onto his back, moved over him, so her knees were straddling his waist, her hands propped on either side of his shoulders.

Lewis pushed sensually and slowly, all the way inside her. She added a soul-searching kiss, then drew herself up, so she was once again on her knees. Lewis caught her by the hips and brought her back down again, letting her do for him, with the most feminine part of her, what he had already done for him. Knowing, even as they neared completion, it wasn't enough. That there could be more…

Much more…

If only he were strong enough to apply the principles he had read about.

Wanting to draw out every second of escalating passion, Lewis sat up, bringing her with him. He knew every moment that they delayed, their mutual gratification would be multiplied tenfold. Their eyes locked. A mixture of tenderness and primal possessiveness filled his soul. She might not trust his intentions one hundred percent yet. She would. "And speaking of pleasure," Lewis teased as their muscles trembled and tensed. He skimmed her body with his fingers, filling his hands with her soft, hot flesh. "I've got a few ideas, too."

The need he had wanted to see glimmered in her eyes. "Oh, you do, do you?" Lexie murmured.

Nodding, Lewis guided her to a sitting position, thighs apart, then sat facing her. Shifting closer, he opened her delicately and moved to possess her, wrapping his legs around her hips, encouraging her to do the same to him. Shock, then pleasure filled her eyes. His body throbbed with need as he brought them together in the most provocative of ways. Lexie gasped as he filled her to completion, seeming as surprised by the tantalizing sensation as he.

Past waiting, as much in her control as she had just been in his, Lewis surged forward and deepened his penetration. He caught his breath as she found him with her hands, never breaking the kiss or connection they had, urging him forward, both hands clasping his inner thighs and buttocks, until he groaned at the pleasure she was giving him.

And then there was no more prolonging the inevitable. Trembling, they succumbed to the swirling, inevitable pleasure. And Lewis knew, in Lexie, at long last, he had found everything he had ever wanted or dreamed, needed or lusted after. The question was, how to convince her of that, too.

"IT WOULD MEAN SO MUCH to me if you and your date could come to the premiere in Austin on Saturday evening," Sydney Mazero told Lexie the next morning, when she stopped by the boutique to pick up her finished dress. The starlet beamed excitedly. "You, and your husband, too, Jenna. I've got tickets for all four of you and made arrangements for you to walk the red carpet with me and enter the theater with me and my family. We can all sit together in the VIP section in front of the stage."

Lexie hedged, appreciating the sentiment behind the gesture, even if she wasn't sure the proposal was in Sydney's best interest. "You know this isn't the way it's usually done," she cautioned. "The stylist for the client stays behind the scenes."

"First of all, Lexie," Sydney said, trying for flip, but the anguish in her eyes was clear, "you're not just a stylist. You're designer. Second, my parents are sooooo nervous. I really need help calming them down or I'm going to freak out. And I don't want to do that and embarrass Beau Chamberlain when he's given me this great chance."

"It sounds like fun to me," Jenna said graciously.

Her heart going out to the nervous teen, for she knew how much scrutiny—and pressure—the young girl was under, Lexie nodded. "Me, too."

"So you'll both come and bring dates?" Sydney asked.

"Absolutely," Jenna and Lexie said in unison.

"Oh, thank you, thank you, thank you!" Looking almost limp with relief, Sydney rummaged in her Kate Spade bag and handed over the envelope with the tickets. "The movie company has reserved a big block of rooms at the Driskill Hotel downtown for the people coming to the premiere. Your names are on the list. All you have to do is call the hotel and tell them how many rooms you'll need."

"I'll call my husband right now and tell him to clear his schedule." Jenna exited.

And I'll try to talk Lewis into going with me, too, Lexie thought. She held the door while Sydney carried her clothing to her car, then ducked into the stairwell to the apartment to use her cell phone in private. She dialed Lewis's office number.

"McCabe," he answered on the first ring.

"Hi," Lexie said, feeling suddenly shy.

"What's up?" Lexie heard the murmur of other voices in the background, which probably explained his somewhat distant tone.

Briefly, she explained.

"No problem. I'd be happy to attend."

Again, Lexie noted how formal his tone sounded. "All right. I'll give you the details later." She hung up the phone, pushing away her sudden niggling doubts, and telling herself not to make too much of his reserve. Their lovemaking the night before had told her everything she needed to know about how he felt about her. Desire that powerful, that all-consuming, was not going to disappear in the course of one business day, Lexie schooled herself firmly. Nor was his tenderness. She was an adult woman. She knew the score. She didn't need guarantees or promises or even declarations of undying love from Lewis McCabe. For the moment, it was enough just being with him, experiencing true physical pleasure coupled with a fast-growing intimacy and a deep sense of belonging.

It was *enough,* Lexie reasoned further, to simply have some fun, and while she was at it, stop and finally figure out who she was and what *she* really wanted out of life. Family certainly. Marriage. And possibly a new career.

Still mulling over the possibilities, Lexie put her cell phone away and walked back into the boutique. Josephine Holdsworth marched in. To Lexie's surprise, Josephine looked loaded for bear.

"Could I speak with you privately?" Josephine asked her.

"Sure." With a shrug, Lexie led her back to the storeroom and shut the door behind them. "What's going on?"

Josephine propped a hand on her hip and scowled. "Look, I know it's none of my business, but after the way you treated Lewis McCabe last night I can't help but get involved…."

"LEXIE WANTS ME to meet her where?" Lewis asked his assistant.

Maxine Cossman consulted her notes. "The Remington Ranch. She said to wear jeans and boots. You might need a jacket for later. To get to where she is, take the dirt access road just south of the ranch to the grove of trees at the far west corner of the property. If you get confused, stop at the barn and have one of the hired hands give you directions."

Lewis handed Maxine a stack of contracts that needed to go out ASAP. "What time am I supposed to be there?"

Maxine took out an express mail envelope. "As soon after work as you can make it. She is apparently there now."

Lewis headed out, not sure whether he was more excited or relieved. He had been trying to reach Lexie on her cell since late morning—to no avail. They had started off the day so well—making love again as the sun came up. Kissing, before he headed out the door. He knew he'd been a little abrupt with Lexie when she telephoned—he hadn't been able to help it. He'd been in the midst of a meeting with a roomful of senior managers. But when he had tried to call her back half an hour later, as soon as the session concluded, she hadn't answered. Too late, he realized he should have nailed down the next "date" before ever leaving the apartment that morning. Now, he saw he needn't have worried. She had been planning to see him this evening all along.

Whistling, Lewis stopped at home to change clothes and then drove on over to the Remington Ranch. He had no problem finding her—although he wasn't prepared for what he saw when he got there. The Remington Ranch pickup truck Lexie had been driving while in Texas was parked beneath a grove of cedar and live oak trees. Lexie had a flat-brimmed hat on her head. Dressed in jeans, flannel shirt, boots and blue denim cook's apron, she was standing next to an old-fashioned chuck wagon. Delicious aromas filled the autumn air.

"I see you got my message," she murmured when Lewis strode over to her.

He tucked a hand beneath her chin, tilting her face up to his. He bent to kiss her leisurely. "I sure did." Wrapping an arm around her waist, he surveyed the area. "So this is what you've been up to all day," he noted, pleased.

She stirred the simmering concoction of beef and vegetables. "I thought I'd cook you dinner the way they did when this land was first settled by our ancestors. Although I have to tell you I cheated a little bit." She blew on the steaming food then lifted a spoon to his lips and let him have a taste. "I got the ranch hands to bring the chuck wagon out here for me. And I'm using charcoal, along with the wood in the fire pit. But the beef stew is made the old-fashioned way."

Lewis savored the rich gravy, tender beef and plentiful vegetables. "Where'd you get the idea to do this?"

Lexie tasted a spoonful, too. "Josephine Holdsworth stopped by the boutique to talk to me this morning," she admitted as she reached for the wooden pepper mill, gave it a few quick twists, then added a little more salt. "It seems everyone in town heard about me walking out on you at the Lone Star Dance Hall last night. The consensus is I've been treating you badly."

As far as he was concerned, it was no one's business but theirs. Lewis followed her over to the hinged wooden flap, folded down and supported on two hinged posts, that served as the chuck wagon's work surface. "Did you set her straight?"

Lexie continued molding biscuits and setting them in a cast-iron skillet. "Actually, I agree with her." Her cheeks pinkened self-consciously. "This relationship of ours, if that is what it is—"

Lewis lounged beside her. "That is definitely what it is."

"—has been rather one-sided up 'til now. You've been doing all the pursuing."

Lewis tucked a strand of hair behind her ear. "I don't mind. I like pursuing you."

Lexie tipped the brim of her hat back. "I like it when you pursue me, too. But no relationship should be one-sided. So, since you gave me a dream date," she concluded, setting the skillet on the grate above the fire.

"Which we never finished," Lewis reminded her.

Lexie flashed him an impertinent grin. "I happen to like the way we finished it very much," she murmured seductively. Clasping his shirtfront, she pulled him toward her. "Making love that way made a lot of things very clear to me."

"To me, too." Lewis wrapped his arms around her waist, brought her against him and kissed her thoroughly. She kissed him back, just as tenderly. Desire seared through him. He knew she might be saying this was all a fling, a temporary connection, but her actions were saying otherwise. The trouble she had gone to this evening said she wanted a future for them, a lasting commitment between them, too.

When they drew apart, both were breathless.

Lewis smiled. "You were saying?"

"Oh. Um. Yes." Lexie cleared her throat and pressed a hand to her breasts. "Anyway, I decided to give you a date to remember, too. I know you like history. And are currently reading up on the late 1800s. So I decided to try and make you as authentic a meal as I could."

What was it his brothers had said? Lewis struggled to remember dating tips he had been given over the years. *When a woman is really interested in a man, one of the first ways she lets him know it is by cooking for him.*

"Excellent idea." He looked at the peach cobbler cooling on the workspace, and the old-fashioned ice-cream churn. He wanted to tell Lexie how much her doing all this meant to him, but wasn't sure how to say it without sounding unbelievably corny and ruining the moment instead. He shot her an equally enamored look instead. "What can I do to help?" he asked her softly, taking her hand in his.

She led him toward the log that was serving as their bench. "You can sit down and relax." Her playful expression turning abruptly serious, she disengaged their hands. "And tell me about Glory Bauer."

Chapter Twelve

Lexie had been wondering all day what Lewis's reaction to that question would be. He looked annoyed but not necessarily emotionally involved.

He sat down on the log, and ever so casually stretched his long legs out in front of him. "Who told you about her?"

Pretending an inner ease she couldn't begin to feel, Lexie set about making a pot of coffee the old-fashioned cowboy way to have with their dinner. "Josephine Holdsworth. She said Glory Bauer trampled all over your heart and that you were still recovering from that love affair gone bad. She didn't want to see me do what Glory had done to you, but she didn't really tell me what that was." Josephine had just implied that Lewis had been crushed, and that in turn had wounded Lexie to the core. Lexie didn't want anyone wounding her man, and he was her man, even if he didn't yet recognize that.

Lewis watched her fill the granite pot with cold water. "Is that all Josephine said?"

"No." Lexie measured out one rounded tablespoon of ground coffee for each two cups of water, and then added it to the pot, too. "She also said that there were lots of single women here in Laramie who would give anything to go out with you, but you were so burned by your previous relationship that you never even saw them." And that in turn had made Lexie so jealous she didn't know what to do. She hung the pot on a metal hook above the fire, right next to the simmering stew. "Josephine didn't think it was fair that I waltzed into town, stole your attentions and did not even appreciate them."

Lewis patted the rough bark to his left. "Did you tell her we made up last night?"

Lexie walked over to sit down beside him. "I didn't think Josephine needed to know that. It wouldn't have really made her feel any better." She paused to regard Lewis slyly. "She has quite a crush on you, you know."

Lewis's lips thinned in irritation. "I like her as a friend."

"And that's it," Lexie ascertained warily, hope rising within her.

"It's never going to happen with me and Josephine," Lewis declared flatly.

Lexie felt enormous relief. "You still didn't tell me what happened with you and Glory. Or even who she is and how you met."

His expression guarded, Lewis studied her. "You want to know everything, don't you?"

You have no idea, Lexie thought wistfully. She shrugged. "Just about."

His eyes roamed her face with disturbing intensity, taking in the contours of her lips, before returning ever so slowly to her eyes. "Glory Bauer is a software designer I know from my days at Stanford," Lewis said reluctantly. "She dated one of my good friends there and they got married when they graduated. A couple years after that, Glory and Isaac split up. She needed a change. She called me. I offered her a job. She came to Laramie. We spent a lot of time together. At first she was just crying on my shoulder, and then we got involved. I should have known better. I should have known, the way she kept trying to make me over into someone else that she wasn't really over Isaac, no matter what she said." He grimaced. "But like a fool I thought her feelings for me were as strong as mine for her. I thought I could be what she wanted me to be, so I asked her to marry me. She said yes. Isaac heard about it, got jealous, came after her and they got back together. End of story."

Aware the biscuits were looking too done on the bottom, and not cooked on top, Lexie took the skillet off the flame and flipped them over to continue cooking. "Except you were humiliated in front of everyone you knew here in Laramie," she guessed as she put the skillet back in place and came back to sit beside him.

Lewis had a distant, unapproachable look in his eyes that hinted just how hurt he had been by the whole debacle. He stared at the horizon. "Anyway, I made a promise to myself never to make the same mistake with a woman again by dating anyone on the rebound, or anyone who wanted to turn me into someone I wasn't. And I haven't," he said gruffly.

She propped her face on her hand and studied him openly. "According to Josephine you haven't dated anyone, period."

He lifted a shoulder in a hapless shrug. "Dating isn't a sport to me. If I don't see it happening for the two of us over the long haul, I don't ask a woman out. Period."

Lexie admired him even more. "That's the way I feel," she admitted straightforwardly.

"Is that why you accepted my invitation last night?" Lewis said.

"What do you think?" Lexie teased.

He swept her hat off, held it behind her and lowered his head for a long, steamy kiss that spoke volumes about his intentions. "I think you are the best thing that's ever happened to me."

"To me, too." Lexie sighed contentedly, shifting over onto his lap. They indulged in another long, spirited kiss. "Which is why I called this morning to ask you to escort me to the premiere of *Calamity Sue* on Saturday in Austin." Briefly, Lexie explained how the invitation had come about. The plans for the event had firmed up since they had talked, and she brought him up-to-date. "My dad wants us all to fly down to Austin together on the Remington jet. Dad took care of the hotel rooms for all of us. All you have to do is show up."

"Dress code?"

"Suit and tie."

He looked as eager to attend the event as she was. "Does this mean your dad approves of you seeing me?"

Lexie kept her face carefully expressionless. "Jenna was convinced we're right for each other, days ago."

He narrowed his blue-gray eyes. "And your father?"

"He just needs to see how happy you make me," Lexie declared, pushing away her nervousness. "This weekend will take care of that."

"AMAZING DINNER, LEXIE," Lewis drawled contentedly, an hour later.

Lexie couldn't believe how much food he had eaten. Two generous helpings of stew, four biscuits, peach cobbler and ice cream. "We're not done yet. We've got two things left."

Lewis tilted his head to one side. "I don't think that chuck wagon is equipped for—"

Lexie wanted to make love, but not amidst the pots and pans. "Very funny."

Lewis bent down to further study their surroundings. He rubbed his face. "Underneath, though, it looks a little cozy."

Shaking her head at his antics, she came toward him with a steaming mug. "Seriously, you have to try my authentic cowboy coffee."

"With pleasure—" Lewis flashed a sexy grin "—if it lives up to the rest of the meal." He took a long draught.

"How is it?" Lexie asked, expecting similar praise.

"Good," Lewis said firmly.

Then why was he avoiding her eyes? Lexie trod closer. She folded her arms in front of her. "No, it's not."

"Yes, it is. It's wonderful."

Lexie'd had her fill of insincerity, working in Hollywood. The one thing she had always expected from Lewis was complete and total honesty. "You're lying. Let me have a sip."

He held the mug away from her, gallant to the last. "You're not supposed to have caffeine, remember? Your reflux…"

"One sip won't hurt." Lexie wrested it from him, tasted a little and spit it right back out onto the grass. "That's the worst thing I've ever tasted!" she declared.

Lewis chuckled, giving up the pretense. "Yeah, it is pretty bad, isn't it?" he commiserated softly.

"Well, no more of that." She dumped what was left into the grass, gave him another spoonful of vanilla ice cream to kill the taste and took one for herself. "We'll move on to the next surprise, a sporting event."

His eyebrows lifted. "We've got tickets to a game?"

She was surprised he looked so excited. She hadn't realized he cared anything about sports. But then, what did they really know about each other except how good they were together, in and out of bed? Hoping this last event wouldn't end up being as much of a wash as the cowboy coffee, she sauntered back over to the chuck wagon and rummaged around inside for the items she needed.

Every woman knew when you planned a special evening for a special guy it had to include two things. No, make that three. Food, sports and sex. The last of which would come much later. "No, silly. We're going to play a game, circa 1886." She popped back out, with a sledgehammer she'd borrowed from the hired hands. "How are you at hammering in stakes?"

Their hands brushed as she passed off the heavy tool, then

ducked back in beneath the wooden top. The stakes had slid toward the center of the wagon, and she had to hoist herself up over the side, legs dangling precariously, to reach them. As she slid back out, she realized he was admiring the view of her backside. He smiled, making no effort to disguise his guilt.

"Depends on what they are going to be used for."

Flushing self-consciously, Lexie strode over to the area she had picked out between the trees and the chuck wagon. Prior to hooking up with Lewis, she had never viewed herself as much of a sexual being. Now, she couldn't seem to stop thinking about sex. Or him.

She laid each stake where she wanted him to hammer them in. "They're going to be used to set up a horseshoe pit," she said, aware his eyes were now making an unabashed tour of the rest of her curves. She rubbed a damp palm down the side of her jeans. "What did you think?"

At last, his gaze moved back to her face. "I had no clue," he murmured dryly.

Lexie paused. Was this a good idea? "You do know how to play, don't you?"

He shrugged, all confident male, then set about completing the task she had set out for him. "I've seen it done. Does that count?"

Lexie sure hoped so. The last thing she wanted to do was humiliate him by being better at a sporting event than he was.

"It's simple." Lexie waited until Lewis finished hammering in the stakes. She measured out twenty-seven feet, marked that as the starting point, then picked up a horseshoe. "Do you want me to help you do it? Or demonstrate the way the game is played?"

Lewis lounged against the end of the antique chuck wagon, arms folded in front of him, no longer looking quite so amused. "Demonstrate."

Reassuring herself that Lewis was so brilliant, he was

bound to pick this up very quickly, Lexie stood opposite the stake. "Okay, pick up the horseshoe and hold it a full arm's length in front of you, caulks side down, at a forty-five-degree angle to the ground. Then you swing the horseshoe up until it is level with your eyes, line it up visually with the stake, then swing the stake backward and forward again, letting it go..." She watched as her horseshoe sailed through the air in a perfect arc and dropped open-end onto the stake.

"All right!" Lexie clapped her hands excitedly. "I got a ringer on my first try!"

"You've done this a lot," Lewis observed, stepping up to take his turn.

"The ranch hands taught me, and every time Dad and Jenna had a barbecue, they hauled out the chuck wagon and the horseshoes."

"Ah, so this is a sentimental thing," Lewis said as he lined up behind the pit. Following her example, he aimed, swung, tossed. The heavy shoe landed a good foot short of the stake.

Scowling, Lewis did his best to contain his frustration. He had never been good at sports. As a kid, he had always been the last one picked for a team. To be shown up by the woman he was trying to impress? Not cool.

"Try again. We'll have a few pitches for warm-up, before we actually start keeping score."

Grimacing, Lewis tried again and hit a good two feet past the stake.

Lexie frowned thoughtfully, watching. "Maybe we should try another style pitching shoe," she said, going back to the wooden carrying box in the wagon that contained half a dozen horseshoes in gold and silver and several more stakes.

Lewis knew it wasn't the shoe in his hand that was the problem. "I think I can do it with this one," he said stubbornly. After all, she had.

"Maybe this wasn't such a good idea," Lexie said, biting

her lip, as he repeatedly tried and failed to get anywhere near the blanking stake.

"Sure it is." More determined than ever to hit the stake at least once, Lewis picked up another shoe and, deciding to get fancy, tried spinning it with a slight turn, like a Frisbee, just to see what would happen. Big mistake, he swiftly realized. The horseshoe sailed way to the right of the pitching area, hit the trunk of a tree and bounced back right toward their heads.

Realizing they were about to get beaned by a flying piece of metal weighing almost three pounds, Lewis grabbed Lexie by the arm and pushed her out of harm's way, then dove down, catching the side of the chuck wagon on the way down.

The shoe clattered past them.

He swore.

Lexie laughed—until she saw the moisture dripping off his arm.

RILEY MCCABE WALKED into the glass-walled ER exam room where Lewis sat, clutching a bloody dishtowel to his arm.

"Tell me again how this happened," Riley said, snapping on some sterile gloves.

Lewis shrugged out of his ripped chambray shirt. "I fought a chuck wagon and the chuck wagon won."

Lexie wanted to kick herself for putting Lewis in a situation where he would be embarrassed. "It was actually all my fault," she said.

Lewis shot her an astonished look. "No, it wasn't. I'm the one who threw the darn thing," he said.

Riley struggled to comprehend. "You threw a chuck wagon?"

"Horseshoe," Lexie corrected.

"We were playing a game," Lewis said, wincing as Riley removed the makeshift bandage and irrigated the wound. "Or trying to—we didn't actually get much past the warm-up stage."

Riley grinned. "I guess no one ever told you Lewis wasn't much for sports that involve pitching, throwing or catching, hmm?"

"The über-athlete in the family is Will," Lewis said.

Lexie recalled what a big football star Will had been in high school, before heading off to join the navy and become a pilot.

"So what ripped open the skin?" Riley asked, bending to examine the deep, three-inch cut.

Lewis winced. "A rusty nail."

"Ahh. Well, you're going to need stitches." Riley gave Lewis a shot to numb the area.

Lexie sat on the other side of the examining table. She slipped her fingers into Lewis's and squeezed. "We figured as much."

Lewis squeezed her hand back. The look in his eyes said he appreciated her moral support.

"And a tetanus shot," Riley continued amiably, already putting in the first suture.

Lewis nodded. "Figured that, too."

The silence strung out, a little uncomfortably. Riley paused and looked at Lexie. "As long as you're here, too, Miss Remington…I thought I told you to take it easy and avoid stress."

Lexie feigned innocence. "So you did."

"Despite all this, you look more rested."

Lexie grinned and squeezed Lewis's hand again. "I *feel* more rested."

Head bent, Riley continued carefully putting in stitch after stitch. "How is the reflux?"

"Better," Lexie admitted. She still had her twinges, but it was nothing compared to what it had been.

"Been adhering to your prescribed diet?"

"Yep."

Lewis chuckled and added, "There was that sip of campfire coffee…"

Lexie flushed, remembering just how awful that had been. In retrospect, she saw she had left the brew on the fire way too long. She stuck out her tongue at Lewis. "Yes, but I didn't imbibe it, remember? I spit it out, so it doesn't count."

Riley shook his head in exasperation. "You two must really have exciting dates. First you're caught sneaking her out of the ranch, then that, uh, parking incident at Lake Laramie, then last night at the Lone Star Dance Hall—which I have to tell you is still the talk of the town—and now this."

Lewis looked at Lexie drolly. "He thinks I'm trouble with a capital T where you're concerned."

"I thought I was the one who was trouble," Lexie said, playfully making her case. "Besides, trouble isn't *always* bad. I mean, look at what they used to say about Riley and Amanda."

"That's true." Lewis winked. "Those two were nothing but fireworks."

"And look at them now," Lexie noted.

"Happily married with three kids," Lewis agreed.

"Which just goes to show," Lexie murmured softly, holding Lewis's eyes, "where there's this much excitement, there's usually something pretty fantastic underneath."

Half an hour later, Lewis was stitched up, inoculated and released. He and Lexie walked out into the parking lot together, where her pickup truck sat. Suddenly, Lexie felt very shy.

"Do you want to go back to the ranch and pick up your SUV?" Lexie asked.

Lewis shook his head. "I think it can wait 'til morning."

"Then what do you want to do now?"

Lewis flashed her a slow, sexy grin. "Guess."

THE APARTMENT ABOVE the boutique was blissfully dark and silent when Lexie and Lewis walked in. She helped Lewis out of the damaged shirt he'd put back on before they left the ER.

It was bandaged from just beneath the shoulder to just above the elbow. He'd been warned not to get it wet in the shower. Aware the apartment had gotten a little chilly since the sun had gone down, she draped the chenille throw over his bare shoulders and went to turn up the heat. "Does your arm hurt?"

Lewis shook his head. "Still numb from the shot."

Lexie toed off her boots, then knelt to take off his. "Well, I guess this makes us even anyway."

Lewis sat back on the sofa. "What do you mean?"

Lexie sprawled on the floor between his legs. She wrapped her arms around his calf, rested her face on his knee and smiled as he reached down and stroked her hair. "Our first date ended with you taking me to the ER. This one ended with me taking you to the ER," she teased gently.

Lewis leaned over and kissed her tenderly on the lips, with all the promise of the lovemaking to come. "Who says it has to end?" he asked her softly.

Her heart took a little leap, and then she tenderly broke off the kiss.

She ran her hands up the insides of his thighs and found her way to his fly. Sheer male appreciation gleamed in his eyes.

"Are you up to what I think you're up to?"

She thrilled at the possessiveness in his low voice. "And what might that be?" she flirted back, kissing him through his jeans.

He groaned as she eased his belt open and brought his zipper down.

Hands hooked in the elastic band of his boxers, she eased his pants down just enough to free the hot, hard length of him. Wanting to feel connected to him, not just physically, but emotionally, she coaxed response after response from him until his hands were on her shoulders, sliding beneath her arms, lifting her up.

"No fair," he murmured, moving her onto his lap. His

blue-gray eyes darkening with pleasure, he took her mouth with his. She could feel his fierce arousal beneath her as he took her wrists in hand and pinned them behind her, making no bones about who was in charge.

She trembled as he unbuttoned her flannel shirt and eased the straps of her bra down. Sensations ran riot through her as he teased her nipples into aching crowns, then moved downward. He stroked her through the fabric of her jeans until she gasped, kissing her full on the mouth all the while. Over and over until neither of them could stand it a second longer.

"I've got to have you," Lexie whispered, feeling deliciously aroused.

He let go of her wrists. "Here?"

"Yes." Willing to do whatever he wanted, however he wanted, she stood on shaking knees and stripped. He did the same. He sank back down on the sofa. She lowered herself onto his lap, thighs on either side of him, kissing him hungrily all the while. Hands on her waist, he shifted her up, the most masculine part of him rubbing ever so gently against the most feminine part of her. Pleasure swept through her body until she could barely breathe. Perspiration dotted her body. Lower still, moisture bathed the insides of her thighs. She writhed against his fingers, letting him explore the delicate folds to his heart's content while his hardness throbbed, hot and ready, against her thigh.

She arched against him, shuddering so they broke off their hot, steamy kiss. And then he was turning her, so she was sitting on his lap, her back to his chest. He was stroking her with both hands, kissing her shoulder, caressing her breasts, tummy, the insides of her thighs, even as they became one.

Loving the unexpectedness of his lovemaking, Lexie tightened around him, matching his movements, surrendering herself completely as she slid toward the brink. Needing him the way she had never needed any man, all fire and heat, need and passion, she cloaked him in tight, honeyed, warmth. Both of them seeking release, they climbed past barriers, finding each other at long last. They clung to each other until the intensity passed, then Lewis was gently disengaging their bodies, shifting her, turning her to face him. He kissed her tenderly once again. His expression showing fierce satisfaction and wonderment, he traced a finger from her cheekbone to her chin.

"This isn't just a fling we're having, Lexie Remington," he told her huskily.

Marveling at the way his body felt nestled against hers, so hard and warm and strong, she wreathed both her arms around his neck. "It isn't?" she whispered, looking deep into his eyes.

He ran his thumb across her lower lip, before kissing her again. "It's something much more serious."

Their glances met. The air between them reverberated with escalating excitement and desire. "Like?"

He stroked both his hands through her hair, still watching her with bright, lively eyes. "Love. The kind that lasts a lifetime."

Pleasure swept through her, even more fiercely than before. She sighed contentedly. "I think so, too," she whispered, basking in the reassurance.

"Good." He flashed her a Texas-sized grin. "Because I love you, Lexie Remington."

"And I love you, Lewis McCabe." It felt good saying the words out loud. Even better knowing they were true.

His eyes glittered mischievously. "We've only got one problem."

"And that is?"

He shook his head in mock ruefulness. "This dream date we keep trying to give each other."

Lexie groaned and dropped her head against his. *Tal*

about a comedy of errors! "I think I'm ready to give up on that."

"I'm not," he vowed softly, pausing to kiss her again. "We're going to have it, Lexie. Sooner than you think."

LEXIE WAS IN THE BOUTIQUE, showing Jenna some of her sketches, when the uniformed delivery man walked in the door. "I have a present for Ms. Lexie Remington."

Lexie's pulse picked up. Aware she was liking her time in Laramie better and better, to the point she never wanted to leave again, she tipped the messenger, then opened the box.

"Is that from Lewis?" Jenna asked.

Lexie no longer cared who knew how serious she and Lewis were becoming. "Obviously." She fought her way through the layers of tissue paper to the gorgeous gown underneath. She lifted it out of the box and held it against her.

"Wow." Jenna looked at the dazzling mauve gown. "That's some new beau you have."

"He is pretty great, if I do say so myself." Lexie knew she was beaming—she couldn't help it. "I'm going to try this on."

"Go right ahead. I can't wait to see it, either."

Lexie slipped into the dressing room.

The clinging silk chiffon evening dress, with its U-shaped neckline, spaghetti straps and flaring floor-length hem was every bit as perfect as she hoped. A scarf, with the same floral imprint as the gown, was designed to be draped across her collarbone and left to flow down her back. Not surprised that Lewis had selected the perfect gown for whatever romantic evening he had planned ahead, Lexie waltzed back out.

"You should call him and let him know how much you like it," Jenna said with an approving smile.

"I will." Lexie plucked her cell phone off the table and called Lewis on his. "Hey, Lewis. Thank you!"

"For what?" Lewis replied, all innocence.

Lexie caught Jenna's eyes and sent her stepmother an amused look. Men! "As if you don't know," Lexie teased back in the same flirtatious tone.

The door behind her opened. Brisk autumn air blew in followed by Lewis, who was still talking on his cell phone "I was on my way over to ask you to lunch. But…maybe it should be dinner?" he said, taking in her dress with the same stunned delight as Lexie felt.

"How about both?" Lexie crossed the distance between them swiftly. Unmindful of the other customers in the shop, she wrapped her arms around his neck. Aware she had never felt so beautiful or joyous in her entire life, she said softly, "You are so incredibly sweet. Thank you!" She kissed him on the cheek.

He looked even more befuddled. "For what?"

Lexie chuckled. "This dress!"

Lewis drew away, his smile fading. "Lexie," he cautioned concern in his eyes. "I didn't send it to you."

Chapter Thirteen

Lexie stared at him, her joy fading as swiftly as it had appeared. "You're not joking, are you?"

"I wish I had sent it," he said with careful politeness.

Lexie turned to Jenna, recognition dawning. "And if you and Daddy didn't send it to me, then…"

Lexie's cell phone began to ring again. Aware Lewis no longer looked as happy as he had when he walked in the door, she picked up.

"Darling."

Lexie's heart sank. Way too late, she began to put it all together. Had she only acted sooner, she could have saved Lewis—and herself—this humiliation. "Mother."

"How did you like the dress that Constantine sent to you?" the Contessa asked.

Lexie's spine stiffened at the victory in her mother's tone. "I don't," she retorted furiously.

"Of course you do," Melinda answered in typical know-it-all fashion. "You're just too stubborn to admit it. But all that can change. I want you to come to Los Angeles today. I'm hosting a party for Constantine at his Brentwood mansion Saturday evening. We would both like you to be there."

The one she had so foolishly put on—and admired! Now that she knew where the dress had come from, Lexie couldn't wait to get out of it. "At your suggestion, no doubt," she grumbled, irritated beyond belief.

"Darling, if he wants you back—and he does—he is going to have to treat you right this time. No more servant hovering in the corner. He agrees that you are going to take your rightful place by his side from now on."

"Too bad I don't want *him* back," Lexie countered sharply, feeling a tension headache coming on. She rubbed her temples. "And just so you know? I'm sending the dress back!" She cut the connection and turned off her phone.

Everyone was looking at her.

"He sent you the dress. Didn't he?" Lewis asked, struggling to curtail his obvious distress with only limited success.

Jenna made herself scarce, as did her saleswoman and the customer they'd been helping.

Lexie took Lewis by the arm. They disappeared down the hall, to the storeroom. She tried not to make too much of the implacable look in his eyes or his newly subdued mood. "Yes. I'm sorry, I thought it was from you."

Lewis shrugged and slouched against the wall, away from her. "I'm sorry I didn't think to send you a dress."

Lexie went toward him, hands outstretched. "I don't care about expensive presents," she told him softly, taking both his hands in hers. "You know that is not what I want from you."

Lewis held her gaze warily. "Then what do you want?" he asked.

"This." Lexie threw her arms around Lewis's neck, kissed him with everything she had, until he was kissing her back just as fervently. Then, she drew back, pleased to see the smile had returned to his face. "And that lunch you promised me," she teased.

Lunch turned into an afternoon spent riding the horses on the Lazy M Ranch, and near dusk, a stop at the home site Lewis had selected for his own ranch house on the property.

They tied their horses to the trees, then walked across the cleared earth to the bulldozed building site. Stakes were set out, indicating the edge of the yard. Within that, a wooden framework had been laid. "They're going to come out and pour the cement for the foundation next week," Lewis said.

Lexie looked around, pleased. "How many square feet?"

"Five thousand."

She paused, close to him. "What's it going to look like?"

Lewis wrapped an arm about her shoulders and brought her in close to his side. "It's going to be Spanish-style architecture, with lots of arches and stucco walls and a red tile roof." He gestured amiably, directing her attention. "You can see I've left room in the center for a courtyard that is enclosed on three sides. I'm going to put a roof over half of it so we can sit outside and enjoy the evening, even when it rains."

Lexie grinned, tilted her face up to his. She loved feeling included in his plans, his life. "We?"

He smiled down at her gently and rubbed his thumb across her cheek before running it over her lower lip. "You are going to be here with me, aren't you?" he asked, looking deep into her eyes.

"That is the plan." Her heart filling with joy, Lexie kissed him again. Then, knowing he wasn't the only one with news about the future, she told him proudly, "I'm going to start looking for studio space here in Laramie next week."

Lewis lifted an eyebrow. Although his expression was carefully matter-of-fact, she could see the interest gleaming in his blue-gray eyes. "You've officially quit your job?"

Lexie nodded, knowing this was a move that had been coming for a long time. Several years, actually, she just hadn't been brave enough to quit a successful endeavor and start from scratch on another. Now, with Lewis—and her family—standing by her side, it didn't seem risky at all. In fact, she lamented not having done this sooner. "I'm going to start calling my clients next week." She laid her cheek on his shoulder. "Of course, a good twenty percent of them have already fired me."

Lewis brought her closer yet and ruffled a hand through her hair. "They sound pretty fickle."

Lexie shrugged, enjoying the intimacy of the moment. It was so nice, just to be with him, talking and spending time together. "Celebrities demand a lot of time and attention from those who work for them. That was fine, when I didn't have much of a life," she said seriously, glad to see he understood how complicated her situation was. "But now that I want to do things like take some time for me, actually take a vacation—my first real one in five years." She sighed heavily. "I understand why they're not happy with me. Just as I understand why I can't keep working at the pace I've been going." She paused and gazed into his eyes. "I want a whole life, Lewis." She smiled. "And I want it with you…"

"Then that makes two of us," Lewis said huskily, bending his head to kiss her. And for the first time in her life, Lexie felt she had everything she had ever wanted or needed.

"YOU SURE ARE BRAVE, agreeing to go to the bimonthly Lockhart family potluck with me tonight," Lexie told Lewis, an hour later.

This evening, the festivities were being held at Lexie's aunt Dani's and uncle Beau's home, in downtown Laramie. All four Lockhart sisters—Jenna, Dani, Meg and Kelsey—would be there, along with their husbands and children. As Lewis and Lexie turned onto Spring Street, they encountered quite a few cars parked up and down the tree-lined avenue.

Lewis parked as close to the century-old Victorian as he could, then got out and opened Lexie's door. She plucked the big bowl of fruit salad—her contribution to the night's buffet—from the back seat, and together they headed up the sidewalk.

"No braver than you," he replied, pressing a kiss to the top of her head, "in agreeing to attend the McCabe family painting party over at Kevin's on Sunday evening."

She shrugged, as excited as she was self-conscious. "It's time our families got used to seeing us together," she stated firmly.

"I couldn't agree more."

No sooner had they walked in the front door, than they were inundated with greetings. Everyone seemed to welcome Lewis with welcome arms—except Susie Carrigan, who walked in carrying several lovely floral planters.

Susie greeted Lexie as warmly as usual. Her hello to Lewis was markedly cooler.

"I don't get why Susie is so...wary of you," Lexie said, after a half hour had passed. Susie had been watching them surreptitiously from the sidelines, frowning more often than not.

"Are you absolutely sure she didn't want to date you, too?" Lexie murmured.

"Positive." Lewis clamped an authoritative hand on Lexie's shoulder and turned her away. "There's no chemistry there."

Lexie sneaked another glance—saw the same disapproving stare—then turned back to Lewis with a beleaguered scowl of her own. "Then why does she keep looking at you like you're not welcome here?"

He shrugged, looking way too innocent. "No clue," he stated flatly, his attention focused on the platters of appetizers set out.

She watched him load a tortilla chip with guacamole, and knew guilt when she saw it. Knowing the two of them the way she did, she couldn't imagine about what. "Did you two have a falling out at Career Night?"

His expression was unconcerned, but the tense set of his shoulders and the cautious slant of his jaw said otherwise. "No."

Her internal radar kicking into high alert, Lexie nibble on a cactus fry. "She wasn't very friendly to you that nigh either. Susie is usually nice to everyone."

Lewis continued to avoid Lexie's penetrating gaze "Maybe she's just in a bad mood," he said off-handedly.

And maybe Susie had a reason to dislike Lewis that Lexi needed to know about. Not that she should be checking u on the man she was head over heels in love with… On th other hand, Lexie had turned a blind eye before, when she ha been involved with Constantine Romeo…and look wher that had gotten her.

Lexie saw Susie head for the kitchen. She picked up platter that needed replenishing and told Lewis she was goin to help out.

Unfortunately, before Lexie had navigated her way out c the packed living room, her uncle Beau intercepted her. A usual, the famous actor-director was wearing jeans and a whit western shirt that belied his international superstar status. "Al Lexie. Just the person I wanted to see," he declared.

"Why?"

Beau plucked the platter from her fingers and handed it o to someone already headed for the kitchen, then guided he to a corner of the room. "First, I wanted to thank you fc taking Sydney Mazero under your wing and going to th premiere in Austin tomorrow night to offer your moral sup port."

His sincere praise made Lexie beam. "It was my pleasur Although, Sydney's going to have to find another stylist t help her from this point forward. I'm getting out of tha business and into design."

"So I heard. Congrats."

"Thanks."

"Second, I heard Constantine Romeo's been bothering yo Do you want me to say anything to him to get him to back off?

"I've got the situation under control," she promised.

Beau narrowed his eyes at her thoughtfully. "You sure?"

Lexie knew the discouragement had to come directly from ıer. Otherwise, Constantine wouldn't take her rejection se- iously and move on to someone else. "Yes." Seeing Lewis oming toward them, Lexie tried to cut the conversation short. Jnfortunately, Beau would not allow it.

"I've known the man a long time," Beau persisted. "He's ne of the most ruthlessly ambitious actors around. When he vants something he doesn't give up."

"He also has a huge ego. I haven't heard from him or my nother since I sent the dress back yesterday." She was hoping ıer slap-down had put an end to Constantine's fantasy about etting her back, once and for all.

Beau frowned. "He promised *Rise and Shine America!* that ıe'd be engaged by Monday."

"And I'm sure he will be." Lexie breathed a sigh of relief as ewis stopped to talk to another of her cousins. "Just not to me."

"I'm being overprotective again."

"You and my dad…" she teased.

"But you can't blame me for feeling somewhat responsi- le for what's happening now since I'm the one who intro- luced you to him years ago," he continued with regret.

Hard to believe she had ever been so naive, never mind llowed herself to be so emotionally vulnerable to such a elfish heartbreaker. Wincing, she said, "You didn't know vhat he was really like then. No one did." Constantine had een an ace at acting like the all-American boy-next-door vith the heart of gold. He still fooled millions of fans. Most f the people in the business knew better.

"But I do now."

"And so do I," Lexie said equably.

Beau patted her on the shoulder fondly. "If you need ıelp…"

"I won't hesitate to ask," Lexie promised.

Beau departed and Lewis took his place next to her.

"How much did you hear?" Lexie asked.

"Enough to know your uncle Beau is worried you haven' heard the last of Constantine Romeo," Lewis replied.

As far as Lexie was concerned, her ex had already spoile too much of her life thus far. "Can we please not talk abou Constantine tonight? I want to concentrate on us."

Lewis scowled, looking McCabe-formidable. "If he show up here again—"

"He won't," Lexie promised quickly, sure about this much "He's in California with my mother. They're planning som big 'to-do' out there while we're at the *Calamity Sue* premier in Austin. He and my mother know I'm not attending it Therefore, he's probably got his next possible fiancée in hi sights already." She shook her head. "And knowing Constan tine's thrift when it comes to spending money on anythin other than himself, she's probably wearing that same mauv dress."

"And you really don't care?" Lewis searched her face.

Lexie rose on tiptoe and kissed Lewis on the lips. "I hav everything I need right here with you."

"SO, WHAT EXACTLY ARE your intentions for my daughter?' Jake Remington asked Lewis, as soon as the Remington je took off from the Laramie airstrip, en route to Austin earl Saturday afternoon.

"Dad!" Lexie gasped.

Jake's assessing glance remained on Lewis. "I think it's valid question."

"So do I," Lewis agreed, to Lexie's surprise.

"You're not helping here," she told him.

Lewis flexed his shoulders and settled more comfortabl in his seat. "Your dad loves you." He paused to regard Jak with respect. "He has every right to know that I intend to marry you one day."

Lexie's mouth dropped into a round "oh" of surprise. Her heart filled with joy.

"This wasn't how I wanted to broach the subject," Lewis continued earnestly, looking first at Lexie, then back at Jake and Jenna, who were seated in two chairs opposite them, with a table in between. "But I have no objection to discussing my feelings for you, Lexie. Heck. I want the whole world to know that we love each other."

Eyes sparkling with a mixture of affection and approval, Jenna elbowed Jake. "Satisfied?" she asked smugly.

"Almost." Jake locked his gaze on Lewis. "About that marriage proposal..."

"Dad!" Lexie cried, exasperated.

"Make it sooner rather than later," Jake continued.

Lewis's face split into a wide grin. "Will do, sir."

To Lexie's relief, the talk turned more casual then. To business, and family. Time went quickly. Before Lexie knew it, the four of them were checking in to the Driskill Hotel, courtesy of her father's prior arrangements.

The clerk handed over three electronic room keys.

One for Jake and Jenna, another for Lexie—both of those on the same floor. Lewis was situated two floors down.

"Somehow I don't think you being so far away from me was an accident," Lexie murmured. She waved Jenna and Jake into the elevator, while she stood with Lewis in front of the cowhide sofas in the lobby. "I'll be up in a minute," Lexie said. "You all go on."

The elevator doors shut.

Lewis steered her to the other side of a large bronze sculpture of a cowboy on a horse. "I think your father is sending us a message that he wants us to behave while we're here."

There was behaving, Lexie thought. And then there was

behaving. Right now she was happier than she had ever been in her life. And she intended to celebrate her new love every way she could—without upsetting her father. She smiled and went up on tiptoe to whisper in his ear, "Wild horses couldn't keep me away from you tonight." She splayed a hand over his chest. The accelerating beat of his heart matched hers. "But we'll be discreet—I promise. Meantime, I have to go get ready for this evening's festivities. So I'll meet you downstairs in the lobby at quarter 'til seven?"

Lewis nodded, looking every bit as ready to make love as she was. "I'll be there."

"See you then." Lexie delivered a sweet kiss to his cheek and dashed off.

Upstairs in the historic hotel, her room was all opulent Victorian elegance, circa the late 1800s. Lexie's suitcase was already on the stand in front of the iron bedstead. She laid out the midnight-blue dress she had brought for the evening's premiere, grabbed her toiletries bag and headed into the luxurious bathroom.

Lexie took her time while in the shower, shaving her legs and shampooing and deep-conditioning her hair. When she emerged some twenty minutes later, the bathroom was steamy as could be. Wrapping herself in the thick white terrycloth robe the hotel had provided, she stepped out into the bedroom and stared in shock at the bed.

The dress she had brought was gone, as well as her suitcase and all her other clothing. On the bed lay the mauve gown she had sent back to Constantine Romeo, as well as the shoes and delicate undies that went under it. Beside it was a single white rose and an embossed envelope with Constantine Romeo's name written in gold across the front. Inside that was another electronic hotel room key and a room number.

LEWIS HAD JUST FINISHED tying his tie when the knock sounded on his hotel room door.

Hoping Lexie was there to steal a pre-premiere kiss, Lewis went to open the door. He was stunned to see Lexie's mother, the Contessa Melinda della Gheradesca, in the hallway. Clad in a stunning white evening gown, a white stole around her shoulders and diamonds adorning her ears, she swept inside.

"I'm here to save you," she announced grandly.

"From what?" Lewis demanded.

She shut the door behind her, a superior expression on her face. "Making an even bigger fool of yourself than you already have."

Dread tightened his gut, along with the worry he was about to lose the best thing that had ever happened to him. "I don't follow." He forced himself to sound casual.

"You can't win." The Contessa flashed a Cheshire cat smile. "Alexandra is going to marry Constantine. The engagement is going to be announced Monday morning on *Rise and Shine America!*"

"In whose universe?" Lewis clenched his jaw.

The Contessa looked down her nose at him. "Scoff now. I guarantee you won't be laughing an hour from now when you see Alexandra walking the red carpet on that gorgeous man's arm."

"Lexie is going to the premiere with me."

The Contessa waved a bejeweled hand in front of his face. "That was the plan. And even I have to admit it was a good one. Constantine is absolutely green with jealousy. He can't bear the thought of losing Alexandra to a nobody like you."

For Lexie's sake, Lewis let that one pass. He shrugged on his suit coat and paused to check his reflection in the mirror. He did not intend to be late meeting Lexie. "Lexie is not using me."

The Contessa stepped behind him and caught his eyes in the

reflection. "Of course she isn't—consciously. But secretly, in the deepest recesses of her heart, you have to know that Lexie never got over Constantine breaking up with her the minute he hit the really big time. His foolishness broke her heart. Now, thanks to my involvement, it can—and it is—being mended."

Lewis had no doubt that Lexie's mother was up to no good. The lady lived for her selfish machinations and social climbing. He could not believe Lexie would be part of any scheme her selfish mother cooked up. He turned to face the Contessa. "You're lying."

"Am I? Then why is Lexie headed for Constantine's suite just about now?"

Lewis grabbed his entry card and put it in the inner pocket of his suit coat. He knew he was supposed to buy this load of bull, and ditch Lexie. No way was he cooperating. He mocked her mother with a look. "I don't believe you."

"Then let's go see. Shall we?"

Figuring there was only one way to shut Melinda della Gheradesca up, Lewis followed her out into the hall, to the elevators. They rode in silence to the appropriate floor and walked past Constantine's suite, where a bodyguard stood sentry. The Contessa's suite was another ten feet down the hall. They entered, leaving the door slightly ajar to afford a view of the entire corridor.

The Contessa glanced at her diamond watch. "Any minute now," she predicted.

Lewis waited and watched, not believing for one red-hot second that Lexie would betray him. Until he saw Lexie striding purposefully down the hall in the mauve dress that he thought she had sent back. She looked gorgeous and fit for battle. Her cheeks blushed with vibrant color, her eyes sparkled. Oblivious to the fact she was being observed, she stopped at the door, murmured something to the bodyguard and was let inside.

Chapter Fourteen

How dare you!" Lexie fumed as she stormed into the suite.

Constantine flashed her his trademark megawatt grin. He auntered toward her, arms outstretched. "I knew you would ook gorgeous in that dress."

Lexie leveled him with a look. "You didn't even pick it out. Ay mother did!"

He lifted his shoulder in an indolent shrug, and thought etter of trying to embrace her. "So I asked the expert on you or a little help," he said softly.

Which was only part of the problem. Lexie regarded him adly. "The Contessa barely knows me."

Constantine arched a finely plucked brow in disagreement. "She knew I could get you up here before the premiere," he pointed out.

He had her there, Lexie reluctantly admitted. "Only ecause you stole my clothes and my suitcase."

He walked back over to pour himself another drink. "I had hem moved up here by a member of the staff. To make things asier, later."

She shook her head no at his offer of a vodka sour for erself. "There is no later between you and me."

Heaving a dramatic sigh, he took a sip of his drink and

moved toward her once again. "Now, Lexie, you know tha you and I belong together."

There had been a time, years before, when Lexie woul have done anything to hear those very words from Constantine, when all she wanted was to have him love her the wa she had once foolishly loved him. But those feelings ha died when she realized how little she meant to him. He n longer had the power to hurt her, she realized, unless she le him. And she darn well was not going to do that. Adaptin the same no-nonsense Texan tone her uncle Beau had use in all those westerns he had acted in, she swaggered clos enough so he could not possibly miss the rancor in her expression. "Now listen up and listen good. I. Do. Not. Love You. Anymore. And frankly, I'm not sure I ever did."

His cocky smile began to fade. Something far les pleasant—though no less determined—flickered in his eyes

Realizing she was in the driver's seat at long last, Lexi folded her arms in front of her. Resolved to make him an his massive ego understand that their relationship woul never be resurrected, no matter what he offered, she continued ruminating out loud. "I think I did love some of the characters you played in the movies, because those people wer genuine. Those heroes had heart and soul and fine characte They fought for what was right. They didn't use and sacrifice others to get ahead." Lexie aimed a lecturing finger hi way, looked him straight in the eye. "That is what you do Constantine Romeo. And this engagement you are about t announce is yet another facet of that behavior."

His face turned red and a vein throbbed in his forehead Still, true to form, he persisted going after what he felt woul be good for his career. "Marriage could be good for both o us, Lexie. You could have the kids you always wanted. Th kind of lifestyle your mother enjoys."

Lexie nodded, pretending to think about it. "All I'd hav

to do is look the other way when you cheat on me with other women."

He released a short, impatient breath and clamped a proprietary hand on her shoulder. "Look, you know I don't prescribe to provincial American attitudes. For a while, a long while, I tried to shield you from that. But now that I've met your mother, and I know what a sophisticated woman she is—"

"Sophisticated or just someone with as few values as you?" Lexie interrupted, shrugging off his grip and stepping away.

He continued as if she hadn't spoken. "I know you have the capacity and the upbringing to be just as tolerant. In exchange, I'll give you as much money as you want. I'll give your mother entrée into the social A-list of filmmakers worldwide. She can even live with us, if you want."

He really thought he was offering her quite a deal. "That way, when you're gone, I won't be so lonely," Lexie guessed sweetly.

"Right."

Lexie whistled, soft and low. "Sounds like you have it all figured out."

"I need you, Lexie. It's just that simple."

Honestly, Lexie wondered, just how stupid did he think she was? "To help you get back on the best-dressed lists."

"And shore up my image," he confirmed, totally serious now. "No one quite gets what is current versus cutting edge more than you do. You were always on the right side of every trend, Lexie," he told her with genuine admiration. "Hell, I think you even started a lot of them."

He was right about that much. "That, I did."

"So what do you say?" He looked at her enthusiastically, sure he had emerged the victor once again. "Do we have a deal?"

"We certainly do." Lexie smiled right back. "And this is what it is. You are going to have your bodyguard return my luggage to my room. You are going to tell my mother that what we had is over—for good. That I am not now or ever going to get engaged to you. And then you will never darken my doorstep again."

He laughed, as if this were just some game they were playing. "And if I don't?" he challenged, still not taking her seriously.

Lexie gave him the deadly look she had saved for just this moment. "Then I start giving interviews to the press. I tell them exactly what kind of man you are. And I promise you, Constantine, if it comes to that, if you force my hand, you'll regret it!"

"LEXIE, WHERE HAVE YOU BEEN!" Jenna demanded as Lexie rushed up to her and Jake in the lobby a short while later. Lexie's normally unflappable stepmother paused to do a double take. "And where did you get that dress?"

No doubt, Jenna recalled the gown and its nefarious origins. Lexie grimaced. "Long story."

Jenna pressed a hand to her chest, looking more maternal than ever. "Oh, dear," she whispered.

"I know." Lexie nodded her head miserably. She looked around at the crowd of movie people gathering in the lobby. "Where's Lewis?" Lexie didn't see him anywhere.

Jake frowned, looking as perplexed as Lexie felt. They all knew Lewis was punctual to a fault. "I haven't seen him," he said.

The feeling of dread inside Lexie increased tenfold. Had her mother and Constantine Romeo somehow set up Lewis, too? She swallowed around the growing knot of emotion in her throat. Her knees began to shake. "Lewis was supposed to meet us in the lobby ten minutes ago."

Jenna touched Lexie's arm gently and continued scanning the crowd anxiously. "Your father and I have been down here for fifteen. We didn't see him," she reported softly.

Lexie refused to let anyone ruin what she had with Lewis McCabe. She rummaged in her evening bag for her cell. "Let me try his cell phone."

Jake sprang into action, too. "I'll go use the house phone to call his room."

Short minutes later, Lexie, Jenna and Jake met in the center of the lobby. "Any luck?" Lexie asked her stepmother and father hopefully, fearing she already knew the answer.

Jake shook his head and Jenna did the same.

Lexie's spirits sank ever lower.

Her uncle Beau stepped out of the elevators and headed their way, her aunt Dani by his side. As always, the famed actor-director and his movie-critic wife made a very glamorous couple. "Everybody ready to go over to the theater?" Beau asked cheerfully, looking outside to the line of limos idling at the curb. He consulted his watch. "They want us on the red carpet in ten minutes."

"I can't find Lewis," Lexie said.

To Lexie's chagrin, neither her aunt or uncle looked surprised about that. "Beau and I saw him half an hour ago, when we got back from the TV station," Dani related matter-of-factly. "He was walking out of the hotel as we were coming in. He said he had to go back to Laramie. He had no choice." Dani paused, perplexed. "I thought he would have told you he was leaving so abruptly."

Lexie shook her head. Had Lewis come to her hotel room and found her missing? She was beginning to have a very bad feeling about this. "Did he say why? Was it a family emergency?" Lexie asked.

Beau and Dani exchanged glances. Dani turned back to Lexie. "Not that we know. All we can tell you is that he was in a hurry to get home."

"MAYBE YOU'RE WRONG about what happened," Brad and Lainey McCabe said as they sat down to watch the video recording of the late night news with Lewis that same evening.

"And maybe I'm not," Lewis muttered, wishing he'd had time to change out of his Hugo Boss suit and tie before jumping in the limo he had hired to drive him back to Laramie. Instead, he was all dressed up with no place to go, and no woman to go with him.... Worse, his happily married brother and his wife knew it. Which meant soon the whole family—hell, the whole town of Laramie—would know it, too.

The call sign of the Austin TV station flashed on the television screen. Thanks to the help of their satellite dish, Brad and Lainey had been able to record what Lewis needed to view.

"Next up," the announcer said, "is coverage of the *Calamity Sue* premiere, held at the Paramount Theater downtown." Lewis fast-forwarded through the commercials and cut back in as the news continued.

"A lot of celebrities were there tonight," the anchor explained over footage of the event. "Beau Chamberlain, the director, and his wife, film critic Dani Lockhart Chamberlain. Right behind them on the red carpet is Sydney Mazero, the young star of *Calamity Sue,* looking gorgeous, with her parents. And to the left of Sydney, in the striking mauve gown, is Alexandra Remington and her parents, dress designer Jenna Lockhart Remington and Jake Remington. And of course we all know Constantine Romeo. And the woman on his arm is former Texan, now Italian royalty, Contessa Melinda della Gheradesca. Now watch...Romeo is moving in, putting his arm around her daughter, Alexandra Remington, too."

"Do you think Lexie Remington is the one he's been hinting he is in love with?" the female news anchor asked.

The news paused on the video footage of the event, showing Romeo casting an adoring look at Lexie, who was looking straight ahead.

"I don't know."

"She was his stylist for almost five years," the female news anchor said. "Obviously they have a connection."

"Maybe," the male anchor replied.

Lewis grimaced. Brad and Lainey gave him pitying looks as the three of them continued to study the footage, frame by frame. Lewis rewound the tape and pointed out grimly, "That dress Lexie is wearing? Romeo gave it to her."

"Jenna told me that Lexie sent that back," Lainey countered, looking just as unhappy about the situation as Lewis felt.

"Obviously not," Lewis growled.

Lainey continued defending Lexie. "I'm sure there's an explanation."

Hurt and humiliation churned through Lewis. He could hardly believe he'd made the same damn mistake again, falling for a woman on the rebound…a woman who had never been his to love. He had just wanted her to be his so badly he hadn't let himself see the truth. "Yes, and the Contessa gave it to me right before I left Austin. Despite the horrible way he treated her, Lexie never stopped loving Constantine Romeo. She was just using me to make him jealous. Obviously," Lewis stood and continued bitterly, "all the drama worked. Their engagement will be announced Monday morning on *Rise and Shine, America!* You can all watch if you want to—I've seen enough."

"I'M TEMPTED TO FIND that young man and give him a piece of my mind, standing you up that way," Jake Remington growled as their jet landed at the Laramie airstrip Sunday afternoon.

Lexie sighed. The last thing she needed was another one of her parents getting involved in her love life. If the Contessa hadn't played matchmaker, Lexie was sure she and Lewis would still be together at this moment. Fortunately, she still had a chance to explain to Lewis what had happened and make things right between them once again.

"Daddy, I can handle Lewis McCabe," she said stonily, even though inwardly she was not sure at all. Especially if Lewis had seen photos of her in that mauve dress….

Jake regarded her over the top of the *Wall Street Journal.* "Can you?"

So she had been up most of the night crying. So her eyes were still puffy, despite the icepacks she put on them, during the flight back to Laramie. So what?

"Maybe you should just track him down and go see him," Jenna suggested with a sympathetic look.

Lexie winced as the jet's wheels touched down on the tarmac. The plane bounced slightly before braking toward the end of the runway. "I just don't understand how he could have told me that he loved me and he didn't care who knew it and then walk out on me that way, without even leaving me a message," Lexie said softly, watching as the pilot turned the jet around and headed back toward the hangar.

"Exactly my point." Jenna put the book she had been reading in her carryall. Together, they disembarked from the private jet. "That doesn't sound like the Lewis McCabe I know," she soothed.

"Maybe you all don't know him as well as you think you do," Susie Carrigan said as she walked toward them.

Lexie tensed, bracing for the worst.

Susie commiserated gently, "Lexie, I'm sorry to have to be the one to tell you this, but…"

Lexie listened to Susie recite the chain of events that had led Lewis to her doorstep in the first place. "You're absolutely sure of this," Lexie said incredulously. "His hiring me was all an inside joke between him and his brothers?"

Susie shoved her hands in the pocket of her overalls and

nodded reluctantly. "I overheard his brothers giving him the business and he admitted it to me the night of the Career Fair at LHS."

So Susie had known Lewis had been pulling one over on her all this time. For what reason? To amuse his brothers? Or because—like Constantine Romeo—he saw a way to use her to make himself even more desirable? All Lexie knew for certain was that anyone who loved her would not have treated her that way. "Why didn't you tell me then?" Lexie demanded, feeling even more miserable and upset.

Guilt flickered across Susie's face. "Because he convinced me that he'd had a change of heart, that he took the whole thing with you seriously. But if he walked out on you last night—"

"How do you know about that?" Lexie interrupted.

Susie shrugged. "It wasn't hard to figure out something was going on. For starters, he was over at the Wagon Wheel restaurant getting breakfast this morning—alone—instead of in Austin with you and your folks, as previously scheduled. So I went up and asked him where you were and he about darn near bit my head off." She paused. "He muttered something about how he should have just stuck to his original plan in the first place and not gotten emotionally involved. Then he said that if it weren't for the McCabe family painting party over at his brother Kevin's house this afternoon, he'd be in California already. And that was when I knew you had to know the whole story behind his hopelessly cruel and self-serving actions as soon as possible."

"UH OH," WILL MCCABE SAID, "here comes trouble."

"What?" Lewis looked up to see Lexie Remington marching through the open front door of Kevin's home. Clad in a pair of black cords, red turtleneck, a cropped black velvet jacket and square-toed western boots, her strawberry-blond hair floating down around her shoulders in wild waves, she looked breathtaking. And ticked off as could be. Which was odd, he thought, as he continued to take in her brilliant turquoise eyes and heart-stoppingly beautiful face, since he was the one who had been heartlessly used and was the only one with the right to be angry.

Hoping for one wildly irrational second that it had all been a big misunderstanding, he put down his paintbrush. The rest of his family followed suit.

"Funny," Lewis remarked tightly, "you don't *look* as if you're about to apologize."

"Me!" She stormed forward and poked a finger against his sternum. "You're the one who needs to apologize!"

Lewis scoffed. "For giving you the space you needed to get back together with Constantine Romeo?"

She jerked her hand from the center of his paint-splattered sweatshirt, as suddenly as if he had burned her. "For hiring me as a joke!"

Lewis swore silently to himself. Quiet fell. Suddenly everyone got very busy painting again. "Go ahead," Lexie demanded, daring him with an imperious look, " just try and deny it."

Lewis raked both hands through his hair, then realized he had just streaked the strands with the pale sage green of the living room walls. Swearing again—this time out loud—he wiped both his hands on his shirt. "Susie told you," he said grimly.

Rosy color brightened Lexie's cheeks. "Yes, and she should have done so a lot sooner. It would have saved us both a lot of grief!"

A delicate cough had heads turning in that direction. "I, for one, like the changes you orchestrated for Lewis's overall appearance and attire," Kate Marten McCabe interrupted, putting her skills as a psychologist and family peacemaker to good use. "It was about time he put that '80s look to rest."

"If only he had been sincere about wanting to do so," Lexie told Kate sweetly.

"I was!" Lewis broke in heatedly, not about to take the blame for something he hadn't done.

She stood with her hands planted on her hips. "You were not. Everybody except me knows your hiring me at all was a joke!"

Forcing himself not to remember how good those hips had felt pressed up against him, he clenched his jaw and went back to painting. "On me, maybe."

She moved so he had no choice but to look at her. "What are you talking about?" she demanded irritably.

Lewis shifted his gaze away from the rapid rise and fall of her breasts. "I went to the Remington Ranch the night you got back to ask you out. Jenna and your dad thought I was there to hire you. I didn't know that. And they didn't know I wanted to ask you out. We were talking at cross purposes and before I knew it, you thought the same thing, too." He took a deep breath. "I didn't know how to tell you that wasn't why I was there without insulting what you do for a living, so I let it ride. Then when you started helping me, I realized how much I needed your assistance in that area. My brothers still thought the whole mix-up was uproariously funny, but I didn't. I didn't like keeping anything from you! I didn't like feeling less than honest. But I didn't see any other way to keep from hurting your feelings."

"Oh." The wind left her sails as abruptly as it had filled them. "But that still doesn't explain why you walked out on me yesterday without so much as a 'See ya later, kid.'"

Aware all eyes were still upon them, Lewis put down his paint roller ever so slowly. The hurt and disillusionment he'd felt then came back at him full-force. "You really want to do this here and now?"

She kept her eyes on his. "Yes."

Lewis did his best to shut out the painful memory. "I saw you in that mauve dress, going into Constantine's hotel suite."

Lexie couldn't help it. She blushed, looking as guilty—and embarrassed—as could be. "It wasn't what it looked like," she protested.

"According to the Contessa it was exactly what it looked like."

Lexie tapped her foot. "Do you see me here with him now?"

"Well. No…" Lewis said reluctantly, still not willing to be played for a fool, no matter how much he loved her.

"And you know what? You're never going to see him anywhere near me again."

Lewis wished he could believe that. The evidence said otherwise. "He was standing next to you on the red carpet last night, Lexie. He had his arm around you and your mother." And much as Lewis wanted to, he couldn't forget that.

A weariness that seemed soul-deep shone in her eyes. "Only because he pushed and shoved his way in while the cameras were going," she said. "Constantine Romeo wasn't invited to that premiere, Lewis. No one had a clue he was going to show up."

Lewis shrugged, unconvinced. "So why wasn't he kicked out?"

Lexie threw up her hands in exasperation. "If they had done that in front of reporters, what do you think today's lead story would be? Once Romeo was there, in front of the Paramount Theater with my mother, no one had a choice. The entire cast and the event's security team had to act like he—and the Contessa—belonged there. Otherwise it would have ruined the premiere of *Calamity Sue* and taken all the attention away from Sydney Mazero and the rest of the cast, after they had worked so hard!"

Relief flowed through Lewis. "So you're not marrying him," he ascertained, the tension leaving his body.

"No! And I don't want anything further to do with *you,* either." Having said her piece, Lexie turned on her heel and stomped back out the front door, across the porch.

Realizing now what a mistake he had made in doubting her, Lewis chased her down the front steps. "Lexie, wait!"

She threw him another withering glare over her shoulder. "Go to hell!"

He raced around to cut her off, aware now she had every right to be upset with him. "I'm sorry."

She ignored his conciliatory gesture. "So am I, that I ever thought we had something special."

"We do." He caught her arm and brought her toward him.

"No. We don't." She flung off his light grasp. "Because if we had anything special between us, you never would have thought so little of me, you never would have walked out on me the way you did. And now it's my turn, Lewis McCabe," she told him, tears shimmering in her pretty turquoise eyes. "I'm the one breaking up with you."

Chapter Fifteen

"I thought I might find you here," Jake Remington said.

Lexie glanced up from her sketchpad to see her dad walking in to the small space she had rented for her new business venture.

She got up from the drafting table. "What do you think?" The space had previously been leased by an insurance agent who had moved to larger quarters. "It still needs to be painted and recarpeted." But in the five days since she and Lewis had called it quits, it had provided a haven for her.

Jake sat down on the only other piece of furniture in the two-room office suite, a heavy mahogany desk. His expression radiated approval. "I think it's great, Lexie. I'm all for it. But—" He paused, his expression as sober as his tone. "That's not why I'm here."

Lexie heard the concern and sensed a fatherly lecture coming on. She made a face at him. "I hope you're not going to try and talk me into moving back to the ranch with you and Jenna."

Jake shook his head. "That would be a step backward."

Lexie relaxed in relief. "I agree. I'm an adult now. I need my own place." *Even when I'm hurting. And I am hurting, more than I ever could have imagined.*

Jake sat with his palms resting on his thighs. "Jenna said you had asked to lease her old apartment."

Lexie nodded and put down her sketching pencil. "She wanted to let me continue to stay there for free but I really think I should pay rent, effective immediately."

Jake shrugged. "Okay. I'll convince her to take it."

Lexie tilted her head, curious. "Just like that?"

Jake sighed and ran a hand across the back of his neck. "The past two weeks have taught me a lot about myself, Lexie. I realize that I'm to blame for a lot of what has gone wrong in your life."

Lexie did a double take. This, she hadn't expected. "How do you figure that?"

Jake flashed a rueful grin and continued in a low voice laced with regret, "I've been way too overprotective of you, for way too long. I should have trusted your instincts, Lexie. Instead, I tried to keep you from getting hurt by forbidding you to see any guy I didn't deem acceptable. As a result, when you were nineteen, you ran off to Hollywood."

Lexie dug the toe of her boot into the carpet. "And to a career you didn't approve," she said, glad they were talking frankly about things that had bothered both of them.

Jake's expression gentled. "I never minded you being a stylist, Lexie. I know what a tough job that is, and how much talent it takes. What I regretted was the interruption to your college education, the fact that you had to grow up so fast."

Lexie shrugged. "That wasn't only because of Constantine, Dad."

"It was also because of your mother," Jake said.

"Yes." The Contessa's attitude about a lot of things had opened Lexie's eyes to the less-Pollyannaish aspects of life and forced her to take off her own rose-colored glasses. And maybe, just maybe, encouraged Lexie to settle for less in the love and romance department than she should have. Now, thanks to her brief involvement with Lewis McCabe, Lexie knew better. There were good men out there with huge hearts. Hearts that could be wounded as easily and permanently as hers.

Jake mistook the reason for her silence.

"Your mother loves you, Lexie," Jake said quietly.

Lexie knew that, just as she knew she would never have the mother-daughter relationship she wanted with the Contessa. She would have it with her stepmother, instead. And that was okay with her.

"Have you heard from the Contessa?" Jake asked.

"Since Constantine announced his engagement to that TV star, last Monday? No." Lexie got up to roam her new design studio restlessly. Hands in the pockets of her jeans she whirled to face her father. "And I don't expect to for a while." It was a relief, knowing she wouldn't have her mother pushing and prodding her toward a much more superficial life. Melinda would be far too busy searching out a glamorous new path for herself, without Romeo's Hollywood connections. Knowing the Contessa, Lexie was sure she would find a way onto the international film community A-list, too.

"What about Lewis McCabe?" Jake asked, standing, too.

Reluctant to think about what a mess her personal life was in, Lexie turned away from her father's probing gaze. "Why would you bring him up?" she asked in a choked voice.

"I don't know," Jake replied drolly, clamping an affectionate hand on her shoulder and turning her around. "Maybe because you're in love with him?"

Fat lot of good it had done her, Lexie thought sadly, tears gathering behind her eyes. Despite the fact that she had given everything she had to him, made herself really and truly vulnerable for the first time in his life, Lewis had been only too quick to dump her when the going got rough. "It doesn't matter." Trying to ignore the aching of her heart, she let her father pull her into a warm, comforting hug. "That's over."

Jake drew away, his concern for her welfare as evident as is abiding love. "Lewis McCabe is a good man, Lexie."

Lexie could not dispute that. "He doesn't trust me, Dad. Vithout trust, there is no love." She couldn't face the possiility of being abandoned again, for whatever reasons. It was imply too painful.

Understanding filling his eyes, Jake commiserated gently, Clearly, Lewis made a mistake. That doesn't mean he oesn't love you or the two of you have no future together. f that were the case, Lexie, Jenna and I wouldn't be toether."

Lexie studied her dad. If anyone knew how to make a isting relationship and marriage, he did. "You're telling me) go after him," she guessed softly.

Her father gave her another encouraging hug. "I'm telling ou to follow your heart."

WORKING LATE AGAIN?"

"As always." Lewis sat back in his desk chair and regarded is stepmother with a rough approximation of a smile. Expeence told him why Kate was here. And although the ist thing he wanted was to talk to anyone about his failed omance with Lexie Remington, he knew he owed his stepiother the courtesy of listening to whatever it was she had to ay.

Kate set the wicker picnic basket down on his desk. "The ecurity guard said I could come on back."

Probably in the hopes that Kate would improve his boss's iood, Lewis thought. Which, given the state of things, was arn unlikely. Lewis breathed in the aroma of roast chicken nd freshly baked bread. "Is that dinner?"

"Actually," Kate said, "it's enough for two."

Lewis peeked inside. In addition to the other items, he saw bottle of wine, a wedge of cheese, grapes, apples and a luscious-looking chocolate cake nestled beside real china stemware and silver. "You're joining me?"

Kate chuckled. "Try again."

"If this is a matchmaking ploy," Lewis warned, droppin the lid back on the basket. He quaffed a sip of coffee that ha long grown cold and bitter.

Kate lifted her hand in an elegant gesture. "I think th match has already been made. It's getting you—" she aime a finger at his heart "—to acknowledge it that is the chal lenge."

Grimacing, he pushed the cup away from him and got u to pace. "I don't want to talk about me and Lexie."

Kate dropped down onto the sofa against the wall. "The let's talk about your dad and me," she said pleasantly. " don't know how much you remember about when I came t help out after you and your brothers moved to Laramie wit your dad."

Lewis met her gaze. "Quite a lot, actually." He pausec "You were our saving grace, Kate."

Kate recalled that difficult time with a soft smile and a even gentler tone. "Eventually, yes, I was, although I can' say you boys welcomed me with open arms from the get-go.

Lewis swallowed, remembering the overwhelming grie he and his brothers had been struggling with at the time "We'd been through a lot. We didn't want another housekeep er-slash-nanny trying to take the place of our mom."

"You were hurting."

"Yes."

"Twice burned, twice shy."

"Exactly."

"And in some ways you are still wary of putting yoursel out there, for fear of what will happen if you experience lov again and then have it snatched from you in such a devasta ing way."

Lewis glared at Kate. "I thought we weren't going to talk about Lexie Remington."

"Listen to me, Lewis." Kate stood and moved gracefully toward him. "I know how much courage it took for you to open your heart to Lexie."

A muscle ticked in Lewis's jaw. "For all the good it did me. She doesn't care that I love her. If she did, she would accept my apology." He paused to clear his throat. "But she won't, so…"

Kate placed a hand on his arm. "What do you think would have happened if your father'd had that kind of attitude when I walked away after deciding that my getting so emotionally involved with him was a colossal mistake? What if he had just given up instead of realizing how scared I was of being hurt and not come after me? What if he hadn't waited patiently until I was ready to take another chance on us?"

They would have all been miserable, Lewis knew.

Kate's love and understanding had helped make them a family again. Her selflessness had brought comfort and security back into their lives.

"No one is guaranteed happiness, Lewis," Kate continued wisely, the love she felt for him and all his siblings shimmering in her eyes. "The luck of the draw, a person's destiny, only takes one so far. It's up to each of us to go out and make things happen and fill our lives with love and joy."

KATE WAS RIGHT, Lewis knew, and it didn't take him long to figure out what he had to do to "make things happen" to get his life—and Lexie's—back on track. He shut down his computer, picked up the picnic basket and was on the way to the door when another shadow crossed his path. Lexie stepped inside his office, looking stunningly beautiful in a snug-fitting black button-up shirt, low slung jeans and boots. She had four or five necklaces of all different lengths and styles glittering in the open vee of her shirt, sexy gold hoops in her ears. She stuffed her hands in her pockets, looking every bit the stubborn-as-all-get-out tomboy she had been in her youth.

He'd had quite a hankering for her then.

That was nothing compared to what he felt now, as he drank in the familiar exotic fragrance of her perfume.

It felt like an eternity since they'd last seen each other. Damn, but he had missed her. And from the tentative—yet resolute—look in her lovely turquoise eyes, she had yearned for him, too.

Not that she'd probably admit it out loud.

"Howdy," she broke the silence to offer the standard Texas greeting.

"Howdy to you, too," Lewis drawled right back, mocking her too-casual tone.

She nodded at the picnic basket and swallowed visibly before tilting her chin back up. She searched his face as thoroughly as he'd been studying hers. "Got plans?" Her voice was lonely-sounding as all get out.

Heart racing, Lewis set the dinner for two aside, then caught and held her gaze. "Very important ones as a matter of fact."

Briefly, disappointment colored the expression on her pretty face. Lexie wet her lips, took a deep breath. "Then I'll make this brief," she stated, moving nearer. She didn't stop until they stood toe to toe. The challenging look he so loved sparkled in her eyes. "I want to start over."

Satisfaction warring with the hope deep inside him, Lewis cupped her shoulders in both hands. He knew this was one battle of the sexes he would win. "Well, I don't," he countered gruffly.

Lexie's eyes widened in shock.

Sure he had her full attention, he continued firmly. "Because that would mean going backward." He felt as if they had already wasted far too much time.

Lexie frowned, impatient. "Then what do you want to do?" she demanded in a taut, sexy voice that sent relief soaring through him.

Lewis stated bluntly, "I want to pick up right where we left off, and have that dream date we've both been longing for—tonight! Only this time, Lexie Remington, when I apologize for being the world's biggest fool, I want you to say you forgive me."

"Done!" she said quickly.

"And then," Lewis continued, not caring how corny it sounded, since it had to be said, "I'll promise I'll never doubt your love for me again. You'll vow you'll never doubt mine. And we'll live happily ever after."

Looking as if she had just won the lottery, Lexie murmured dryly, "I think I can handle that, Lewis McCabe."

"Good." Giving in to the desire that had been plaguing him from the moment they'd laid eyes on each other again, after years spent apart, he wrapped his arms around her waist and tugged her against him.

Lexie splayed her soft, delicate hands across the hardness of his chest. She regarded him steadily. "But first, I have some things I need to say to you, too."

Willing to do whatever it took to set things right between them once again, Lewis nodded. "Go right ahead."

Lexie gulped. Moisture glimmered in her eyes and her low voice shook with emotion. "I'm sorry I didn't ask you to go see Constantine with me, instead of trying to handle it on my own."

"I would have, you know." More than anything, Lewis wanted to protect her.

Lexie nodded. "I was trying to spare you. Instead, I only ended up hurting you more. And—" Lexie drew a shaky breath and pushed on "—I'm especially regretful I didn't accept your apology when we both figured out just how expertly we were both set up."

Lewis knew that had he and Lexie just stuck together whe it counted, instead of falling victim to their doubts, they neve would have succumbed to the trap that led to the misunde standing, and break-up. He was as determined as she that woul never happen to them again. Lewis pressed his lips to he temple. "Whatever happens from here on out, we're in it togeth er."

"A couple," Lexie declared, just as resolutely.

Lewis wanted to be a lot more than simply friends an lovers. Needing her to want that, too, he delivered a lon soul-searing kiss that left them both aching for more. "Mo than that, I hope," he said huskily, looking deep into her eye

Her breath coming rapidly, Lexie waited for him to go o

Lewis cupped her face in his hands. "I know it's soon," h continued hoarsely, more sure than ever they were on the rig path now, "but it's like I explained to you last week. Whe something feels this right—"

"It is this right," Lexie agreed happily.

"In a forever kind of way," Lewis affirmed tenderl "Which is why..." Swallowing hard, Lewis got down on h knees in front of her. "I want you to marry me, Lexie Ren ington."

Lexie's turquoise eyes sparkled as much as her wid winning smile. "And I want you, Lewis McCabe, to marr me," she volleyed right back. "So the answer," she vowed she dropped down to her knees, too, wreathed her arn around his neck, and passionately returned his kiss, "is yes

Turn the page for an excerpt from
Cathy Gillen Thacker's
latest book, A Laramie Christmas,
coming in December 2007 only from
Mills & Boon® Special Edition.

A Laramie Christmas

by

Cathy Gillen Thacker

‹evin McCabe knew thirteen and one half days of pure un-dulterated bliss were too good to be true. It figured he would ·e something that just had to be investigated on his way back › Laramie, Texas. Spying the unmarked white van currently acked up to the rear door of Miss Sadie's Blackberry Hill ıansion, he pulled over to the side of the winding rural road nd watched a woman carry armloads of stuff out of the ouse, stash it in the van, then dart back into the residence ia the side door. Just his luck that he was driving his battered ›ur wheel drive vehicle instead of his police car and had no mergency communication system.

Keeping an eye out for anything else suspicious, he crept ›ward the house, stopping just short of the white van. Vishing he had a way to check the license plates, he cut the ngine and got out to scope out the situation. He started ›ward the still open side door and paused to look in the ·indows of the rented van. It was loaded with the vacation-ıg Miss Sadie's valuables, he noted grimly as Christmas ıusic floated merrily from the interior of the house. Every-ıing from a Tiffany lamp to her jewelry box and favorite ›cking chair.

"May I help you?" a feminine voice asked coolly from the ›p of the eight weathered wooden steps.

Time to appear clueless about what was going on. Kev turned away from the loot with his best "Aw, shucks, ma'r I'm just a dumb country boy" grin, and immediately notice several things about the woman standing beneath the portic She wasn't a local. He was sure of that because had he ev encountered this very beautiful woman, even in passing, h definitely would have remembered her.

Reminding himself he would need to make a positive I later, Kevin estimated the interloper was around five feet si one hundred and twenty pounds, and curvy in all the rig places. Her copper hair fell to her chin in a riot of sprin loaded curls he found incredibly sexy. And his attraction the perpetrator didn't end there. She had an angelically rour face with full apple cheeks, a straight, slender nose and a th upper lip countered by a full lush lower lip, just right f kissing. Her peachy skin was fair and flawless save for th freckles sprinkled lightly over her face, her savvy blue ey intelligent, wide-set and long-lashed.

Not surprisingly, she was incredibly nervous—and pr tending not to be, even as she stood there with a five-foo high plastic candy cane standing upright beside her. Althoug what she was doing with that, he didn't know. The faded re and-white plastic lawn ornament didn't look like somethin you would want to steal.

Reminding himself she could be a lot more dangerous tha her sweet and sexy appearance indicated, he paused at th bottom of the stairs. Tipping his hat in her direction, he pr tended to be every bit as oblivious to the criminal wrongdoin going on as the situation demanded. "Hello. I'm Kev McCabe."

THAT WAS THE PROBLEM with agreeing to do a last-minute jo like this, in an unfamiliar part of the state, Noelle Kring thought. You never knew who was going to show up, bringin he kind of "trouble" she just didn't need two weeks before Christmas. And the six-foot hunk in front of her was heartache personified.

Or at least he would have been if he'd bothered to clean up. The golden brown hair peeking out from beneath the brim of a Stetson hat needed to be both combed and cut. She estimated it had been weeks since his boyishly handsome face had been shaved. And that, she couldn't help but note a little wistfully, was a shame. The scraggly dark brown whiskers on his face detracted from his nicely chiseled features and the sexy cleft in his chin. Not that she should be admiring this handsome stranger who was obviously scoping out the place—and her.

He moved closer, drawing her attention to the implicit threat in his impossibly broad shoulders and scrappy, streetfighter's build. This was not a man she'd want to meet in a dark alley. This was a man she would want on her side. Although for whatever reason, despite his outwardly laid-back manner, he did not seem to be. "I stopped by to see Miss Sadie, if she's available," he began, casually enough.

He might think he was good, but after the way she had been raised, Noelle could spot a pretender a mile away. Not that he needed to know she was on to his game. "Actually, she's not," she replied with another cool smile.

He kept his eyes on hers. "Do you know when she'll be back?"

"No, I don't." Determined to give as little information as possible, Noelle chanced a look behind her into the interior of the house. To her immense relief, she heard nothing but the strains of "Oh Come All Ye Faithful'."

"I see." He propped one boot on the bottom step. Leaning forward, he rested an elbow on his thigh. Settling in for the duration, he charmed her with a sexy smile. "And you are…?"

Noelle ignored the shiver of awareness that sifted through

her. There was no way she was giving out that informatio in this day and age. She glanced at the wintry gray sky wishing for a burst of rain that would send him on his way "Too busy to stand here chatting with you," she said sweetly turning to go back in the house.

"You seem stressed," he remarked.

You don't know the half of it.

"Is there a problem in there?"

Noelle listened hard and, to her continued relief, still hear no "suspicious" sounds coming from inside the house.

He paused, offered another ingratiating look. "Anything can help you—or Miss Sadie—with?"

Wishing she had followed the advice given her, instead o trying to handle this "interruption" alone, she moved awa from the door once again. She stopped at the edge of th landing and gripped the big plastic candy cane in front of he "No. And there won't be a problem if you leave now." Sh made no effort to disguise the warning.

As she had suspected, the sexy stranger did not respon well to the veiled threat. "And if I don't?"

She let him squirm for a few minutes. "Then I'll be force to make a citizen's arrest."

Something shifted in his gaze, his choked laughter turne into a mannered cough. "On what grounds?" he asked i disbelief.

Noelle kept her expression composed. "Coming onto Mis Sadie's property without an invitation and then refusing t leave when asked."

He tipped his hat back, letting her see every nuance of hi insulted expression. "I am not trespassing."

"We'll let the sheriff's department decide that. Frankly, think they're going to be on my side."

The corners of his lips crooked up. "Doubtful, since work for the sheriff's department."

She tilted her head and gave him the look she reserved for nyone who tried to snow her. "Really."

"Yes."

She paused to look him up and down, beginning to enjoy ıis matching of wits and wills. "Then they must have some ery peculiar uniforms."

He took off his hat and shoved his hand through clean, umpled hair. "Obviously, I'm not on duty now."

"If you ever were," Noelle muttered beneath her breath. She hould have just stayed inside and hoped he didn't do anything razy—like break a window or jimmy a door lock—while she vaited for help to arrive. Instead, she was out here, with only plastic candy cane to protect her, talking to a smooth-talking ottie whose self-confidence apparently knew no bounds....

* * * *

Don't forget A Laramie Christmas *is out in December.*

New York Times bestselling author Linda Lael Miller is back with a new romance featuring the heartwarming McKettrick family from Mills & Boon® Special Edition.

Sierra's Homecoming
by Linda Lael Miller

On sale December 2007 wherever books are sold.

Turn the page for a sneak preview!

Sierra's Homecoming

by

Linda Lael Miller

Soft, smoky music poured into the room.

The next thing she knew, Sierra was in Travis's arms, close against that chest she'd admired earlier, and they were slow dancing.

Why didn't she pull away?

"Relax," he said. His breath was warm in her hair.

She giggled, more nervous than amused. What was the matter with her? She was attracted to Travis, had been from the first, and he was clearly attracted to her. They were both adults. Why not enjoy a little slow dancing in a ranch-house kitchen?

Because slow dancing led to other things. She took a step back and felt the counter flush against her lower back. Travis naturally came with her, since they were holding hands and he had one arm around her waist.

Simple physics.

Then he kissed her.

Physics again—this time, not so simple.

"Yikes," she said, when their mouths parted.

He grinned. "Nobody's ever said that after I kissed them."

She felt the heat and substance of his body pressed against hers. "It's going to happen, isn't it?" she heard herself whisper.

"Yep," Travis answered.

"But not tonight," Sierra said on a sigh.

"Probably not," Travis agreed.

"When, then?"

He chuckled, gave her a slow, nibbling kiss. "Tomorrow morning," he said. "After you drop Liam off at school."

"Isn't that…a little…soon?"

"Not soon enough," Travis answered, his voice husky. "Not nearly soon enough."

* * * *

Don't forget Sierra's Homecoming *is a December novel.*

Special moments

We hope that the Special Edition novel you have just finished has given you plenty of romantic reading pleasure.

We are thrilled to have put together a section of special free bonus features, which we hope will add to the entertainment in each Special Edition novel from now on.

There will be puzzles for you to do, exciting horoscopes glimpsing what's in your future, author information and sneak previews of books in the pipeline!

Do let us know what you think of these special extras by emailing specialmoments@hmb.co.uk

For you, from us…
Relax and enjoy…

Cathy *Gillen Thacker*

Dear Reader,

Working out what to wear is something that has stumped us all from time to time. The "look" you eventually end up with usually depends on how and where you spend most of your time. For instance, my office is in my home and I place a premium on comfort, so you're more likely to find me in jeans, trainers and a cotton shirt than a dress and heels. Fortunately, no one really cares how a writer is garbed when he or she is writing – people just want to read a good story. Celebrities and CEOs, on the other hand, are held to a different standard.

Globe-trotting Lexie Remington knows this and has made a career of helping clients work out what kind of image they want to present to the world. Whereas the brilliant – but style challenged – computer genius Lewis McCabe is too much of a man's man to employ anyone to tell *him* how to dress. And this puts the fun-loving millionaire in a quandary. Lewis wants Lexie's attention. He won't get it if he doesn't at least pretend to respect what she does for a living. So following a small misunderstanding, he inadvertently gets himself in a Texas-sized mess. One his four brothers think is a hoot…

I hope you enjoy *Blame It on Texas* as much as I loved writing it. For more information on this and other books, please visit my website at www.cathygillenthacker.com.

Happy reading!

Cathy Gillen Thacker

Author *Biography*

CATHY GILLEN THACKER

is a full-time wife, mother and author who began writing stories for her own amusement during "nap time" when her children were toddlers.

Twenty years and more than fifty published novels later, Cathy is almost as well-known for her witty romantic comedies and warm, family stories as she is for her ability to get grass stains and red clay out of almost anything, her triple layer brownies, and her knack for knowing what her husband and children are up to almost before they do!

When writing, Cathy's greatest goal is to entertain and uplift. "To give people the power and courage to dream."

Cathy's books have made numerous appearances on bestseller lists and are now published in seventeen languages and thirty-five countries around the world.

She says the most satisfying aspect of being a writer is hearing from her fans. "I love hearing from readers. Knowing just one person really enjoyed a book makes all the hard work seem worthwhile."

Krisskross

E-Beginnings

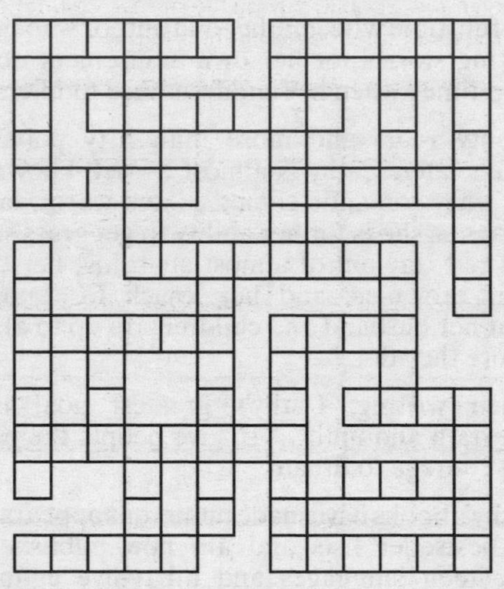

4 letter words

Else
Epic
Erin
Exit

5 letter words

Earns
Earth
Elope
Equal
Excel
Eyrie

6 letter words

Editor
Effect
Effete
Either
Elapse
Exempt

7 letter words

Ebonite
Embrace
Enemies
Entreat
Evil eye

8 letter words

Emperors
Estrange
Eventide
External

Special moments

Sudoku

To solve the Sudoku puzzle, each row, column and box must contain the numbers 1 to 9.

8	3		7				4	2
	1			5	9			
7						6		
	4				3			5
	9			2			8	
6								
	2		3	7	8		1	
				6		3		
			4		1			

Horoscopes

Dadhichi is a renowned astrologer and is frequently seen on TV and in the media. He has the unique ability to draw from complex astrological theory to provide clear, easily understandable advice and insights for people who want to know what their future may hold.

In the twenty-five years that Dadhichi has been practising astrology, face reading and other esoteric studies, he has conducted over 8,500 consultations. His clients include celebrities, political and diplomatic figures and media and corporate identities from all over the world.

Aries

21 March - 20 April

You can successfully bring your plans and projects to completion this month. You need to control your nerves and also your reaction to co-workers, however. On the 1st, 2nd, 14th and 15th, you may lose your temper with those who are actually trying to help you. Patience seems to be the key word this month to assure you of success. Problems with money are clearing up and a better bank balance is also assured after the third week of August.

Taurus

21 April - 21 May

Unusual people will be part of your life this month and your popularity will be strong when you least expect it. You'll seem to be more in demand and this has everything to do with your forceful and vibrant personality. Between the 4th and the 10th you'll be riding the wave of social popularity. Enjoy it as much as you can.

by *Dadhichi Toth*

Gemini

22 May - 22 June

Although your work seems set to reach a new plateau, you mustn't let your health or that of someone else become an obstacle to greater achievements. On the 6th and the 14th, listen to your body signals and have that check-up to reduce your worry, if nothing else. A friend will invite you to travel, but your work commitments may not allow you the freedom you would like.

Cancer

23 June - 23 July

Positive news from someone at a distance will amuse and lift your spirits. After the 5th, your communications with others will be cordial, if not humorous. Practical jokes and novel circumstances break the tedium of day-to-day life. Friends' problems will be greatly relieved by your own sense of humour. An opportunity is presented by a rival or opposition company and is worth considering.

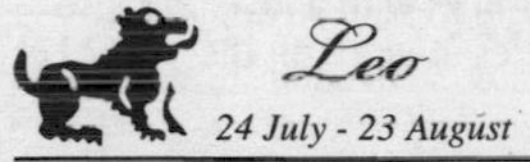

Leo

24 July - 23 August

Many happy returns, Leo! The Sun will revitalise your personality and all your relationships during the coming three or four weeks. Although greater responsibilities are indicated from the 12th, your happy disposition is likely to meet these challenges with a can-do attitude. Money or valuables that are suddenly lost will reappear just as mysteriously.

Virgo

24 August - 22 September

Sudden infatuations are likely to excite but also confuse you, as others won't show their hand. Honesty will be necessary to keep you on the right track. Your service-orientated personality will be called upon to assist people in dire straits, especially after the 10th. Playing the compassionate game to genuine people is commendable, but you need to sift the wheat from the chaff. Don't be a sucker for a hard-luck story.

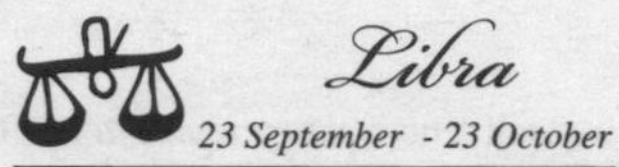

Libra

23 September - 23 October

Extra debts make the first week of August difficult for you. You have to work hard to overcome worries and use your creativity to dig yourself out of a financial ditch. Discussions with bank managers on the 4th and the 6th will work magic and restore your confidence. Collaborative interviews with employers are also set to change the complexion of your work after the 17th.

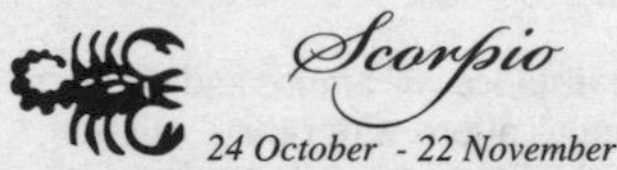

Scorpio

24 October - 22 November

Favourable karma from younger people is a great start to the month. Your advice is useful and is based upon solid experience. You may not be paid for your assistance, but will get satisfaction from working for a good cause. Sexual relationships are hot and spicy on the 5th, 6th and 7th. Journeys with a lover are also light-hearted and rejuvenating. Obstacles at work on the 14th? Let others know just where you stand!

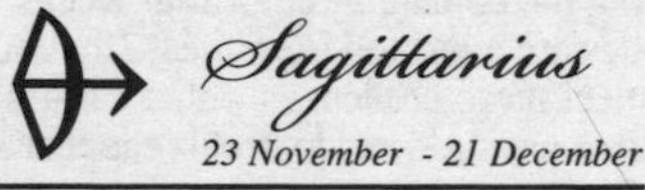

Sagittarius

23 November - 21 December

Don't be too clever in the way you communicate. You could be trying to impress others with your know-how, only to find yourself all tangled in knots. Actively listen to what others have to suggest and quietly agree even if you don't. Make your moves after the 18th, when you'll be better informed for an attack. Between the 20th and 22nd, an emotional experience could set you up for a new friendship. Don't play hard to get.

Capricorn

22 December - 20 January

Even if you receive threatening correspondence or harassing phone calls, keep your cool on the 1st. Others will be testing your mettle to see how far they can push you. On the other hand, trouble on the home front will cause you to react excessively, thereby throwing you off-centre and negatively impacting upon your professional responsibilities. Some meditation or the company of calmer people will help you in finding inner peace. Good news on the grapevine can be expected on the 19th.

Aquarius

21 January - 18 February

Your work will find you whizzing here, there and everywhere, especially between the 1st and the 6th. Delegate some responsibility to those who aren't quite as busy. Rumours on the 8th will ruffle your feathers if you read too much into the gossip. Rely on a friend to feed you the correct information before retaliating. A temporary cooling-off of your relationship should be an opportunity for you to re-examine your values this month.

Pisces

19 February - 20 March

Stop interfering in a relative's personal affairs if you want peace of mind. On the 4th, 5th and 6th be a minimalist in your advice and let your actions speak louder than words. A nice relief from antagonistic issues can be expected around the 15th, when you're free to engage in intimate moments with the one you love. An increased social agenda is likely after the 27th.

Word Search

Freshening Up

J	B	A	E	S	L	I	O	H	T	A	B	G
J	B	T	O	Y	A	N	N	E	H	G	D	E
D	R	T	O	K	E	K	E	G	U	O	R	Y
P	M	A	P	N	M	L	B	L	U	S	H	E
C	H	R	M	B	I	B	I	P	K	H	K	S
O	N	B	A	W	P	L	E	N	S	H	C	H
N	K	L	H	K	S	R	O	I	E	B	I	A
D	M	T	S	R	F	T	L	N	R	R	T	D
I	L	M	C	U	E	O	N	C	A	G	S	O
T	K	K	M	O	P	D	O	E	D	L	P	W
I	T	E	G	L	L	L	W	Y	C	R	I	A
O	G	T	I	H	O	D	S	O	P	S	L	R
N	V	A	W	G	R	K	C	A	P	A	V	A
E	N	Z	N	E	N	H	J	R	L	J	O	C
R	K	E	N	K	H	N	H	D	E	T	Z	S
B	X	O	L	O	T	I	O	N	Q	A	S	A
N	T	O	O	T	H	P	A	S	T	E	M	M

ATTAR	EYE SHADOW	POWDER
BALM	HENNA	ROUGE
BATH OILS	LANOLIN	SALTS
BLUSH	LIPSTICK	SCENTS
COLD CREAM	LOTION	SHAMPOO
COLOGNE	MASCARA	SOAP
CONDITIONER	NAIL POLISH	TONER
EYELINER	PERFUME	TOOTHPASTE

Special moments

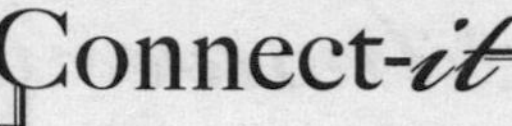

Sherlock Holmes Fill-In

Each line in the puzzle below has three clues and three answers. The last letter in the first answer on each line is the first letter of the second answer, and so on. The connecting letter is outlined, giving you the correct number of letters for each answer (the answers in line 1 are 4, 6 and 6 letters). The clues are numbered 1 to 8, with each number containing 3 clues for the 3 answers on the line. But here's the catch! The clues are not in order - so the first clue in the line is not necessarily for the first answer. Good luck!

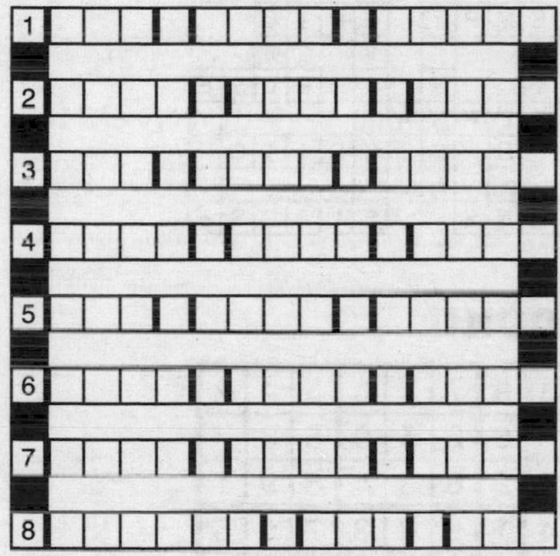

Clues:

1. Test. *The Reigate* ___. African equines.
2. *The* ___ *Face*. Look for. Humorous.
3. Peer group. Quiet. *The* ___ *Carbuncle*.
4. *The Engineer's* ___. Macaw. Sharp.
5. Long poem. *The* ___ *Beeches*. Cure.
6. *The* ___ *Bachelor*. Happening. Die.
7. Soak up. Dutch cheese. *The* ___ *Coronet*.
8. Scepticism. *Man with the* ___ *Lip*. Snare.

KRISSKROSS

E	F	F	E	C	T		E	F	F	E	T	E
L			M				N			A		M
O		E	B	O	N	I	T	E		R		P
P			R				R			T		E
E	Q	U	A	L			E	I	T	H	E	R
			C				A					O
E			E	V	E	N	T	I	D	E		R
N					S					X		S
E	X	E	M	P	T		E	P	I	C		
M		X			R		V			E		
I		I			A		I		E	L	S	E
E	X	T	E	R	N	A	L					Y
S			R		G		E	D	I	T	O	R
			I		E		Y					I
E	A	R	N	S			E	L	A	P	S	E

SUDOKU

8	3	9	7	1	6	5	4	2
4	1	6	2	5	9	8	3	7
7	5	2	8	3	4	6	9	1
2	4	1	9	8	3	7	6	5
5	9	3	6	2	7	1	8	4
6	7	8	1	4	5	9	2	3
9	2	5	3	7	8	4	1	6
1	8	4	5	6	2	3	7	9
3	6	7	4	9	1	2	5	8

WORDSEARCH

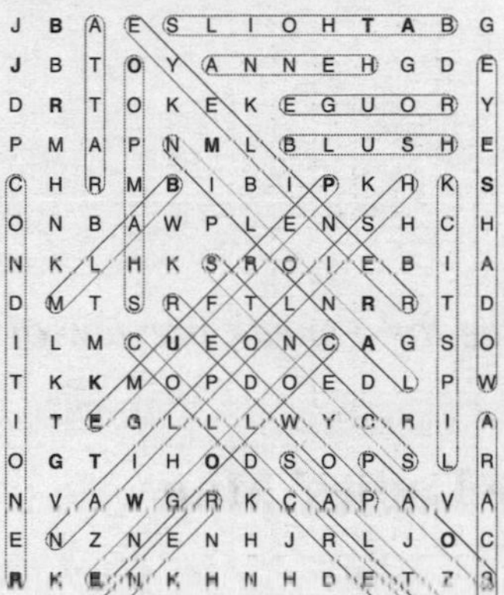

CONNECT-IT

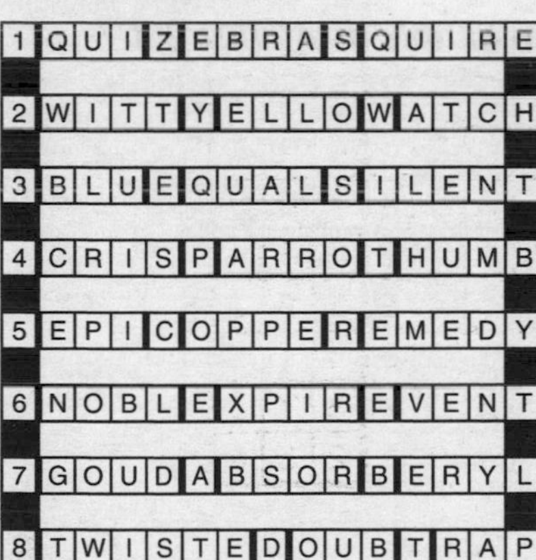

1 Q U I Z E B R A S Q U I R E
2 W I T T Y E L L O W A T C H
3 B L U E Q U A L S I L E N T
4 C R I S P A R R O T H U M B
5 E P I C O P P E R E M E D Y
6 N O B L E X P I R E V E N T
7 G O U D A B S O R B E R Y L
8 T W I S T E D O U B T R A P

Turn the page for a sneak preview of

The Ladies' Man

by

Susan Mallery

Available in August 2007

The Ladies' Man

by

Susan Mallery

Carter Brockett eyed the curvy brunette in the prim dress and knew he was seconds away from all kinds of trouble. The cool, logical side of his brain reminded him that all the pain and suffering in his life could be traced back to one source: women. Life was always better when he walked away.

The part of his brain—and the rest of him—that enjoyed a warm body, a sharp mind and a purely feminine take on the world said she looked interesting. And that last bit of consciousness, shaped by a very strong-willed mother who had drilled into him that he was always to protect those weaker than him, told him that the attractive brunette was in way over her head.

He could be wrong of course. For all he knew, she was a leather-wearing dominatrix who came to the Blue Dog because of the place's reputation. But he had his doubts.

The Blue Dog was a cop bar. But not just any hangout for those in uniform. It was a place where guys showed up to get lucky and the women who walked in counted on that fact. Carter usually avoided the place—he worked undercover and couldn't afford to be seen here. But one of his contacts had insisted on the location, so Carter had agreed and prayed no one from the force would speak to him.

No one had. He'd concluded his business and had been about to leave when the brunette had walked in with her friend, who was currently involved in a heated conversation with Eddy. Eddy wasn't exactly a prince when it came to his dating habits, so Carter had a feeling the chat wasn't going to go well. He nodded at Jenny, the bartender on duty, then pointed to the brunette. Jenny raised her eyebrows.

Carter didn't have to guess what she was thinking. Jenny, an ex-girlfriend, knew him pretty well. Yeah, well, maybe after a few months of self-induced celibacy, he was ready to give the man-woman thing another try. Even though he knew better. Even though it was always a disaster.

He glanced around and saw he wasn't the only one who'd noticed the contrast between the brunette's made-for-sin body and her Sunday-school-teacher clothes. So if he was going to protect her from the other big bad cops, he'd better get a move on.

He walked to the bar, where Jenny handed him a beer and a margarita. He ignored her knowing grin and crossed to the brunette's table.

"Hi. I'm Carter. Mind if I join you?"

As he asked the question, he set down the margarita and gave her his best smile.

Yeah, yeah, a cheap trick, he thought, remembering all the hours he'd spent perfecting it back in high school. He'd taught himself to smile with just the right amount of interest, charm and bashfulness. It never failed.

Not even tonight, when the woman looked up, flushed, half rose, then sat back down, and in the process knocked over her nearly empty drink and scattered the slushy contents across the table and down the front of her dress.

"Oh, no," she said, her voice soft and almost musical. "Darn. I can't believe I…" She pressed her lips together, then looked at him.

He'd already sopped up the mess on the table with a couple of napkins. He completely ignored the dampness on her dress. Sure, he was interested, but he wasn't stupid.

"You okay?" he asked, curious about a woman who actually said *darn.*

"Yes. Thank you."

He passed over the drink he'd brought.

She glanced first at it, then at him. "I'm, ah, with someone."

He kept his gaze on her. "Your girlfriend. I saw you come in together."

She nodded. "She's breaking up with her boyfriend and wanted moral support. I don't usually… This isn't…" She sighed. "She'll be back soon."

"No problem," he said easily. "I'll keep you company until she's finished."

Even in the dim light of the bar, he could see her eyes were green. Her long, dark hair hung in sensuous waves to just past her shoulders.

Carter held in a snort. Sensuous waves? He'd sure been without for a little too long if he were thinking things like that.

She shifted uncomfortably and didn't touch the drink.

"Is it me or the bar?" he asked.

"What? Oh, both, I suppose." Instantly, she covered her mouth, then dropped her hand to her damp lap. "Sorry. I shouldn't have said that."

"It's fine. I'm a great believer in the truth. So which is more scary?"

She glanced around the Blue Dog, then returned her attention to him. "Mostly you."

He grinned. "I'm flattered."

"Why? You *want* me to think you're scary?"

He leaned forward and lowered his voice just enough to get her to sway toward him. "Not scary. Dangerous. All guys want to be dangerous. Women love that."

She surprised him by laughing. "Okay, Carter, I can see you're a pro and I'm way out of my league with you. I cheerfully confess I'm not the bar type and being in this setting makes me horribly uncomfortable." She glanced at her friend. "I can't tell if the fight's going well or badly. What do you think?"

He looked at Eddy, who'd backed the blonde into a corner. "It depends on how you're defining 'well.' I don't think they're actually breaking up. Do you?"

"I'm not sure. Diane was determined to tell him what she thought, once and for all. In 'I' sentences."

He frowned. "In what?"

She smiled. "*I* think you're not treating me with respect. *I* think you're always late on purpose. That kind of thing. Although she did say something about wanting to kick him in the head, which is unlikely to help. Of course, I don't know Eddy. He may like that sort of thing."

Carter was totally and completely charmed. "Who *are* you?" he asked.

"My name is Rachel."

"You don't swear, you don't hang out in bars, so what do you do?"

"How do you know I don't swear?" she asked.

"You said 'darn' when you spilled your drink."

"Oh. Right. It's a habit. I teach kindergarten. There's no way I can swear in front of the children, not that I ever used a lot of bad words, so I trained myself to never say them. It's just easier. So I use words like 'darn' and 'golly.'" She grinned. "Sometimes people look at me like I'm at the dull-normal end of the IQ scale, but I can live with that. It's for the greater good. So who are you?"

A complicated question, Carter thought, knowing he couldn't tell her the truth. "Just a guy."

"Uh-huh." She eyed his earring—a diamond stud—and his too-long hair. "More than just a guy. What do you do?"

That changed with the assignment, he thought. "I'm working for a chopper shop. Motorcycles," he added.

She straightened her spine and squared her shoulders. "I know what a chopper is. I'm not some innocent fresh out of the backwoods."

Her indignation made him want to chuckle. She reminded him of a kitten facing down a very large and powerful dog. All the arched back and hissing fury didn't make the kitten any bigger.

"Not a lot of backwoods around here," he said easily. "Desert, though. You could be an innocent fresh out of the desert."

Her lips twitched, as if she were trying not to smile. He pushed her margarita toward her.

"You're letting all the ice melt," he told her.

She hesitated, then took a sip. "Are you from around here?" she asked.

"Born and raised. All my family's here."

"Such as?"

Now it was his turn to pause. He didn't usually give out personal information. In his line of work, it could get him into trouble. But he had a feeling Rachel wasn't going to be a threat to much more than his oath of celibacy.

"Three sisters, a mom. Their main purpose in life is

to make me crazy." He made the statement with equal parts love and exasperation.

Rachel looked wistful. "That's nice. Not the crazy part, but that you're close."

"You're not close to your family?"

"I don't have any."

He didn't know what to say to that and reminded himself too late that he was supposed to be charming her, not reminding her that she was alone in the world.

"Are you from around here?" he asked.

"Riverside?" She shook her head. Her hair swayed and caught the light and, for the moment, totally mesmerized him. "I moved here after I graduated from college. I wanted a nice, quiet, suburban sort of place." She sighed. "Not very exciting."

"Hey, I've lived here all my life. I can show you the best spots for viewing the submarine races."

She grinned. "Where I grew up, we went parking over by the river. Well, not really a river. More of a gully. Part of the year, it even had water in it."

"Parking, huh?"

She shrugged. "I had my moments."

"And now?"

Her gaze drifted to where her friend still talked to Eddy. "Not so much." She looked back at him. "Why'd you come over?"

He smiled. "Have you looked in the mirror lately?"

She ducked her head and blushed. Carter couldn't remember the last time he'd seen a woman blush. He wanted to make her do it again.

"Thank you," she said. "I spend my days with five-year-olds whose idea of being charming is to put glue in my hair. You're a nice change."

"You're comparing me to a five-year-old?" he asked, pretending outrage.

"Well, a lot of guys have maturity issues."

"I'm totally mature. Responsible, even."

She didn't look convinced. "Of course you are."

* * * *

Don't forget The Ladies' Man
is available in August.

0807/23a

THE LADIES' MAN

by Susan Mallery

Rachel Harper wasn't the one-night-stand type, but when sexy Carter Brockett offered the stranded teacher a ride home, one thing led to another… And now Rachel had news for this ladies' man…

A LITTLE CHANGE OF PLANS

by Jen Safrey

Pregnant after a fling, Molly Jackson's business and reputation were on the line. So she turned to her best friend, Adam Shibbs, for a quick marriage of convenience – but would real love spring from their short-term charade?

CHASE'S PROMISE

by Lois Faye Dyer

For years, Raine Harper had hated Chase McCloud, but when her brother disappeared, she needed the bounty hunter's help. Their search yielded more than they bargained for – the truth about the past… and the promise of a future together.

Available at WHSmith, Tesco, ASDA, and all good bookshops

www.millsandboon.co.uk